Acclaim for the Work of JAMES M. CAIN!

"America's greatest writer."
    —*Albert Camus*

"Nobody else has ever quite pulled it off the way Cain does, not Hemingway, and not even Raymond Chandler. Cain is a master."
    —*Tom Wolfe*

"Cain can get down to primary impulses of greed and sex in fewer words that any writer we know of."
    —*New York Times*

"Good, swift, violent."
    —*Dashiell Hammett*

"The poet of the hard-boiled school of the American novel."
    —*Washington Post*

"One of the most remarkable storytellers in the U.S."
    —*Time*

"Lean, muscular, punchy."
    —*Washington Star*

"Brisk and involving."
    —*Kansas City Star*

"Cain is a superb storyteller, his pages breathe excitement."
    —*Saturday Review of Literature*

It was twilight dark, a large room with booths all around, with heavy curtains drawn close, shutting them off. And the girls were oddly dressed, if you could call them dressed at all. The hostess had on a buckskin coat with fringed bottom, but the waitresses were practically naked—they were topless, and except for a skimpy swimsuit bottom in the French bikini style, bottomless too. By looking at them, I knew those girls were for sale. I knew that such things went on, and yet I began to feel nervous. But I didn't want to show it—I wanted to come off as a woman of the world, not a waitress. So I smiled through my narrowed lips, and tightened my grip on Tom's arm.

One of the girls came with our drinks. She said: "When I go I'll close your curtain, and won't bother you after that—fact of the matter, nobody will. You want me, I mean you want service, like more drinks or something, there's your light, that button there." She showed us a fixture on the table. "Just press it, and pretty soon, I'll come. Or if not me, some girl. I could be tied up, but if I am, one of the girls will come, just give her a minute or two."

"...You could be busy, you say?" asked Tom. "Doing what, like?"

"Well the customer, he can get lonely."

"And you keep him company?"

"Something along that line."

I didn't much care for her, and couldn't resist the temptation to ask her: "Still wearing that bikini bottom? Or do you take it off?"

"It all depends..."

The
COCKTAIL
Waitress

by James M. Cain

A HARD CASE CRIME NOVEL

A HARD CASE CRIME BOOK
(HCC-109)
First Hard Case Crime edition: September 2012

Published by

Titan Books
A division of Titan Publishing Group Ltd
144 Southwark Street
London SE1 0UP

in collaboration with Winterfall LLC

Print edition ISBN 978-1-78116-034-3
E-book ISBN 978-1-78116-035-0

Design direction by Max Phillips
www.maxphillips.net

Typeset by Swordsmith Productions

The name "Hard Case Crime" and the Hard Case Crime logo are trademarks of Winterfall LLC. Hard Case Crime books are selected and edited by Charles Ardai.

Printed in the United States of America

Visit us on the web at www.HardCaseCrime.com

THE COCKTAIL WAITRESS

I

I first met Tom Barclay at my husband's funeral, as he recalled to me later, though he made so little impression on me at the time that I had no recollection of ever having seen him before. Mr. Garrick, the undertaker, was in the habit of calling Student Aid, at the university, for boys to help him out, but one of those chosen that day, a junior named Dan Lacey, couldn't come for some reason, and his father asked Tom as a favor to go in his place. Tom, though he'd graduated the year before, did the honors with me, calling for me and bringing me home in a big shiny limousine. But he rode up front with the driver, so we barely exchanged five words, and I didn't even see what he looked like. Later, he admitted he saw what I looked like—not my face, as I was wearing a veil, but my "beautiful legs," as he called them. If I paid no attention to him, I had other things on my mind: the shock of what had happened to Ron, the tension of facing police, and the sudden, unexpected glimpse of my sister-in-law's scheme to steal my little boy. Ethel is Ron's sister, and I know quite well it's tragic that as a result of surgery she can never have a child of her own. I hope I allow for that. Still and all, it was a jolt to realize that she meant to keep my Tad. I knew she loved him, of course, when I went along with her suggestion, as we might call it, that she take him until I could 'readjust' and get back on my feet. But that she might love him too much, that she might want him permanently, was something I hadn't even dreamed of.

I caught on soon enough, though, when she came over, at

graveside. Leaving Jack Lucas, her husband, and Mr. and Mrs. Medford, her parents, who of course were also Ron's parents, she first shook hands with Dr. Weeks, and I suppose thanked him for the beautiful service he'd conducted, and then came over to me. "Well, Joan," she began, "you got what you wanted at last—I hope you're satisfied."

"What's that supposed to mean?" I asked her.

"I think you know."

"If I did I wouldn't be asking. Say it."

"Well the police certainly thought it funny, as everyone else did—you putting him out in the rain, in nothing but his pajamas, so he had to drive somewhere to get taken in, and if he crashed on a culvert wall I don't think you were really surprised—or much upset."

"I put him out," I told her, "after he came home drunk at two o'clock Sunday morning, woke me hollering for another beer, and then got the bright idea of punishing Tad for something he did week before last—and Tad still healing from the last time. I knew nothing about the car he had borrowed over the week-end, which must have been at the curb, keys still in the ignition, for him to be able to drive off the way he did. Nor did I pay much attention when I looked out and found him gone. By that time, nothing he did or could do would surprise me, and as soon as I got Tad quiet I went to bed. It wasn't until the afternoon, when he was finally identified, that I found out what had happened to him. So if you think I planned it that way, you're mistaken."

"So you say."

"And so you'll say too."

"…I beg your pardon, Joan?"

"Say it, Ethel, what I told you to say, that you're mistaken— or I'm slapping your face right here, in front of Dr. Weeks, in front of the Medfords, in front of Ron's friends, in a way you won't forget. Ethel—"

"I was mistaken."

"I thought you were."

"I said it. I don't think it."

"What you think means less than nothing to me. What you say does, and it better correspond." We stood there glaring at each other, but then ice water began to drip down my back. It crossed my mind, suppose she really gets mean, and tells me to come get Tad? I thought: I can't take him yet, as I can't work if I have to stay with him, and I had to get work to eat, and also pay for him, as of course I couldn't just sponge his keep off Ethel. I felt myself swallowing, then swallowing again, and at last swallowing hard. I said: "Ethel, I apologize for my tone. I've been through quite a lot, and being accused of murder, or something that sounds a lot like it, is more than I can take. So—"

"It's O.K. I make allowance."

"Now, may we get on?"

"If you're talking about Tad, everything's taken care of, and there's nothing to get on to."

"Then, I thank you."

But I sounded stiff, and she snapped: "Joan, there's nothing to thank me for, Tad's my own flesh and blood. He's welcome and more than welcome, for as long as may be desired. And the longer that is, the better I'm going to like it."

That's when she overshot it, not so much by what she said, as by the look in her eye as she said it. And that's when I woke up, to the fact it was not at all like her to take things lying down, especially an insult from me, and if she did take it, there had to be a reason. It brought me up short, but what could I do about it, especially here by the side of Ron's grave, with his father, mother, and friends still whispering nice things about him? There was nothing that I could think of, as slaps wouldn't cover it, or make any sense at all—they never made sense actually, as I had often found out to my sorrow, and would shortly find out again. All I could do was blink, and I heard myself ask, very meekly: "Where is Tad, by the way?"

"Joan, I thought best not to have a three-year-old child at the service, but he's in good hands and there's no need for you to worry."

What made me turn I don't know—she may have glanced over my shoulder—but anyway, I did, and there not far away was my son, playing beside Ethel's car, still favoring his left arm when picking up his ball, while Eliza, the woman who did Ethel's cleaning, looked on. I started for him, remembered, and lifted my veil, throwing it up on my hat. About that time he saw me, and came running, but in the way a three-year-old runs, leaning over forward, his feet having a hard time keeping up with his head. They didn't quite, but as he toppled I caught him. He wailed at the touch of my hand against his shoulder. I moved my hand and held him close and kissed him and loved him. When we'd had our beautiful moment Eliza assured me: "He's been like a lamb, Miss Joan—no trouble at all. I was so sorry, what happened to Mr. Ron."

"Thanks Eliza, that helps."

"Want me to take him now?"

"Please."

When I got back, Ethel had rejoined her parents and Jack. I thanked Dr. Weeks, shook hands with Ron's friends, men he knew from the bars mostly, a none-too-refined bunch in work pants and windbreakers, but very well behaved. Then I nodded to Mr. and Mrs. Medford, who nodded in return, coldly, and it was easy to see they believed Ethel's nonsense. Then I rejoined Tom, who had withdrawn a few feet when Ethel came to me. "Are we ready?" I asked him.

"Any time you are, Mrs. Medford."

And so, on an afternoon in spring, I left the cemetery in College Park, Maryland, and headed for my home in Hyattsville, some five miles down the line, a suburb of Washington, D.C., to face the rest of my life, with a living to make, for myself and my little son, and no idea at all how to do it. So who am I, and why am I telling this? My maiden name is Joan Woods, and I was born in Washington, Pennsylvania, a suburb of Pittsburgh. My father, Charles Woods, is a lawyer and a community leader, with only one fault that I know of: He does what my mother says, always. At seventeen, I entered the University of Pittsburgh, but then opportunity knocked at my door: a boy from a steel family fell in love with me, and presently asked me to marry him. My mother was quite excited, and my father yessed her completely. But Fred bored me to tears, and a situation developed. To give it a chance to clear up, I took myself off to Washington, where a girl I knew had a job on "the Hill," as it's called. She thought she could work me in too, and after taking me into her apartment, had me "stand by" for her call. Actually, it was "sit by," all day long, which can get tiresome, I found, as well as murderously lonesome. When the boy down the hall knocked I let him in, and one thing led to another. Next time, I was pregnant. But I knew nothing at all of anything that could be done. So far as I was concerned, a pregnant girl got married, which I did. To call Ron a reluctant bridegroom would be the understatement of the year. He hated getting married, hated little Tad, and I think hated me.

My mother hated me, and my father cut me off. I was left at the mercy of the Medfords, who I think hated me too, just to make it unanimous. Mr. Medford gave Ron a job, as a salesman in his real estate firm, and Ron did quite well—except he kept getting drunk. Then Mr. Medford would fire him, but hire him on again the following week. He fired and rehired him so often that Ron began gagging about it, calling himself Finnegan Medford, though that ended for good when Ron ruined the sale to the Castles, turning up drunk the way he did and putting his hands on Mrs. Castle, accidentally he claimed. There was no hiring him again after that, and Ron spent the months that followed cursing his father's name, and my name, and our son's, but not earning any income, so that our savings ran out and the utility companies wouldn't hear excuses anymore and turned off service at our house.

The house—Mr. Medford also gave us that, or half gave it to us, leaving a $7,500 mortgage dangling, as an "incentive" to Ron, he said, to straighten himself up and accept responsibility. It had no such effect, but it did make me gray in my teens, finding $110 each month for the amortization payments, back when there was still money to be found. Now there was none, and the foreclosure warnings had begun to arrive by mail.

It was in front of this house, a bungalow from the 1920s, that we stopped that day of the funeral, with Tom jumping out, handing me down, and waiting on the sidewalk while I ran up on the porch, found my key, and unlocked the front door. Then I turned, waved, and (he insisted later) blew him a kiss (which I don't believe), having no idea at all that at that moment I was looking straight at my job, in a restaurant down the hill, and at the man I would come to crave as I crave life itself.

So what's the fly in the ointment, and why am I taping this? It's in the hope of getting it printed to clear my name of the slanders against me, in connection with the job and the marriage it led to and all that came after—always the same charge, the one Ethel flung at me of being a *femme fatale* who knew ways of killing a husband so slick they couldn't be proved. Unfortunately, they can't be *dis*proved either, at least in a court of law, for as long as the papers say "it is alleged," you can't sue anyone. All I know to do is tell it and tell it all, including some things no woman would willingly tell. I don't look forward to it, but if that's how it has to be, it's how it has to be.

Whatever *I* did, Tom blew *me* a kiss, and drove off.

2

I had put on the veil, not from old-fashioned ideas about what a widow should wear, but to hide the side of my chin, which was black and blue from the bruises Ron had put on it, by hitting me that night, while we wrestled for Tad. I could have covered them with makeup, but knew the Medfords, to whom I couldn't explain the reason, would disapprove, and the veil was a simple way out. So now I opened my jar of Max Factor and went to work. But first of all I undressed, taking off the dark suit, pantyhose, black bra, and dress shoes I had on, then working in front of the mirror, there at my dressing table. And as to what I looked like naked: This was thirteen months ago, and I was just twenty-one. I'm just under medium in height, normally a bit on the slender side, and heavy-busted, as they say. But my legs are my best point, as I've been told often enough. They are straight, round, soft, and gracefully formed. My face is thick and my features stubby, but shadows under my eyes do something for me, so I'm not too bad-looking. My hair is blonde, but dark blonde, "corn-husk blonde," some call it, with the gray streaks I've already mentioned. My eyes are green and a bit large, so with the shadows I do have a cat look, that I have to admit.

I put the makeup on, then powdered and used my rabbit's foot, finally coming up with a reasonably decent face. Then I dressed, putting on white bra, white panties, red socklets, flat shoes, Levis, and a rough blouse, as being suited to the work I had in mind, of which more in a moment. I had just finished when I heard the front doorbell. It didn't ring, as my current was cut off for non-payment of bills, but it clicked, and then there came a knock. I went down the hall and opened, expecting some bill collector, and rehearsing something to say. But the same two men were there as I'd talked to before, down at the county building, police officers. "Sergeant Young, Private Church, come in," I told them.

"You remember us, then?" said the older of the two men, the sergeant, taking the cap of his uniform into his hands as he came inside.

"Well, I wouldn't forget you *so* soon."

"I mean, our names."

"I have them right, haven't I?"

"Yes, but it's unusual."

By that time, I'd brought them into the living room, that I wasn't any too proud of, as the sofa had had one of its legs pulled off, on one of Ron's lively nights, and the broken corner was held up by a pile of books. However, I seated them with their backs to it, sat down myself, and asked: "So? What can I do for you gentlemen?"

"Tell her," the sergeant told Church. The younger officer eyed him with what I thought was a little reluctance, but finally turned back to face me.

"We're off duty, Mrs. Medford," said Church, "but you were so cooperative before, when we questioned you on what happened, that we stopped by this time to *tell* you, 'stead of *asking* you, something you ought to know—that we think you ought to know. And why we're free to tell is, the woman who called last night didn't give her name, so she can't claim confidentiality—as they're calling it now. Hey, there's a word and a half."

We all laughed and I felt guilty inside, seeing anything funny on this day of days, but then I said: "O.K., Private Church, I'm listening. What did you come to tell me?"

"About this call we got. In reference to a guy, a guy so happens you know, name of Joe Pennington."

"Now I know who called you!"

"As we think we do too."

"What did she say about Joe?"

"That he was here, that he was with you Saturday night, at the time your husband came home. That instead of your little boy, he was the cause of the fight, and helped you do it, push your husband out on the porch, that—"

"I haven't seen him in over a year!"

"As we found out, Mrs. Medford."

"Why it's all a silly lie!"

"We know that, Mrs. Medford—we checked Joe Pennington out, he was doing the Block that night, the Block over in Baltimore, as he had a witness to prove, a very pretty witness, who really went into detail—"

"What we came about," the sergeant interrupted to say: "Why would this woman tell it, such a made-out-of-the-whole-cloth tale? Well, after we checked out Joe, we think we came up with the answer, and as it kind of concerns you, we thought we'd stop by and tell you. She kept talking, this woman who called, about your sister-in-law, who had taken in your little boy, for a reason she said over and over—"

"'Out of the goodness of her heart.'"

"That's what she said, we expected you to know, as it sounded like kind of a habit, something she said pretty often. And the thought crossed our mind that the woman who called us up and the kind sister-in-law were one and the same woman. So, where do you come in, and what was the point of Joe? You wouldn't come in at all, and Joe wouldn't have any point, unless, unless, *unless*, she was trying to egg us on, to move against you somehow, to have you declared unfit, an unfit mother that is, of the child she's now taking care of. In other words, if she could prove that you were immoral, she could keep the child herself—something of that kind, we both thought was in her mind, and that's what we came to tell you. Now does it tie in, at all?"

"She practically told me so, no more than an hour ago. At my husband's graveside she stood and all but admitted she wanted my boy for herself. If she loves him, I can't blame her for that—I do, and everyone does, and she's had a blow, a terrible tragic blow. And she can't have a child anymore of her own, and no doubt it's affected her mind. But—"

I couldn't go on, and sat there, trying to regain control. "It's what we came to tell you," said Sergeant Young, very gently. "We thought you ought to know."

I still sat there, but caught his eye running over my clothes. "I'm dressed for work," I explained. "I have to get started today."

"…What kind of work do you do?"

I hated to answer, but felt I had to say something. "Well, as of today," I said, "I hope to do some. There's a power mower out there, under the back porch, and a can of gasoline, and up the street a ways, at houses where I'm not known, are lawns that haven't been cut yet, and I thought I could do a couple, that is if the people will let me—it would bring in a few dollars, and with that I'd buy something to eat and then take a day to think. If I could gain a little time, I might get a job at Woodies, or Hecht's, or Murphy's—I mean as a salesperson. I'm not trained for any special work—in high school I took English composition, and in college had barely got started before I withdrew—and then how'd you guess it, got married. Then my little boy came, and—that's where I'm at, now."

Why I talked so much I don't know, but they seemed so concerned I wanted to. And I was nervous, too, I suppose; anyone would be, talking to the police.

After a moment the sergeant asked: "Had you thought of restaurant work?"

"How do you mean, restaurant work?"

"Like waiting on tables."

A look must have crossed my face, as he went on, very hurriedly, and a little embarrassed: "O.K., O.K., O.K.—just asking, no offense intended. There's one thing about it, though: Compensation is mainly in tips, and them you bring home every night. You don't wait till Saturday—or the first of the month, as some jobs make you do."

"...Keep talking, please," I said.

"Well, another thing is, that the Garden of Roses down here is just down the street from you. For Woodies you'd need a car, as you would for the Hecht Company, or Murphy's, or any place at the Plaza. And Mrs. Rossi might need someone. She often does—and you could refer to me."

"Who's Mrs. Rossi?"

"Bianca Rossi, the owner. Her husband, who died, was Italian, but she's not. And, she's O.K. Kind of a sulky type, but decent and not at all mean."

"...She sounds like my girl."

"You being good at names would help, specially on tips."

"My mother," I explained, "went to private school, where they specialized in manners, especially the importance of names, and she drilled it into me. They didn't think to tell her that the essence of manners is kindness."

"We could ride you down."

"If you'll wait till I put something on."

"What you have on is fine—you look like a working girl, and a working girl is what's wanted—that is, if anyone is. If Bianca takes you on, she'll give you a uniform."

"Then what are we waiting for?"

It was that quick and that unexpected, the most important decision of my life. Until then, I'd never thought of waiting on tables—and I didn't have time to question if I was too proud to take tips, or to think about it at all. The main thing was: It meant money, quick. So in ten seconds there we were rolling, in Sergeant Young's car, down the hill to the restaurant.

3

The Garden of Roses is on Upshur Street in Hyattsville, across from the County Building, which is on Highway No. 1 at the south of town, "The Boulevard," as it's called. It's one story, of brick painted white, and with its parking lot sprawls half a block. It's in two wings, with a center section connecting: one wing the restaurant, the other the cocktail bar. The center section is half reception foyer, really a vestibule as you go in, with a hatcheck booth facing, a half-door in its middle. Sergeant Young handed me down and walked me to the front door while Private Church waited in the car.

"This is very kind of you, helping me when you didn't need to and had no reason—"

"I didn't need to, but I had reason."

I caught his eye running over my clothes once more, and I thought perhaps over what was beneath my clothes as well, and I stiffened slightly, which he must have seen because when he next spoke it was with a greater formality. "Mrs. Medford, I have an idea what you have been through. I saw the records from when you brought your son to the hospital to have his arm seen to. I can see the marks on you, and in your home. If you'll forgive me saying so on the day you buried him, your husband was a brute, and you're well rid of him—provided that it doesn't cost you your child as well."

I nodded my thanks. We stood a moment longer, and it appeared to me that Sergeant Young would have wanted to say more, but not with his partner looking on. He returned my nod and walked back to his car.

When he and Private Church had driven off I went inside to the foyer. No light was on and for a moment, after the sun, I couldn't see. But then a girl, a waitress, popped out of the dining room, and said: "We're closed till five o'clock—try the Abbey at College Park."

"I'm calling on Mrs. Rossi."

"What about?"

"That I'll tell her, if you don't mind."

"I got to know what you want with her."

Now my temper, as perhaps you've guessed, is one of my life problems, and I stood there for a moment or two, trying to get myself under control, when suddenly a woman was there, middle-aged, no taller than I was, but big and thick and blocky. The girl said: "Mrs. Rossi, this girl wants to talk to you, but won't say what about. I tried to get out of her what she wants of you but she won't—"

"Sue!"

Mrs. Rossi's voice was sharp and Sue cut off pretty quick. "…Sue, curiosity killed the cat, and what's it to you what she wants of me?"

Sue vanished, and Mrs. Rossi turned to me. "What do you want of me?" she asked.

"Job," I told her.

"…What kind of job?"

"Waiting on table."

She studied me, then said: "I need a girl, but I'm afraid you won't do—I don't take inexperienced help."

"…Well—since I've barely said three words, I don't see how you know if I'm inexperienced or not."

"The three words you said, 'Waiting on table,' were enough. If you'd ever done this kind of work, you'd have said 'on the floor.' …Are you experienced or not?"

"No, I'm not, but—"

"Then, I don't take inexperienced help. Have you had lunch?"

"…I wasn't hungry for lunch."

"Breakfast?"

"Mrs. Rossi, you make me want to cry—I'll tell Sergeant Young, who suggested I come to you, that at least you have a heart."

"…You know Sergeant Young?"

"I do. I think I can call him a friend."

"And he sent you to me?"

"He said you might need someone."

"What made him think I could use you?"

Well, what had made him think she could use me? I tried to think of something, and suddenly remembered. I told her: "He was struck by my sureness on names. He thought in this work it might help."

"What's my name?"

"Mrs. Rossi, Mrs. Bianca Rossi."

"What's the girl's name that was here?"

"Sue."

She put a hand in the dining room, snapped her fingers, and when Sue reappeared asked me: "What's *your* name?"

I started to say, "Mrs. Medford," but caught myself and said: "Joan. Joan Medford."

"Miss or Mrs.?"

"I'm a widow, Mrs. Rossi. Mrs."

Then to Sue: "This is Joan, and she's coming to work on the floor. Take her back, give her a locker, find a uniform for her—from the back-from-the-laundry pile, there on the pantry shelf." And then to me: "When you're dressed, come back to me here and I'll tell you what you do next."

"Yes, Mrs. Rossi. And thanks."

"Something about you doesn't quite match up."

"It will, give me time."

✳

Sue led through the dining room to a kitchen with a chef and two cooks in it, chopping and slicing and stirring, to a corridor that led to a room with lockers on one side and benches down the middle. She opened the locker with a key she took from a rack, then disappeared, and by the time I'd taken my things off was back with my uniform, the short skirt and apron in one hand, the jersey in the other. She watched while I hung up my clothes in the locker, and put on the things she had brought me. The key had a wrist loop on it, and when I had locked up and slipped it on, I must have made a face at my legs, which of course were bare, as she said: "It's O.K.—some of the girls don't wear any pantyhose. On some things, like fingernails, Bianca's strict as all get-out, but on others she don't care."

She led on back to Mrs. Rossi, who was still in the dining room. But with her was a gray-haired, rather good-looking woman perhaps in her forties, in peasant blouse, crimson trunks, and beige pantyhose that set off a pair of striking-looking legs. "Be with you in a minute," Bianca told me, and went on talking. But the woman asked: "Hey wait a minute—who is *she*?"

"New girl," said Bianca. "But about the imported bubbly—"

"Wait a minute, wait a minute! Why's she dressed for the dining room?"

"It's where she's going to work."

"Oh no she's not. Here you've been promising me a girl, and now when she's here you put her to work on *this* side."

"She's new, she's never been broken in, she can't work in the bar, she's not qualified."

"Oh yes she is!" And then, to me: "Show her your qualifications, to work in the cocktail bar. The gams, I'm talking about."

I turned to show my bare legs, and she went on: "*And*, by her looks she's been broken in." Then to me again: "Haven't you?"

"If you mean what I think you mean," I admitted, "yes. I'm a widow, so happens. A recent widow with one child."

"So, Bianca?"

It wasn't the first time, and wouldn't be the last, that I'd see her take a position and then reverse herself when pressed. "O.K., take her over."

"Come on," said the woman to me, leading me back toward the lockers. "Name, please?"

"Joan. Joan Medford."

"Liz. Liz Baumgarten."

I couldn't help liking Liz, I don't think anyone could, but suddenly I asked: "When does the cocktail bar close?"

"One o'clock. Why?"

"How I get home is why. The restaurant, I know, closes at nine o'clock, and I could walk home at that hour. But at one in the morning—"

"No problem—I'll ride you, Joan. I have a car."

We'd reached the changing room, and Liz closed the door behind her. I took off the skirt, apron, and blouse, and she brought the same trunks as she was wearing, and another peasant blouse. Then, opening a locker, she took out a package of pantyhose. "They're beige—O.K.?" she asked.

"Oh my—and thanks, Liz."

"In the bar, bare legs get kind of cold at one o'clock in the morning. But, if you'll accept a suggestion from me, with what you've got to go inside this blouse, I'd leave the bra off."

"You sure about that?"

"Well, I do. It kind of helps with the tips."

"With me, tips are the main thing."

"And with everyone, Joan. Don't be ashamed."

And then, explaining: "In case you've been wondering, why I would want competition, when I've had it all to myself, well, it kind of works backward, there in a cocktail bar. Because, swamped with work, I've been slow, and in a bar, it's one thing you don't dare to be. They'd wait for food, but drinks to them are important. And when I slow down from being swamped, they get real sore about it. And when they get sore they don't tip. What I'm trying to say, beyond a certain point, a whole lot of people don't help, not with the tips they don't. Vice versa, you could say." And then, when I'd put on the pantyhose, trunks, and peasant blouse, which drew tight over two points in front: "You'll do. I'll say you're qualified."

"You're not bad yourself."

"O.K. for an old lady—pass in a crowd."

She was a lot better than that, and as to what she was actually like: I never did guess her age, but whatever it was, it was enough to give her gray hair all the way through—beautiful gray hair, silver almost, that she wore cut at her shoulders, and curled. She was medium in size, with features slightly coarse, I have to say, and yet damned good-looking. Her eyes were a light blue, and wise but not hard. And her legs were different from mine—where mine are round and soft, hers were full of muscle, but with keen lines and a graceful way of stepping.

She led on out again, to the dining room, to the foyer, and to the bar, where a blocky-looking man in a white coat was polishing glasses with a cloth and arranging them in neat rows. "Joan, Jake, Jake, Joan—she's our new girl, Jake. Go easy, she's never worked a bar before." With that, she headed off for the kitchen.

"Haya, Joan."

"Jake, hello."

It turned out that on alternate weeks, I was due in at four o'clock instead of five, to fix set-ups for Jake, as well as get the place ready, putting out Fritos in bowls, and setting the chairs down, where they'd been put up so the place could be swept. The sweeping was going on now, by a boy with a push mop, so I got at the set-ups first.

"First set-up is for the old-fashioned. You know what an old-fashioned is?"

"You mean the orange slices and cherries?"

"…Yeah, them." He gave me a long look, then went on: "And for Martinis?"

"I turn the olives out in a bowl and stick toothpicks in them."

"For Gibsons—"

"Onions, no toothpicks."

"O.K. Now, on Manhattans—"

"Cherries."

"No toothpicks if they have stems on them. But sometimes the wrong kind is delivered, and them without stems take picks. On Margaritas—"

"Salt? In a dish? And a lemon, gashed on one end, to spin the glasses in?"

"Speaking of lemon—"

"Twists? How many?"

"Many as three lemons make. Cut them thick, put them in a bowl, and on top put plenty ice cubes, so they don't go soft on me. I hate soft twists." He looked at me like I was a dancing horse or some other marvel. "You sure you never…?"

I explained: "My mother used to give parties, and my father fixed the drinks. I was Papa's little helper."

"Christ, you have a father—I should have known. Well, it takes all kinds, don't it?"

It was the sort of remark I could have taken poorly, but he was smiling as he said it, so I smiled back at him. "What else?"

"The Fritos—they're for free, and you keep the bowls filled at all times. They put the customers in mind of having a drink."

"You mean they're salty."

"I don't and you don't. I mean they're compliments of Bianca, and you know what's good for you that's what you mean, too."

"They're special from Mrs. Rossi."

"And don't you forget. She's a nut about it." He tossed his cloth down on the bar, untied his apron, and came around to my side. "Let me show you the rest."

He showed me my pocket totalizer, my cash register, and my book of slips, and explained to me how to keep the slips in separate piles, and then when a check was called for, to tote it up on the totalizer, present it to the guest, take his money to the register, put it in and ring up the amount of the check, then take out his change and bring it back to him. "And for Christ's sake don't make a mistake," he growled, looking me in the eye. "Bianca's easy on some things, like wind blowing free in the blouse, but on others, like clean fingernails and money, she's a bitch. You make a mistake, it's on you."

"I won't make a mistake."

I had just got the chairs down and was putting the Fritos out when Liz came back again, from where she'd been in the kitchen. "So let's split up our stations now," she said. "How you say we split it right down the middle and alternate: one week I'll take the near station, the one by the door, while you take the one near the men's room, next week, vice versa. Fair enough?"

"O.K., suits me fine. But this week you take the station next to the door, so you can greet them when they come in, the patrons I mean—they'll all be strangers to me."

"That's how we'll do it, sure," she said. Then:

"Got to go—here comes Mr. Four-Bits, always our first customer. You'd think, the way he rolls out his two quarters, they were solid silver, from the Philadelphia mint."

I looked, and Mrs. Rossi was bringing a customer in, an important-looking, middle-aged man in gabardine slacks and sport shirt. Liz motioned, and Mrs. Rossi started to seat him at her station. But when he saw me he stopped, stared, and said something. Bianca looked surprised, and brought him over to me. It was my first meeting with Earl K. White, and I was just as startled as Liz.

4

He was a tall man, rather pale, and obviously someone important. I went over, handed him a wine card, with of course the cocktail list facing, and asked: "May I get you something, sir?" He asked for a tonic on the rocks, without even opening the card, and when I turned to the bar, Jake was already opening a bottle, and putting it out beside a highball glass with one rock in it. "Hold on to your tray at all times," he said, "and watch the cork center. It's to keep stuff from sliding around, but if you're not used to it, tricky." I went back to the table, put down the glass and poured, and took the bottle back, throwing it into the box under the bar. Then I walked past Mr. Four-Bits to my place near the men's room. But he turned and motioned me to him. "You're new here?" he asked.

"Yes, sir—this is my first night…If you have to know, you're my first customer."

"What's your name?"

"Mrs. Medford."

At last, after watching it all day, it slipped out on me, but at once I corrected it. "Joan."

"You gave yourself away."

"…I already said it's my first night."

"I can't say I've found many cocktail waitresses called 'Mrs.' It sounds more like the way a lady announces herself."

"I am a lady, I hope."

"That may be; not every waitress is." He said it with a glance in Liz's direction. I couldn't imagine what he found unladylike in her deportment or manner and not in mine, unless it was that I had called him sir. We were wearing the same outfit, after all, with the same fraction of the buttons on our blouses unbuttoned and the same lack of concealing fabric underneath.

"The ones that I know are," I said. "And I imagine most of them are. Being a waitress and being a lady are not incompatibles."

"That's a very big word for a waitress."

"I'm sorry, sir, if you prefer smaller ones, let's say a person can be both."

"…Well, then, what do you want me to call you?"

"Whatever you wish, sir."

"Mrs. Medford?"

"…I admit in a bar it sounds a bit silly."

"I agree. I'd rather call you Joan."

"Then, please do."

We both were sounding self-conscious, and our eyes locked. His gaze wandered down to my legs, and then locked with mine again. I knew that, in spite of our small clash, or perhaps because of it, this man was attracted to me. I waited, and then, in a faintly personal way, asked him: "What do you want me to call *you*?"

He waited, while his mouth twitched in a smile, and then very solemnly said: "I'm Earl K. White the Third."

He spoke as though I should know who Earl K. White the Third was, and perhaps even fall down from surprise, but I'd never heard of Earl K. White the Third. However, hating to disappoint any man well-off enough for there to be three of him, I pitched my voice as though greatly impressed: "Oh? Really?"

"Yes. Now you know."

"Mr. White, I'm honored."

"Mrs. Medford, Joan, likewise."

Then, after looking me up and down once more, especially

down, he added: "If I may be personal, Joan, I'd say your husband's a lucky man."

I knew it was really a question, and I waited a moment before answering. Then: "Mr. White," I told him, "I don't have a husband—I'm recently widowed, I'm sorry to say. But I do have a child that I have to support, a little boy three years old, which is why I took this job, and came out in this outlandish garb. I may say I applied for work on the restaurant side, but then was told I was wanted in here, or more qualified for work in here, whatever it was. I don't myself quite know the reason for my transfer—unless they thought I looked well in the uniform. Or costume. Or lack of costume—whatever it is."

"Whatever it is, it's most becoming." Then: "Joan, I judge you've been through the wringer—may I express my sympathy? Belated, but sincere. I've been through the same wringer. I'm widowed too—my wife died a few years ago."

"Oh? Then I express my sympathy too."

"Thank you, Joan. Thank you very much."

It was all stiff, self-conscious, but we managed to get it said: I was free, and he was. Then, as though to switch to casual things, he said: "Beautiful weather we're having."

Now my mother had said to me once, "You'll be told: Don't talk about the weather. Joan, always talk about it. It's the one thing everyone has in common with everyone else, and often the only thing to talk about. Talk isn't always so easy—talk about what you *can* talk about."

"Oh it certainly is," I answered. "I read somewhere there are more quotations about June, about the weather we have in June, than about any other month. A day like today you know why."

"That's fascinating, Joan, I'll have to look it up in Bartlett."

Who Bartlett was I had no idea, though next day I found out. We talked along, about the difference a fine day makes, and then suddenly he asked for his check, and I went to the bar and wrote it. When I brought it to him, he took out a five-dollar bill and put it down, but when I reached for it he covered my hand and put it aside. Then he picked up the five, returned it to his wallet, and took out a twenty that he put down in its place. I took it to the bar, rang up 85 cents on the register, and took out his change, three fives, four ones, and 15 cents in nickels. Then remembering about the four bits, I put one of the ones back and took four quarters out. Then I put the fives, ones, and change on a pewter change tray that was there, and went back to the table with them. I confess it was in my mind, as a way of being on purpose quite personal, to decline the two quarters he'd give me—"Please, Mr. White, not from *you*." Because, I don't mind saying, a rich widower who liked me wasn't someone to treat as a customer. "I think of you as a friend," I was going to let myself stammer—but he crossed me up. When I put down the change he waved it off, being already on his feet. "That's even, Joan—thanks for a most pleasant visit. I'll probably be in tomorrow, and look forward to seeing you then."

I couldn't make myself give back $19.15, I needed it so.

He left, and I noticed for the first time a man in chauffeur's uniform waiting for him in the foyer. I knew I'd made a strike that could be important to me, but what stuck in my mind was: I wished I liked him better.

5

If Jake saw me stuffing the bills in my pocket, the pocket I found in my trunks, it didn't show on his face, but Liz saw me doing it, and gave me a squint-eyed look, that wondered at once what the meaning of it was. Maybe I wondered too, just a little. However, the time for wondering passed, as all of a sudden the place began filling up, and there was no time for anything except drinks. Of course, some of those people, instead of moving on to the dining room, decided to eat where they were, and I had to serve them dinner. For that, I had to meet the chef, a barrel-chested Lithuanian named Bergovizi whom everyone addressed as Mr. Bergie, so he could explain how things were done in the kitchen, especially how to "call it" for him, as he said. It had to be done in a certain way, especially on stuff like sauce—if the customer wanted it separate, like the *meuniere* on fish, I had to say "boat it," not "serve the sauce separate," or anything complicated. Or if the customer didn't want sauce I had to call: "Hold the sauce." I knew there was a reason for things like that, and put my mind on it to remember, but it was all quite a strain and soon, after all I'd gone through that day, I began to wilt. Jake noticed it, and whispered: "Take it easy, Joan. There's no rush—let 'em chaw on their Fritos."

It made me laugh, and helped, and it helped still more when Liz gave me a pat, telling me: "You'll get a break around eight, then go have dinner yourself—Mr. Bergie will fix you up." Still, they kept coming, as Mrs. Rossi kept bringing them in, being her own maître d', or maîtresse d', I suppose I should say. Around eight-thirty things slacked off and Liz told me to eat, and I did, seating myself at a folding table set up between the six-burner stove and the propped-open pantry door. It was the first proper meal I'd had in months. Mr. Bergie cut me a thick slice of roast beef, and I had it with a baked potato, a dish of vanilla ice cream I dipped myself from the freezer box, and coffee, and it freshened me, especially the coffee, so I felt I could go through the rest of the night.

I was doing all right until just before closing time, when a man with a party of six began to give out about oil, and said it with gestures, one of which swept every glass off the table onto the floor. I wanted to scream, and couldn't face getting that mess up. But then Jake was there with towels, and Liz was down on her knees, mopping up before I could start. I got down on my knees too, not being upset anymore. When the man paid his check, which with drinks and food for six had come to just about $50, he left an extra $15, and I split it with Liz and Jake, feeling warm and close and friendly. By the time we had it clear Mrs. Rossi locked the front door, toted the registers and counted the cash. Mine checked out O.K., and next thing I knew, I was in Liz's car, and she was backing out of the lot. I still had on my uniform, as she had suggested I wear it home, "so you can dress for work there tomorrow, and skip the locker-room bit."

We were halfway home, and she hadn't said too much. But then suddenly she started to talk. "Joanie," she began, "something happened tonight, that made me wonder about you. You know, how you feel about things."

"Liz, make it plain. What happened tonight? What are you talking about?"

"I'm talking about Mr. Four-Bits. One girl's tips are strictly no other girl's business, and girls don't tell what they get, even to other girls. Just the same, I happened to see what he gave you—a lot more than he ever gave me. Well, all right, you're less than half his age and pretty as hell, he's entitled to like what he sees. But, I notice you took it."

"…Well? Wouldn't you have?"

"Are you being funny?"

"Well, you would have, wouldn't you?"

"The point is, you did. And of course I wondered why. I mean I have that kind of mind. So, I get to it. Joan, do you take a broadminded view? I mean, when he ups and propositions you, you're not going to smack him down?"

"I hadn't got that far with it."

She stopped talking and kept on driving, but then started up again. "What I'm leading to, Joanie: I get propositioned, myself. Time to time, I mean. And some passes I don't turn down. Well? It's fifty bucks. So what I'm leading to: Often, the guy, the one that likes my looks, has a pal, and wants to know if I have a sidekick, some girl who would care to make it four. Well, Joanie, what do you say? The comment I got tonight, you stirred up plenty of interest, and the subject is bound to come up. So, hit the nail on the head, what do I tell that pair that asks? Do I have a sidekick or not? Or in other words, it's nice work if you can get it, and does it appeal to you?"

"You catch me by surprise. I never thought about—" Then: "You really do this? Let a man take you out and, and…"

"When opportunity presents, Joanie, and assuming I don't mind his looks."

"But don't you ever get…in trouble?"

"If you mean what I think you mean," she said, throwing my words back at me, "any girl can, whether there's money involved or no. You just have to know where to take care of it if it happens."

I thought back to my situation three years earlier, my ignorance of such matters. I'd lived a lot since then, and not all of it good, but I still was an innocent on some topics. "You can get that done here?"

"Here? No, of course not. But up in New York, if you know the doctor to call, and I do. But if you're careful it never comes up. Hasn't for me but once."

"I...I don't know what to tell you."

"O.K., take your time. Think about it, Joan."

And then, after perhaps three seconds: "O.K., you've thought it over, what do you say? Yes or no? You want one of them dates or not?"

By now, she had pulled up in front of my house, and sat there looking at me. And I sat looking at her, with a mixed feeling of love and terrible pity, that she'd even think of such a thing, and wondering why. In the bar she must have done well, as I was doing so far, and she was certainly good-looking enough to have a man of her own, without having to be dating strangers on the basis of passes made in a bar, by men she barely knew. And then suddenly, I thought I'd better tell her how things were with me, and why I couldn't say yes, "at least at this time." So I started off: "Liz, I couldn't. I just buried my husband today. I'm Joan Medford—the girl that was in the papers this week, that put her husband out, and—"

I got no further.

"...Oh! Oh! Oh! The one who died in the car wreck? And they said his wife was—oh!"

She was warm, tender, and wonderful, taking my hand in hers, kissing it, patting me on the knee, doing the things you would want. "I read about it," she said. "You don't have to tell me the rest—*and you're her*? You came down today, *and worked*?"

"Liz, I had to. I had to get money, quick."

"Well you got some, Joanie. I'm proud of you."

"I tried to do as you showed me."

"You did wonderful. Now Joanie, would it help if I came in

with you? I mean, put you to bed? Made you a cup of tea? Or—
you got some Scotch in the house?"

"I don't drink, Liz."

"Me neither. I got weaknesses, but not booze."

"Just let me sit here a minute."

"Sit all night if you want."

She kissed me when I got out, then waited while I unlocked the
front door before driving off. I went in and lit a candle, as of
course my lights were cut off, and started to count my money.
But then I collapsed into tears, as a crying spell hit me, not from
feeling bad, but from feeling so happy all over. That may make
no sense, but it did, in a way, because from feeling so utterly
sunk, so unable to think what to do, except to get some work
mowing lawns, here I was with a job, with friends that warmed
to me, and money, cash money, bulging my velveteen pocket, in
these silly trunks I had to wear. By candlelight I knelt, by the
side of my bed all alone, and counted the money I'd brought
home. With the $19.15 I'd got from Mr. White, my $5 share of
the last tip I had got, from the man who knocked over the glasses,
and the other tips, I had $61—an amount I couldn't believe.
And I had the prospect of making more the next day, the day
after that, the day after that, and as many days as I wanted. It
seemed too good to be true. I tried to remember Ron, how I
had felt for him once, when I'd first met him and he was at his
most charming, and I suppose I did manage to summon some
memories suitable to the day of a man's funeral—but my tears
of joy kept coming. At last I put the money under my pillow,
took off my trunks and blouse, crept into bed with no clothes
on, and slept.

6

Next morning I got up, made coffee for myself over the flame of a chafing dish, a skill I'd learned ever since the gas had been discontinued, and put on pants and a blouse. Then I sat down at the dressing table and wrote three checks, one to the gas company, one to the electric, and one to the phone. Two of them I put in a drawer, as I wouldn't have money to cover; but one of them, to the phone company, I put in my bag and I went out. I walked down to the bank, reserved $10, and deposited the rest, more than $50 in all. Then I walked up the hill to the phone company, which had offices near the bank. They sent me up to Mr. Wilson, on the second floor. I handed him my check, tucked into the last bill we'd received, marked "Third Notice," and asked him: "Mr. Wilson, how soon can the phone be turned on?"

"...Just a second. I'll see."

He left the room, but then in a short time was back. He sat down and pushed me his phone. "Will you dial your number?" he asked.

"Mr. Wilson, my phone is cut off. Perhaps I should have mentioned, it happened some time ago, when I didn't pay my bill, and—"

"Well, try it anyway."

I dialed my number. "Oh!" I yelped. "It's ringing."

"I thought it would."

He laughed, and I hung up so I could clap my hands, though I loved hearing the ring. He gave me a little pat on the arm, and once more I felt happy and friendly. Then I walked down the hill, crossed the street, and a half block up went into a luncheonette in the middle of a big parking lot, where I ordered breakfast—a big, real breakfast, of orange juice, fried eggs sunny side up with a slice of ham, buttered toast, and coffee. For the figure, it's not recommended, but for the soul, when you haven't eaten like that, at least at breakfast time, for so long you can't remember the last time you did, it's wonderful. I took my time, and chewed every bite. When she brought me my check, the girl asked me: "Didn't I see you last night at the Garden? Didn't you serve us our drinks? Me and my friend?"

"That's right, I remember. You were in the blue dress."

"First night out in a while."

"Did you find the service O.K.?"

"Little too good, I'm sorry to say—especially how well the friend liked it. He's not my boyfriend, exactly, but since he was taking me out, I could have done with a little less looking. Not that it was *your* fault."

"I'm sorry. I didn't notice."

"Well, he sure did. That boy liked you."

"They make us wear those things, you know."

"I imagine it helps with tips, from male customers anyway."

"It seems to."

She looked down at her own torso and shook her head. "And I'm working here. If I had what you have…"

I left her a dollar as tip. It wasn't her fault she couldn't fill out a blouse the way Liz and I could.

Back in the house I looked up Elizabeth Baumgarten in the phone book and dialed her number. When she answered I said: "Liz, this is Joan. I got my phone turned on, and in celebration thereof, called you first of all." She took it big and flung off a couple of gags, then said she'd stop by around 3:30 and run me down to work. I told her: "Make it three, so we can visit a little while," and she said she would. Then I set the alarm and lay down for a little nap, to let the breakfast digest. I got up just after two, put on light tan pantyhose, the trunks, flat-heel comfortable shoes, and a peasant blouse of my own, as the other wasn't fresh anymore, and needed a dunk in the basin. I was hanging it up on the shower rail when the doorbell clicked, with a knock following, and I skipped down the hall to answer. But instead of Liz it was Ethel. Her eyes opened wide at my costume. "Oh," I said. "Hello, Ethel."

"I'm here for Tad's things," she told me.

"Well come in, why don't you? Act sociable."

"...If he *has* any things, that is."

I didn't appreciate this crack, but I still played it friendly and took no notice. "Of course he has things," I assured her, motioning her inside.

"I only say so because you seemed to have so little, when I first came here on Sunday. It was truly a shock."

"So you said at the time."

She continued to speak, not bothering to face me, as she walked past me to the living room: "I mean, not even electricity, Joan! I don't see how you could live that way, how you could raise a child that way."

Before I followed I glanced at her car, which she'd put in the drive, to make sure Tad wasn't in it, locked up to bake in the sun. He wasn't, and I went in the living room. By then she'd taken a seat, but resumed her stare at my outfit, especially my trunks. "I see you've noticed my uniform," I said. "I've taken a job. I work in a cocktail bar—the Garden of Roses, down the street."

"...Joan, I'd be ashamed!"

"Of what? Working for a living?"

"There are livings that don't require you to dress like...a tramp."

"Find me one that'll have me and I'll apply. In the meantime, I'm earning good money and all I'm doing for it is bringing people drinks and a bit of food, and a smile to go with them."

"Might as well have nothing on but that smile."

"The more they admire what they see, Ethel, the more they tip—and tips are the object of the game. They have to be, when you have a little boy and have to pay board for him."

"You don't have to pay board, I've told you."

"Oh, but Ethel, I do. I can't be beholden to you."

She stared some more, then broke out: "Joan, don't you have any pride? If not for your own sake, Joan, you could think of Tad."

"You mean, to be a fit mother for him?"

"...Yes! That's what I mean, exactly!"

"And you're not the only one, Ethel. Would you believe it, some woman called up the police about it, talked to the officers who handled Ron's case, trying to get them to move, to have me declared an unfit mother. Can you imagine something like that? This woman even mentioned Joe Pennington—you know, that boy you spread rumors about, as being something more to me than just an acquaintance. Who do you suppose would have done a thing like that?"

She didn't answer, and I sat there kicking my foot. Then the doorbell spoke again, and when I opened the door Liz was there. She came in and I presented her: "Ethel, Miss Baumgarten, my very good friend. Liz, my sister-in-law, Mrs. Lucas."

Liz waved her hand, and as Ethel nodded her head, threw off the spring coat she had on, standing forth in her cocktail-bar outfit, which of course was identical with mine, except for the blouse not quite the same. Seeing Ethel's expression she said: "If the clothes kind of startle a little, Mrs. Lucas, they're O.K., we work in a ginmill, Joanie and I. We serve drinks in a cocktail bar, and our bunch, they kind of like legs. They shouldn't but they do. Mine aren't terrific, like Joanie's, but for an old lady, they'll do. At least, so I've been told."

"They're—quite striking," said Ethel.

"I'll get Tad's things," I said, "and then we can have some coffee."

I went back to the kitchen, started water in the chafing dish, then went in the little room that I had used as a nursery and got Tad's things from the chiffonier drawer. Most of them were clean, but in one corner were the things he'd had on since the day Ron got killed, and those I had in my hand when I took the clean ones, which I put in a grocery bag, back to the living room. I handed the bag to Ethel, waved the others, and told her: "These aren't clean, I'll wash them out and bring them Sunday, when I go over to visit my child—if I'm invited, that is."

"I'll wash them," said Ethel, reaching for them.

"No, I'll do it, of course."

"I'll wash them!" she snapped, and took them from me. "And how about his medicine, for the pain…?"

"All gone," I said. "Used up in the first two weeks."

"But Ron said the doctor gave you a month's worth!"

"It might have been a month's worth," I said, "if Ron hadn't continually aggravated things by pulling Tad around by the arm, or slapping him when he got mad."

"And you didn't buy more?"

"With what money?"

By that time Liz was camped down by the sofa, having a look at the broken leg. "I don't get this," she announced. "It's not any bust-off, Joan—it's a pull-off, has to be, as all the pins are here, and nothing's really been broken. Only time I've seen the like was in the bar when a drunk got to rolling around one night and gave a yank to a table leg."

"Oh, those things happen," I said.

Ethel said nothing, as of course Liz was so close to the true explanation, involving Ethel's brother, my husband, that it wasn't at all funny. I said: "I'll see if the coffee's coming on for ready," and went back to the kitchen. I made the coffee, put it in the pot, put sugar lumps in a bowl, and opened the last tin of condensed milk. But when I got back to the living room with it, Ethel was ready to go, and did, shaking hands with me, and bowing coldly to Liz. Liz was still in front of the sofa, sitting tailor-fashion on the floor, and when Ethel had gone, said: "I'll bring my do-it-yourself kit over and fix this thing—it'll be no trouble at all, just a glue job, with twenty-four hours in a clamp —I have the glue, I have the clamp, I have the book of instructions. The kit was a gift from my boyfriend, my regular boyfriend, that is, the one who comes on Sundays and pays my rent, kind of. At least most of the time. And if you think it funny he'd give me such a kit, so do I—but the real funny part is that he'd give me anything, so I'm thankful for small things." She saw me about to say something and interrupted before I could. "…And if you think it funny that I have a regular boyfriend when I told you I sometimes go with other men, too, picked up in the bar, well—so do I. I don't pretend to understand it. But I keep doing it, and I won't tell you it's just for the extra money."

"What else is there?"

"Their asking, I guess," she said. "They're so eager sometimes. It takes the curse off gray hair. You know what I mean, Joanie? At a certain age, we need assurances."

I set down the coffee things. "At any age, Liz."

"I suppose so."

She poured herself a cup, and I was glad to see her do it, since I hated for the milk to go to waste.

"Joanie, explain something to me, please."

"If I can. What?"

"It's about your sister-in-law."

"She's not too friendly, Liz. She blames me for what happened to her brother—my husband, Ron. And then there's my son. She's taking care of him now, supposedly to help me, but what she really would like is to keep him."

Liz nodded as though I'd just confirmed something she'd been thinking. "She didn't think I could see her, but I could, out of one side of my eye. And that bundle of soiled clothes, the ones you were going to wash that she grabbed out of your hand, she was holding them to her face, burying her nose in them, and smelling them, Joan, I'd swear that's what she was doing— I can't be mistaken about it. She was smelling your little boy's clothes, not the clean ones, the dirty ones."

"It doesn't surprise me at all."

"Well, what would make her do that?"

"She's hipped on him, Liz. She always was, but even more since Ron's death. I'm telling you, she's trying to steal him off me." I explained about Ethel's surgery, the hysterectomy I suppose it was, and she sat thinking that over. Then: "Are you willing, Joan? You want to give the boy up? Is that how you want it to be?"

"I'm here to tell you it's not."

"Then you got a thing on your hands."

"I know I have, but as of now I'm helpless to move in and block it."

"Why'd you let her take him in the first place?"

"She forced it," I said, "made it clear I could go along willingly or she'd call the state and have him taken away from me permanent, by showing them how we were living. Never mind that it was Ron that reduced us to it. She'd just show them we had no gas, no electric, no money in the bank, that I had no income and no prospect of earning any…"

"Well, she'd have been wrong about that."

"That's so," I said, "but now that I'm working, it means I

couldn't take Tad back even if Ethel were willing. Not while I'm out eight or nine hours a day, six days out of seven, and Tad still so young. He needs care and attention, and if I'm not around— I *have* to leave him with her, whether I like it or not."

"She's got it bad, Joanie."

"Don't I know it."

Liz had a second cup while I finished my first, and when I'd washed up she said we should be getting started, "so you get there by four o'clock. Jake's particular about his set-ups."

"O.K., but there's something I have to do first."

What I had to do was look up Earl K. White III in the phone book. I did, and he was listed, at least his residence was, on one of the streets of College Heights Estates, the swank part of University Park, but no phone. I looked in the District book, and sure enough he was there, in boldface type, with "Investment Secs" after his name. What that meant I didn't quite know, but I looked under that head in the yellow book, and lo and behold there was a big ad that went something like this:

Earl K. White III
Investment Securities
Successor to Earl K. White, Jr.,
And Earl K. White—
Three Generations of Financial Stewardship
Since 1913
MEMBER, NEW YORK STOCK EXCHANGE

That seemed to cover everything. At last, I knew who Earl K. White III was. I rejoined Liz, telling her: "O.K., let's not keep Jake waiting."

7

Mr. White came in at five on the dot, and Mrs. Rossi, or Bianca, as she now told me to call her, brought him directly to my station, giving him the same table as he'd had the day before. He ordered tonic as before, and of course Jake had the bottle open and was pouring by the time I got to the bar. I took it to the table, served it, disposed of the bottle, and took my place by the men's room, all in just a few seconds. But he beckoned me over, telling me: "If you tried, you could be more sociable, Joan."

"I come when called," I answered.

But we both laughed, and knew we'd been playing games. "I thought about you," he remarked. "All during the night."

"And perhaps I thought about you."

"How long have you been widowed, Joan?"

"...Four days."

"Four—what did you say?"

"Days—since late Saturday night. Sunday morning, really."

He stared, and I thought I'd better tell him a bit more, at least enough to avoid making a mystery out of it, which I saw no need to do. I went on: "I'm the Joan Medford you probably read about in the papers, who put her husband out of the house, and then was told next day he'd driven off in a borrowed car and crashed it on a culvert —or culvert headwall, I guess it was."

"Why—yes, I did read about it. I'm sorry." And then, as he seemed to remember more: "The police figured in the item I read about it—facing them isn't so good."

"You could say that, Mr. White."

And then, since I'd got that far, I went on: "We'd had an argument before I put him out, and I knew nothing about the car, the one a friend had lent him before going off for the weekend, that he drove off in. He was in pajamas, so he had no driver's license on him, or anything to identify him. So the police, after checking out the car plates, assumed he was Leland Brooks, the owner. But then, when Leland was finally found, at Annapolis where he was spending the weekend, and he came in to the undertaker shop where Ron was, and made identification, it was Sunday afternoon. Then they got me down there, and for two hours I had to face them, answering all sorts of questions. Did I know about the car? Why did I let him drive away? Didn't I know he'd been drinking?" I shook my head. "Did I know. He announced it at top volume when he walked through the front door and wouldn't stop announcing it until I brought him a beer, even after it woke our son and started him bawling. And then he was ready to take a belt to him, not just for this crying but for breaking a jar the week before, which he'd done by accident, and anyway it wasn't a special jar, we just used it to store change, back when we had enough change to be worth storing."

"…And you told all this to the police?"

"All of it, three or four times over. It was a young private and a sergeant, and I could see they weren't bad people, but they had a bad job to do, and they did it."

"You have my sympathy, Joan. I can't imagine anything worse."

"Oh, I can—and you could too if you'd ever been hungry, ever had to stretch a dollar to feed three people. The worst was that I couldn't possibly bury him, and had to ask help of his family. And on top of that was my little boy, and what to do about him. My sister-in-law took him, and to have any chance of getting him back I had to find work, at once. My coming here was accident—the police suggested this place, and from the bottom of my heart I thank them. It may seem queer to you, but to me it's been a godsend. I don't even mind these clothes."

"You shouldn't. They're very becoming."

"At least they fit."

"And rather well."

We both laughed again, but then he sat shaking his head, his face becoming quite solemn. "Bereavement's a terrible thing," he said, in a low, faraway voice, as though meaning it double extra. "It's not so bad in itself—a black shadow at the time, but it lifts, give it time, and becomes a memory. But always it has its after effects, which can be very ugly. Joan, my wife died five, almost six years ago, a blow I still haven't recovered from. But the worst of it wasn't her, losing her I mean, it was the effect her passing had on her children, my stepchildren, to transform them from a seemingly loving son and daughters into three vultures, who think nothing but money, money, money. Morning, noon, and night, they and the lawyers they have do nothing but hound me ragged, for their shares of their mother's estate. Joan, my wife left a will, leaving a fourth to me, and a fourth to each of them, but we had everything together and to divide it would mean the liquidation of my business, my property, my holdings of various kinds—it would take a year to do it and would leave me completely disorganized, so I'd have to start in business all over again—I'm simply not going to do it. They can wait till I die." And then, in a very dark and mysterious way: "Joan, there are things about me that you don't know, that perhaps you'll never find out. But I have to suspect, that the badgering these three have given me could well be the reason I'm in the condition I face for the rest of my life."

He was making me somewhat uncomfortable, talking that way of his stepchildren, and perhaps to change the subject I heard myself say: "Oh you don't have to tell me. Because the bereavement, the hours with police, even asking for help with the funeral were nothing to what came later." I then told about Ethel and her schemes to steal Tad from me, ending with how she'd acted that very afternoon. "I suppose I can understand it," I said. "My child is a joy to be with, and he is her flesh and blood, and all she has left of her brother. Just the same, allowing for everything, I'm sick at the idea she wants him, wants to steal him off me, I mean—and still don't know what to do. Just for now, I have to let her keep him, as without money I can't get him back and couldn't keep him myself if I did. Not without savings to fall back on, and with a mortgage hanging over me for good measure, which is how my loving husband left me. *But*—be thankful for little things. For the time being I have a job, and believe it or not, it pays. Not many treat me as you do, or did yesterday, I mean—but I'm not doing too badly. Compared with other things, other kinds of work, I mean, even allowing for this outfit I have to wear, I'm better off than I thought I was going to be."

I may have said more, especially about Ethel, all the time wishing I hadn't, as I wished he hadn't said what he did about his stepchildren and what rats they were—one of the first things I had learned at home was: Don't wash family linen in public, or with anyone except family. And I wish I could say I got to talking that way because of the way I felt, the way Ethel was bugging me, but it wouldn't be true. I did it because I knew without being told, from the way he was lining it out, it was the kind of talk that he liked. So, from the beginning, I knew there was something about him I didn't accept. But I also knew, would have been dumb not to know, that he was falling for me—that he was interested in more than just talk, and that I was playing for very big stakes. And for a stake like that you close your eyes to things—or at least a woman does. I was playing up to him, with whatever kind of talk it took. So when he paid his check with another $20, and waved the change at me, I said: "You don't have to do that. I'm doing all right, Mr. White. And I'd like to feel you're my friend—"

"I am your friend, Joan. I hope."

"Then friends don't tip each other—"

"If they're really friends, and one has more than the other, he tries to equalize—just a little bit. But don't worry, if it's so very little, *that* can be fixed."

We both laughed and I took the money.

That was Wednesday, and he came Thursday, Friday, and Saturday, each time leaving me $19.15. So, also on Thursday, I could put more money in the bank, and mail out my other two checks, the ones to the gas company and the electric company. And, still on Thursday, Liz came with her kit and glued the sofa leg on, putting a clamp on to hold it, so it would set firmly and hold. Friday she came and took the clamp off. Saturday, the men came from the gas company and electric company, to unlock my meters again. So Saturday, all of a sudden, from being a poor thing on Tuesday, with no job and no idea where to get one, I had a job, money in the bank, a living room that was decent again, gas, light, and phone—and had to do something about it. I mean, I wasn't a thing, I was living. I took a cab to Woodies, the big store at Prince George's Plaza, and bought Tad a tricycle, a blue one, more than I could afford but I wanted him to have the best in the store. And on Sunday I took a cab over to Ethel's and came in with a smile on my face.

Not that she acted so friendly toward me. She protested against the tricycle, seeming to resent that anyone but her might buy Tad toys while he was under her roof, and really being objectionable when I took out my checkbook to pay her, a week's board for Tad already boarded out and another week in advance, plus extra toward a new prescription for his pain pills. At first she refused to take it, but Jack Lucas, her husband, got in it, wanting to know: "When did we get so rich we don't need fifty bucks? Take it and thank her, Ethel, and stop acting silly with her."

So, she took it.

They lived in Silver Spring, perhaps six miles from me, in a house up on a terrace, and when I got there Tad was out back, with two other children, splashing in a backyard wading pool, a rubber thing with red stripes, that they'd filled with a garden hose. But of course the tricycle was news, and they all rolled it out front, where they took turns riding in it. Then Ethel, Jack, and I sat in the backyard, on recliners, and Ethel tried to be agreeable, unsuccessfully—and I tried, successfully. I felt positively angelic, even to her. Once, there were screams from the street, and I raced around the house to see what was going on. The little girl, who was a bit older than the two little boys, had ridden the tricycle off, so she was down at the corner with it, while the boys were screaming their heads off to her. Ethel, who followed me out, denounced the girl as a pest, explaining that she was always muscling in on what the other children had. But I knelt down, took her in my arms, and asked if she'd like a pair of skates. When her face lit up I promised to send her one. I promised the little boy a ball and glove, and Tad a new hat. Then everyone was happy, and I was the fairy godmother.

So, when we resumed our seats out back, I felt happy and pleased with myself. However, that didn't last long.

Ethel asked, her voice like ice: "Where did you get the money you're spreading around so generously to every child in sight? Working at your cocktail lounge?"

"That's right."

"I didn't realize a waitress gets tipped so well, just for waitressing. Or are you doing more now, on the side?"

"I'm sure I don't know what you mean."

"I'm sure you do."

"My customers have been generous with me, and I choose to share it. I won't apologize for it."

"It's not the generosity you should apologize for, but what you have to do to make it possible."

Her husband had a trapped looked on his face, as though he wished he could have been somewhere else, not watching his wife light into me.

Suddenly Tad was there, sidling up to Ethel. "What is it, darling?" she asked him.

He pulled her head down, and whispered.

She patted him, picked him up, and carried him into the house.

"You got to go, you got to go," said Jack.

He rode me home after that, very sociably, and I felt grateful to him. But for some reason my day wasn't nice anymore. Not because of what Ethel had said to me—she'd said as much before, and I could overlook it. But all because my son had gone to his aunt when he had to go to the bathroom, instead of me, his mother.

8

Whether the need to do something about it was vividly in my mind when Mr. White next came into the bar would be hard to say. But I certainly lost no time in making myself agreeable to him, offering him the cocktail list as always but adding: "But perhaps you don't really need it, if you're having the same as you regularly do."

"Please. It's very pleasant, Joan, having it remembered what I regularly have."

"Well, Mr. White, I wouldn't forget it so soon."

Jake had already opened the tonic and was filling the glass with rocks. I toted, then poured, taking the bottle back to the bar. Did I put an extra sway in my step as I walked away, to make my hips jog and my bottom twitch? I may have. I know I unbuttoned an extra button on my blouse before turning around, tray in hand.

"Joan, there is something I'm curious to ask you."

I rejoined him at his table, and swapped a full bowl of Fritos for the half-full bowl in front of him. It was no more than I'd have done at any of the dozen other tables in the bar. But perhaps I bent slightly lower doing it than was absolutely necessary. "What's that, Mr. White?"

"Earl, please."

"I'd feel too familiar."

"Please."

"Earl, then."

"I…"

"What is it? What do you want to ask me?"

"I'm not usually tongue-tied, Joan, I just find myself some-what distracted at the moment."

I smiled and lowered my gaze, and said softly: "Pleasantly, I hope?"

"Most pleasantly."

"But all the same, I don't want to make it hard for us to have a conversation, Mr.—Earl." I fastened up the lowest open button on my blouse. "Better?"

"From a certain point of view."

I walked around behind him. "Better still?"

"From the same point of view, yes."

There were no other customers in the bar just yet, and Jake had vanished into the storeroom on some errand. For the moment we were alone. I thought of what Ethel had accused me of, and of what Liz had proposed, and about how physically unap-pealing this man was to me—tall and ungainly, pale and middle-aged. But I thought, too, about Tad, sleeping in Ethel's home, her kisses comforting him instead of mine when he cried out in the night, her face the one he woke to each morning, and I knew I'd do anything to have him back.

I leaned over Mr. White's shoulder from behind, reaching forward to polish a spot on the table with a napkin, as though wiping up a spill. Through the thin fabric of his shirt and the thinner fabric of my blouse, my breasts pressed warm and heavy against his shoulder blade.

I heard his breathing change, becoming rapid, even ragged.

"There was something you wanted to say, Earl?"

He swallowed. "You make me so excited I can't talk."

I stood upright again, and came around to face him once more.

His face was red, less like a blush than a man suffering after long exertion. He took a swallow of his tonic. It was a minute before he regained his usual color—that is, his usual pallor—and his breathing resumed its normal rhythm. "I like you, Joan. I hope you know that. Perhaps I like you too much. It's not good for me to get too excited."

"Why not?"

"Can we just say doctor's orders and leave it there?"

"I don't know if I'll be able to leave it there, if it means we need to stay at arm's length."

"Joan, you must."

"We'll see," I said. Then: "What did you want to ask me?"

He took another swallow. "Your husband, who died this past week—how long were the two of you married?"

"Four years," I said. "Just under."

"…And your son is three, you said?"

"That's right. Just over."

"And how old are you?"

"Twenty-one."

"I see."

"What do you see?"

"I just wanted to understand your situation better, Joan."

"And do you, now?"

"You were seventeen…?"

"A little over," I said.

"And can I ask why you married him?"

"I'm sure you can guess."

After some time he said: "It's not a good reason, Joan."

"I found that out."

"…You don't like to talk about it?"

"Would you?"

"I would like to know what happened, as perhaps I can help."

"I was in Washington, waiting to start a job. Ron was there, too, living in the same apartment building. He had a record-spinner in his apartment and we would slip over there when we had nothing else to do. Of course we quickly found other things to do—and then I had to get married. That's all. You need to understand, I was happy about it at the time. But alas, Ron had to get married too, and he wasn't happy at all. He hated it. He hated it, he hated me, and he hated our little boy. His family hated me too, but didn't hate little Tad, especially Ron's sister didn't. So she has him now, and I have this job."

"Well, don't hate the job."

"Hate it? I was down on my knees the other night, thanking God that I had it."

"After all, it introduced us. You give me something to look forward to each evening, which I haven't had in a long time, not since my wife died."

There came a pause, while I stood there before him, holding my tray balanced on one hand, the half-filled bowl upon it. We neither of us said anything.

"Is the situation really so dire?" he asked. "With your son and your sister-in-law, I mean."

"Yes," I said simply. But then, not wanting to walk away on a sour note, I smiled and said: "But things are looking up. Thanks to you especially. Each night brings me one small step closer to my goal."

"But only a small step, Joan. I'd like to do more."

"Well, then, we're even, because I'd like to do more for you as well."

I was surprised to see a look of pain cross his features. But I couldn't ask him about it because Bianca appeared then with another man on her heels, and I recognized him at once, even out of uniform.

*

Bianca seated him at a table in my station, the small one at the far end of the room.

"Mrs. Medford."

"Sergeant Young—can I thank you again, for suggesting I come here, for recommending me to Bianca, or vice versa, whichever is the right way to say it?" I handed over the wine and cocktail list, though obviously he knew the Garden better than I did and probably already knew what he liked to have.

"I'm glad she had an opening for you, and that you took it." He handed back the card. "You can ask Jake to make me up a smash."

Jake mixed a whiskey sour and poured it into a highball glass with some muddled mint leaves at the bottom. Sergeant Young took a long sip and set it down, then looked me over from head to toe. This time I didn't stiffen. A week can make a difference.

"Mrs. Medford, I came partly to see how you are doing, and partly to sample Jake's handiwork—but also because there's something I want to let you know. It regards your case, and the matter of your husband's death."

"I thought that was all behind us," I said.

"It ought to be, and I wish it was. If it was up to me it would be. But Church—you remember Private Church—he's young and eager and stubborn, and out to make a name, and for some reason he's not satisfied with the verdict of accidental death."

"Why?"

"They train you at the academy to find crimes, Mrs. Medford. When you're new in the job, you never want the answer to be that there wasn't one. Let a few years pass and you know better —you're thankful when a case can be closed without fuss. But he hasn't had those years yet and is still burning to solve murders."

"And he thinks Ron was—"

"He thinks we should keep the investigation open. He didn't even want to come tell you about your sister-in-law's call last Tuesday, but I convinced him it was the fair and proper thing to do, seeing as how the accusation against you was so clearly false."

"For that I thank you. But—what can I do about the rest?"

"It's not a question of your doing anything, just be aware that as far as the police are concerned, the matter's not closed."

It shook me, even though I knew I'd done nothing wrong, that no amount of investigation could show I had. You hear stories of people being railroaded, of innocent men and women sent to the chair. I asked: "What's he got to be unsatisfied about?"

"Nothing, if you ask me. But he doesn't like how some of the facts line up. Your husband was a heavy drinker—we got that from all the interviews we did—and he'd been drinking quite a lot that night, yet he was sober enough afterward to manage a drive home of more than forty minutes, in the dead of night, on some fairly twisty roads, without any mishap. Why, then, after you put him out of the house, does he crack up the car just ten minutes from home—presumably no more tired, no more drunk, the road no darker?"

"It was raining by then," I said. "And we'd been arguing—he might have been distracted."

"You see, now, that's exactly what I told him." Sergeant Young spread his hands. "But—all the same. Church insisted that the car be checked for signs of tampering, he asked the medical examiner who performed the autopsy about any signs of violence to the body that might not have been caused by the accident…"

"And?"

"And nothing. None of these inquiries turned up anything. But he still insists we not close the file."

"Aren't you his boss?"

"His partner, Mrs. Medford. It's not the same thing."

"So: what does this mean for me?"

"You might have to answer some more questions, at some point. You might be asked to sign paperwork permitting your husband's body to be exhumed."

"Exhumed!"

"I'm sorry, Mrs. Medford." He genuinely seemed to be.

"It's a horrible thing to suggest," I told him. "But if it has to be—O.K. I've got nothing to hide. He can ask all he wants." The tremor in my voice gave the lie to the confidence I was trying to portray.

Sergeant Young leaned across the table toward me and dropped his voice. "I wish you could be spared all of this, Mrs. Medford. Really I do. You don't deserve it after what you've been through. Your husband drank, and he ran off the road, and he was alone in the car when he did it. Even if you did have a hand in it somehow—"

"Sergeant Young!"

"—I say *even* if you did—"

"I didn't!"

"—but *even if you had*, I wouldn't like to see you hounded for it, much less punished."

"Please don't say anymore. You make me very uncomfortable."

"I regret that very much, Mrs. Medford. My intent was the opposite." His eyes held mine, and I could see kindness in them. Or what I thought was kindness—you can never be certain. "As I say, they don't teach it at the academy, but you learn it on the job: not every man's death is a crime."

I was relieved to see I had other customers to serve now. Making apologies, I headed for a table of three men in business suits, and felt enormous relief when they placed an order for club sandwiches to go with their drinks, since it gave me an excuse to retreat to the kitchen, to call it to Mr. Bergie.

I stayed in the kitchen as long as I could. When I got back to the bar, the sergeant was gone, having left behind just the mint leaves in his glass and a dollar tip.

9

I come now to Tom Barclay, but before I tell about him, what he did to me and what I did to him, I have to tell about our pants, the hot pants Liz went out and bought, for her and me to put on, without telling Bianca we would, thereby causing a situation. It might sound frivolous, coming on the heels of such serious matters as potentially being accused of murder—but everything else stemmed from it, however trivial it might have seemed at the start.

It was the first week of July, and murderously hot in the Garden, even with air-conditioning. That was unusual in Hyattsville, because Prince George's County doesn't have it hot like in Washington, or in Montgomery County in Maryland, alongside Prince George's but north of it; and vice versa, not such cold weather in winter. But we had it hot this time, and not being used to it, our clientele was feeling it more than some other clientele might. And of course all the girls were feeling it, especially Liz. During a lull one night she said to me: "Joanie, not to get personal, but are you getting damp, like? In a certain intimate place? That we don't mention in mixed company, but between girls could be called the crotch?"

"Liz, it's these velveteen trunks—"

"They're nothing other than *murder*—"

"And, Liz, the pantyhose make it still worse."

"Joanie, we're doing something about it, but don't ask Bianca's permission, because she could say no for some reason, and I'm not sure what I'd do about it. I could blow my top, but don't want to. You know what I mean, Joanie? I like it here."

"What are you going to do?"

"You'll see."

So I saw, because next night here she came in with four pairs of chambray hot pants, in the same color the velveteens were, crimson. Or almost the same color—they were really more like maroon, which of course had some black mixed in, instead of blue. When I'd paid her for my two, one to wear, the other to wash overnight, she led the way back to the locker room, where we made the switch. "And Joanie," she whispered, when we both had the velveteens off, "we take off the pantyhose too. And we don't put them back on."

"Are you sure we shouldn't ask Bianca?"

"No, Joanie, we should not."

"Why not? Why go looking for trouble?"

"That's it, she might say no."

And when I'd peeled the pantyhose off, and had put the hot pants on, pulling them up over skin, she said: "And, with the legs you got, Joanie, it could also be a nice feature. It could attract trade, you know what I mean."

"Speak for yourself, why don't you?"

"O.K., then, O.K."

Under pantyhose I wear panties—there's two schools of opinion about it, but decency, it seems to me, as well as personal cleanliness, wants that layer of silk, in against your personal parts. So, silk panties inside, chambray pants outside, both kind of loose, don't forget—and topside the peasant blouse as I always wore it before to go out on the floor, when who should come in but Bianca. We had it hot for some minutes—she didn't really have a good objection to offer, but insisted she should have been asked.

I said: "O.K., then we ask."

"And the answer, Joan, is no."

Liz cut in: "No, Bianca, on this we don't ask you, we tell you. Did you hear what I said?"

Bianca was looking furious, but I could see her sense of affront warring with her native preference to give in when pressed. Liz must have seen it, too, and pressed harder.

"O.K., then, we strike. As of right now, if you say we have to wear those velveteens in this heat, we're on strike. We're going to letter us up some signs and parade up and down in front. And we'll wear these when we do it."

"But those hot pants'll get wrinkles in them," Bianca said. "All pointing front and center and down. They won't be decent."

"Wrinkles are good for business. Wrinkles like you say we'll have." Liz went on: "Anyhow we *won't* have wrinkles, Bianca, these pants are made out of chambray—chambray the shirting material, made on purpose not to get wrinkles." She pulled out the label on her extra pair. "Hey, these are Burlington pants. Wake up—Burlington wouldn't make wrinkles."

It gave her the excuse she needed, to save face: "Then—I guess it's O.K."

"Then, Bianca," I told her, "we graciously call the strike off."

"O.K., Joan."

She kissed me, and Liz gave a little cheer, and that was the end of the matter.

So I thought.

I guess it was 11:30 that night, when Tom came in with his friends, three other guys and two girls, the men all young and rugged and both the women beauties, and all of them half crocked when they got there. Liz had overflow business, and Bianca gave them to me, putting them in a booth, which made a pretty tight fit. It was so tight that Tom had to push one girl in just a little bit tighter before wedging in himself, on the left side of the booth as I faced it, which of course put him next to me, one leg jutting out into the aisle, when I stood in to serve. He grinned naughtily at me, in a way clearly meant to make my heart race, and it annoyed me that, being a rather handsome grin, it did, just a little. Then they all began ordering doubles—bourbon and ginger ale, I suppose the worst combination ever, not only to make them all drunker, but also to make them sick. However, Bianca said go along, give them what they wanted. "He's an old friend, Tom Barclay is, so don't hurt his feelings, please." I tried to imagine how this young buck with the rakish grin could be an old friend of a woman Bianca's age, and I suppose it showed in my face because Bianca said, "His father was a regular here from the time my husband built the place. Tom's grown up here."

He didn't seem to have grown up too much, judging by the way he was carrying on with his friends. But Liz got in the act, saying how nice he was, "except of course when slopped, but even then no worse than somebody else. Who is nice slopped?"

"I couldn't think of anyone."

Serving drinks to the slopped is no work to write home about, no matter how nice when sober. The girls got louder and louder, and the guys more personal with me, meaning they said things no one should say, to any girl any time anywhere. But Tom, being next to the aisle and to me, didn't confine it to saying. He also did some doing, pawing me over whenever I came to the table, especially around the bottom, which he patted a number of times. I fixed that by stepping away, and no great harm was done. But then, as I was reaching across to pour one of the girls her drink, he put his hand on my leg, on my bare leg, above the knee on the inside, and began sliding it up. You can see now why I've gone into such detail, about the hot pants, the silk panties underneath, and how loose they both were. I'm trying to say I all but turned to ice, and reacted automatically: I clamped both legs together, so his hand couldn't move, and at the same time turned away, on my heel or something. But that pulled his hand around too, and I suppose threw him off balance, because all in the same split second, there he was on the floor, pulled out of the booth when I turned. Then, in a flash, there was Liz. And then, there was Bianca. It was she, not me, who saw what the fall had done to him—reacted on his stomach, so he was holding on to his mouth, gulping and gagging and trying not to throw up on the floor. And I was standing back, his hand off me at last, wondering what I should do.

It was one of his friends, sliding out of the booth, who got him to his feet and began rushing him back to the men's room, growling into his ear: "Not here, Tommy, not here! Hold it! Hold it three more steps, and then let it come, the whole goddam bellyful!"

He got to the men's room without letting go in the lounge, and after a long moment of silence, somebody laughed and conversation went on. Bianca, for once in her life, showed some spine, and said to the bunch at the table: "You've all had enough. When you've drunk out, you can get. I said get, I mean get the hell out."

She came, stood by me, and waited while Jake went back in the men's room. He came out and came over. "We're in luck," he reported. "He let go all right, five and a half gallons—but in the toilet. He flushed it, and not none went on the floor."

He went back to the bar.

The friend came out of the men's room, and rejoined his other two friends and the girls.

Then at last, here came Tom.

He started for the booth, but changed his mind and sat at a table, the same one Mr. White sat at every day when he came. I brought him a cup of hot coffee from the kitchen, black, and said: "Maybe this will help."

"You bet," he whispered. "Thanks."

He sipped it, flinched at how hot it was, then sipped again. He kept on sipping until it was all gone, then wiped his mouth with a cocktail napkin. He took out a pocket comb and combed his hair, and then picked up the napkin again and wiped his face, where it was covered with sweat. "Feel better now," he said with a smile more subdued than the grin he'd given me before, but no less handsome, and don't think he didn't know it.

"Wouldn't you like a little more coffee?" I said.

"No, I'm O.K. now."

"You sure you are?"

"Oh yeah. I feel good now."

"Then in that case—"

I stood off and let go at his cheek with one hand, I guess on my right-hand side, then with my other hand on his right—on his left and his right. Then I let go all over again, as he half stood and tried to grab my hand. But I yanked them clear and kept on slapping, with everything I had. The guy who had gone to the men's room with him came diving over and grabbed me, "wrapping me up" as it's called, but I jerked loose and let him have it too, so he staggered and fell. Then I turned back to Tom, and really went to finish him off, and trying to duck me he fell too, beside his friend on the floor. By then, as Liz told me later, the whole place was in an uproar, with Bianca grabbing at me, and Jake grabbing at me, everyone grabbing at me, trying to make me lay off. Of course, with Tom on the floor, I had to lay off, and did. But it was some seconds before I realized what Bianca was saying, as she kept backing away from me, where I must have made a swipe at her too. "You're fired!" she kept screaming at me. "You're fired!—now get out, you get out of here! Didn't you hear me? I said get out!"

By that time I'd come to my senses, a blend of indignation on the one hand and shame on the other; that, and rage at myself for losing my temper and, with it, the job I needed so badly. I'd told myself I'd do anything to get my son back—but one drunk's wandering hands had been enough to make me a liar. I cursed my temper as I headed back to the locker room.

I'd come to work in my uniform, but I'd worn a spring coat to hide it, and I had left some other clothes in my locker besides—the denim pants that I'd worn that first day, and a plain white linen top. I was there, peeling off, when Liz appeared, and she began taking her uniform off too. "She's not doing it to you, baby! You hear what I said? I told her—told her to her face she's not. So we're both out, same like. It's how it always winds up, these goddam jobs in a ginmill, but tomorrow we'll look up another."

Then Bianca was there, and Liz let her have it direct, with what she told me but more, expressed in potent language, at which Liz was quite good. And Bianca just stood there and took it, by the benches in the middle, while I kept on changing my clothes. And then lo and behold, who should be there but Tom. He looked hangdog and pale, but passably sober now that he had some coffee in him, and perhaps my slaps had knocked some of the drunkenness out of him as well. "What's going on?" he wanted to know.

"What do you think's going on?" Bianca answered. "I'm sorry, Tom. But the kind of help I get now, these things can happen, and do. Please overlook it, this once. It won't happen again, I promise you."

"I asked what's going on?"

"She's fired, that's what's going on."

"No, Bianca, she's not. Not over a smack or two."

"A smack? She was giving it to you like Floyd Patterson in the fifth round, and not only you. She'd have decked me if I hadn't stepped back at the right moment."

"But you did."

"Your friend didn't, and got a right to the jaw."

"From a southpaw," Tom said. "He'll recover."

"Listen, Tom, I can't have a girl in this place that treats you the way she did. Treats any customer like that, but especially you. That—"

"Goddam it, I said she's not fired." He advanced on us both and Bianca shrank away.

"She'll apologize, and it won't happen again. Isn't that right?"

"She's not apologizing for anything," Liz shouted, but I put a hand on her arm.

"I was out of line, Bianca, and I'm sorry. I lost my temper."

Liz was having none of it. "Joanie! I saw what—"

"Oh, he deserved it, and worse. But I still shouldn't have done it."

"Bianca?" Tom said. "I'm satisfied, are you?"

"Three broken dishes! And a stain in the carpet—"

"I'll pay for it."

"I can't take your money, Tom—"

"*I'll pay for it.*"

She looked as though this might finally be her breaking point, the time she put her foot down and wouldn't be moved. But finally she muttered, "O.K., O.K., Tom. If you want it that way."

"She stays?"

"If she controls that temper in the future."

Liz snapped: "How about if Tom here controls his hands? And after I vouched for you, too!"

That began another round of it. It took us ten minutes to get it all settled down, with Tom leading Bianca back to the bar and Liz and I changing back into our uniforms. When Liz and I went back there, things were going as usual, only with Bianca serving the drinks as Jake mixed them. In a half hour or so we closed, but when Tom and his party went, he still hadn't paid his check, never mind the extra for the damage I'd caused. "Don't worry," Bianca told me, still mad, it seemed. "He promised he will. You won't be out anything."

"You bet she won't," Liz told her. "Did you hear me?"

"Liz, I heard enough for one night."

10

Next day nothing was said, by Liz when she drove me to work, by Bianca after I got there, or by Jake when I got ready his set-ups, about what had happened the night before, somewhat I confess to my relief, though the fact that nothing was said meant I was still in the doghouse. Things went along as though nothing had happened at all, until lo and behold, who do I see sitting there, around eleven o'clock at night, at the same table he'd been at, the one Mr. White always sat at, looking at me, but the man who had grabbed my leg. I asked: "Can I serve you something, sir?" as though I'd never seen him before.

"Fizz water," he answered. "Seltzer. Straight."

I brought it, and he said: "And, my check, please. From last night. I should have paid and forgot."

I had it, under an ashtray, at the end of the bar, and got it for him. It was forty some dollars, almost fifty. He put down two twenties and two tens. I handed one of the tens back, but he pushed it at me again. "For you," he said. "I forgot you last night, too. Or at least, forgot to pay you."

I put the $10 down again, and told him: "I'll get you your change," and did, putting a dollar and something, forty or fifty cents in silver, on the change tray in front of him. He pushed it, with the $10 added again, toward me, telling me: "I said, that's for you."

"Sir, I'm sorry: I want nothing from you."

"...That how you treat an old friend?"

"Sir, you may be Bianca's old friend, but you're not mine—

not an old friend or any kind of a friend. I don't care for your money, and frankly I don't care for you."

I went back to my station, but he followed me over. I noticed some customers had started to stare, as perhaps I'd been louder than I'd needed to be. Quieter, I told him: "Will you please go back to your place? You're attracting attention here."

"I have something to say to you."

"You have nothing to say to me."

"As an old friend, I have."

I led on back to his table, and he followed, at last sitting down again. To put an end to the wrangle, I said: "What is it you wish to say?"

"I want to apologize, for not knowing you at first—last night I'm talking about. I'd never seen your face, you see, and didn't know it was you till I took a flash at your legs, from where you'd tossed me on the floor. They're so beautiful I knew you then. They're the most beautiful legs in the world—anyway, the most beautiful I ever saw."

I could feel my face getting hot, and asked him: "Can I serve you something else, sir?"

"After last night, I think I'd better stick to seltzer for a while." Then, staring down at my legs—my bare legs, don't forget, as I was wearing the chambray hot pants Liz had bought me the day before—he half whispered, as though really shook: "They're really quite unforgettable, Mrs. Medford."

"…How come you know my last name?"

"I said: We've met before."

"We haven't—I've never seen you before."

"It's possible you didn't notice me that day—but we met, I assure you. You live in a bungalow, just up a ways from this place. I called for you there, took you home there, and stayed by your side in between."

"…When was this?"

He named the day in June, and I felt the blood leave my face, for it was the day Ron was buried. I stared at him, and suddenly asked: "Who are you? And what is this, anyway?"

"Barclay's my name," he said in a casual way. "Thomas Barclay —Tom. I took the place of a friend's son, Jim Lacey's son Dan, who couldn't respond to the undertaker's call because he'd been out with me the night before. We'd gotten to drinking, I'm afraid—and you've seen for yourself how that can end up. But if Dan had simply failed to show, he'd have gotten the one more black mark the school had told him he couldn't afford— in a word, he'd have been expelled. So his father asked if I would sub in: go for you in the car, pick you up and ride you over to the cemetery that day, and then ride you back. I didn't much want to, I'll admit, but his father's an important man and I did it. And I was awfully glad I did. When you waved me good- bye, then blew me a kiss from the porch—"

"*I?* Blew *you* a kiss? You blew one to me, I recall, but I did no such thing."

"I'm here to tell you you did. I couldn't see your face as you had on a veil. I never did see it, that day. But I saw your hand move, under it and out."

"Do you hear? I did not blow you a kiss."

"I'm sorry, I was sure you did."

"I may have fussed with the veil."

"But you did see me blow you one?"

"I couldn't very well help it. And I confess I was greatly sur- prised. It seemed a piece of insolence, to a woman bereaved as I was."

"I wouldn't have done it if you hadn't done it first. It was only polite to respond in kind."

"I see, so you were being polite."

"If that makes you happier to receive it, certainly, let's say it was politeness."

"I'd believe it more if you hadn't made so much just now of how unforgettable my legs are."

"Can't a man have two reasons?"

"He can have as many as he wishes. It's no concern of mine."

"Mrs. Medford, I apologize. I've made a terrible impression. I'd like to make it up to you. But I see here is not the place to do it—not with you waiting on me, and people watching. What would you say to my taking you out? Somewhere private, when you get through, some place where we can talk and get better acquainted."

"Thank you, that wouldn't please me."

He had a way of smiling, a way of holding his head cocked slightly, that defied you to dislike him. "It might. You never know."

I struggled not to show any response. It was more of a struggle than it should have been. My heart had been warring with my head since the first moment I'd seen him, or perhaps it was something lower down inside me than my heart, and the battle wasn't over yet. "Will there be anything else?"

He put up his hands in surrender. "What do I owe you?"

"I'll get you your check for the seltzer."

Taking me home that night, it was Liz who began talking about him. "Not to be nosey," she said, "but did Tom Barclay settle that check? The one he walked out on last night?"

"The young man I slapped, you mean?"

"I'd say you more or less beat him up, but yes he's the one I mean."

"Yes, he paid it."

"I saw him, drinking seltzer for a change."

"And quite an improvement, I would say."

"He really is O.K.," Liz said, and drove along a while further. "Look, I saw what he did. And I'd have been hot, too. I hate that kind of stuff, always have, always will. It's one thing if they pay for the privilege, but…" She smiled over at me. I had a hard time smiling back. "But, boys will be boys, way I look at it—they got hands, and what God gave them to use, they're going to use come hell and high water—nothing's going to stop them, let's face it. *But*, if they apologize, if they show they got some respect, then O.K., life can go on—no use being sore. What I'm trying to say is, now he's been in, now he's apologized, you could think that guy over, Joan. I mean, for kind of a steady, go out with him after work, maybe ask him up to the house, you might like it, just for a change. And who knows? It might really lead you somewhere. Things like that happen, occasionally. I wouldn't smack him out."

"You trying to sell me this guy?"

"He's hardly unpleasant to look at, and he's got prospects. You could do worse, Joanie."

"And who says he's sold on me?"

"He could have done some talking. His talk could have got to me. O.K., then, I spill it: He told one of the guys last night he'd met you before—and that you made quite an impression on him. Supposedly he didn't realize it was you in the Garden, first off, but then from your legs he knew you. I don't get it, Joanie, why your legs, not your face—"

"He escorted me to Ron's funeral."

"And why wouldn't he know your face? It's pretty enough, I'd say. If I was a guy, I wouldn't forget it, I don't think."

"I was wearing a veil."

"Oh? Then it checks out, Joanie!"

"Yes, he was telling the truth. He took me."

"O.K., then, I'd think him over if I was you."

"Why? Is he anybody special? Or just because you and Bianca have known him since he was a pup?"

"He's nobody special—not yet. But he's one of those you just know will be. Tom Barclay's got an ambition that means some-thing. He's got all sorts of big ideas."

"Like what?"

"I don't remember them all. There was one about clearing all the nettles out of Chesapeake Bay using the hot-water over-flow from one of those atomic energy plants."

"That's his idea? We'd all be irradiated in no time."

"Well, he's had others."

"Any that succeeded?"

"Some he said have come close."

"He said."

"Don't count him out," Liz said. "He's a thinker, our Tom, and one of these days he'll think up something that'll turn the world on its ear."

"I'll wait till he does."

"Oh, then it'll be too late! He'll be in such demand!"

"I'll stand my chances."

"You don't like him at all?"

"…I could stand to look at him."

"That's the spirit."

"But Liz, he put his hand—"

"—where you've put it many a time yourself, let's not kid ourselves. There are worse things than a handsome man with his hand down there."

I lay there in bed that night, thinking him over. If he really did have prospects, that might put things in a different light, though of course 'prospects' was only a way of saying he might some-day have some fraction of what Mr. White already had for sure today. At the same time, he did have, in spades, what Mr. White did not, what we might term a physical appeal, not just being good looking and young but having a presence to him, a scent almost, that took something loose inside a woman and coiled it up tight. And I thought, perhaps it does make sense, what Liz said on the way home, that if they apologize, then life can go on, and no use being sore. I began feeling less bitter towards him. But then all of a sudden I thought: When did he apologize? I thought over the whole conversation, and remembered his apologizing for not knowing me until he looked at my legs, but for what he did he never apologized at all, and fact of the matter, never even brought the subject up. And then I wondered: Why? Why, if he did something like that, that calls for an apology if anything ever did, didn't he come out and say it? It seemed there had to be a reason. Matching it in with the fact that he made me a pitch, tried to date me up for the night after I got through work, it had to mean something, it couldn't be accident, something he didn't have manners to do, or forgot about, or would have said if something else hadn't come up. I mean, it was deliberate, had to be. I slept all right, didn't lie awake over it, and yet it was there, whenever he crossed my mind.

II

He was in several times, always alone, always ordering seltzer, and always taking the same table, the one Mr. White had sat at a few hours before. And always he pitched some more, that we should go somewhere, after the Garden closed, and as he said, "get better acquainted." I waited and waited and waited, that he should bring up the subject, of what he had done to me, and say he was sorry for it, but he never did, not once. And, naturally, it wasn't something that I would bring up myself. But on going out with him, I kept putting him off. I would say, "Give me a raincheck, please. There's things in my life that hurt, and I'm not quite over them yet. Little later on, I may like to go out with you. Just right now, I'm not going out with anybody." Something like that—just what, I'm not really quite sure. Because something happened at that time that stood my life on its head, and kind of mixed things up in my mind, as to just what happened, and how.

It was an afternoon like any other, so far as I knew at the time. I'd just got done filling the bowls on all the tables when here came Mr. White, so prompt you could set your watch by when he'd come in. And I brought him his usual order, then stood keeping company with him, expecting the conversation to be his usual, what louses his children were, and my usual, the thing I had on my hands, with Ethel—which I didn't like myself for, but kept banging at just the same. But today he just sat there sipping his drink, looking out toward the foyer, and not saying much, about his children or anything. And then, all of a sudden: "Joan, could you be dressed and ready, eleven o'clock tomorrow morning, if my driver calls for you? To take you on an errand that will be to your advantage?"

"...What kind of an errand?"

"You'll see. I have a reason for not telling you in advance—a very compelling reason, one I'd rather not discuss, but that I think you'd accept if you knew what it was."

"Well you're certainly mysterious about it."

"If you knew why, I'm sure you'd not be offended."

"Be ready to go at eleven?"

"That's it. Jasper will call for you."

"I'm flying blind, but—"

"You'll not regret it, I promise you."

"Then if you say so, O.K."

"Fine. Fine. Fine. And, Joan, if you'll have a deposit slip with you? Your personal deposit slip, from your bank. One of those things in the back of your checkbook?"

"...What is this, Mr. White?"

"You'll find out in due time."

It sounded as though he was giving me money, and yet I was annoyed in spite of myself. Why all this mystery about it? He said he had a good reason, that I wouldn't mind if I knew it, and yet I wanted to know it before getting into that car. Still, though I pressed him about it quite hard, I'd have been a fool to tell him no, mystery or no mystery. So, I said I'd be dressed and ready, when Jasper showed up in the car—and spent the night wondering what he was up to, and why he acted that way. Turned out that from his point of view, he did have a reason, a real one, not unfriendly to me, but I didn't find out till next day what it was.

I put on a suit I'd bought, a dark green one that went with my hair, and was out on the porch waiting when Jasper showed up, right on the stroke of eleven. He drove me up to the Estates, and presently turned into one that took my breath, it was so beautiful, like a fairy castle, almost. It was in the colonial style, the Maryland colonial style, with a pair of "hyphens" between the center section and the wings—one-story passages, connecting things up so the line is broken, and better proportion gained than is possible with wings jammed up tight to the center. The whole house was of brick, painted light yellow, with dark olive-green shutters and white trim. Four low chimneys rose from the center section, and two each from the wings, making eight in all, and matching the white trim was the drive, which was dead white, but luminous somehow, with a sparkle to it. Later, when we left and I commented on it, Jasper said the reason was that it was made of oyster shells.

There were no pillars or gewgaws in front, just a plain entrance with portico and a brick platform one step up, in front of which we pulled to a stop. But before I could get out, Mr. White was there, bareheaded, tapping the window of the car. When I put it down, he greeted me, then dropped an envelope into my lap, marked "Mrs. Medford," and stepped away. I felt distinctly rebuffed at not being asked inside, but he said: "Jasper'll take you to the bank, whichever one you want—and you can make out your deposit slip. You brought one, I hope?"

I said I did, and he waved Jasper on. I waved to him as we rolled off, I'm afraid a bit coolly, as I had never had such a thing happen in all my life. However, it was time I found out what was going on, and I got the flap of the envelope open by running my finger inside it, and took out what was inside. On top, attached by a clip, was a check drawn to Joan Medford, for $50,000.

To say I was stunned would be the understatement of the century. I actually pinched myself, to make sure it wasn't a dream. When I made my head stop spinning around, Jasper had slowed down, and was asking me where to: "Mr. Earl, he said you wanted a bank. Like in College Park? Hyattsville? Say where, Mrs. Medford. I ain't headed nowhere right now."

I looked at the check again. What it said was unchanged. Under it were four duplicate copies, each marked COPY TO ACCOMPANY TAX RETURN. In the lower left-hand space of the check was typed the word GIFT.

"College Park, please. Suburban Trust."

"Drive-in window?"

"No, I'll be going inside."

"O.K., Mrs. Medford. Now I got it."

I chose College Park as I wasn't known at that branch. I wanted to avoid the whistles and surprise and excitement it might have caused in Hyattsville, at my regular branch I mean, to bring in such a check for deposit. When we arrived, I made out the slip I had brought, put it in the window under the glass barrier, and watched while the teller stamped it and gave me my receipt, as though it was just one other deposit—which to him no doubt it was. Then I went out and asked Jasper to take me home.

I sat in the living room, looking out at the street and trying to get used to what had happened to me. I was still numb, though. When the doorbell rang, I was sure it was Jasper again, come to say there had been a mistake, that we had to go and retrieve the money somehow.

But it wasn't Jasper. It was Private Church, standing on my doorstep, a brown cardboard folder of papers in one hand and the cap to his uniform in the other. The expression in his eyes was purely neutral, impossible to read, but I felt my heart leap as though he were holding a pair of handcuffs out toward me. For weeks I'd been anticipating this visit and it hadn't come; now it was here, and it was impossible not to link it in my mind with the money I'd received, even though of course there was no way they could be connected, no way anyone could know about that other than Mr. White and me. Unless the police had asked the bank to notify them if I made any large deposits…? But what would it mean if they had? There wasn't anything improper in what Mr. White had done for me—I hadn't asked for it, and he was free to spend his money as he saw fit. But how could I explain that to the police, if they got suspicious? What could I say the money was for? Some sympathetic conversation each night over tonic water?

"Mrs. Medford, may I come in?"

I wanted to shut the door on him, keep him outside, perhaps telephone his partner to ask what I should do—but what I had to do, and did, was stand to one side and let him come in.

"I'm sorry to trouble you, Mrs. Medford—"

"No trouble. None whatsoever."

"—but I'm afraid we need your signature on a document, so that we can complete the investigation into your husband's death. Finalize it, as they're saying these days."

Having set down his cap on the back of the sofa, he fished a single sheet out of the folder and laid it on top, handing me a pen from the breast pocket of his jacket.

I took it from him, consumed with relief that it wasn't about the bank or the money after all. But the feeling was short-lived. Looking at the paper, my vision blurred so that all the words on the page ran together, except for one that stood out near the top: EXHUMATION.

It was Liz's week at doing Jake's set-ups, so she didn't stop by for me. I walked instead, my light coat thrown over my uniform. All the way down to the Garden, my thoughts kept racing from the money to the paper Private Church had made me sign and back again. He hadn't known about the money—yet. But he might find out at any time, and if I didn't have a good explanation when he did, it could go badly for me. But there weren't any good explanations, not as long as Mr. White and I were strangers to one another. Of course, if that could be changed… But did he want it changed, or could he be persuaded to? It would mean a new life if so, not just an answer to Private Church but a new start for me, and a way to get Tad out of Ethel's hands. It could solve all my problems quite neatly. But there was a world of doubt in those two words, *if so*. And in the meantime the police would be digging up Ron's body, and subjecting it to tests—of what sort, Private Church hadn't said, but I knew what the purpose was. It was to show that I'd had something to do with Ron's death, that it hadn't just been an accident.

As best I could, I forced Private Church and his papers and his tests from my mind. There was nothing I could do about any of that. I just had to trust that the police couldn't possibly discover anything that wasn't there—though I knew as well as anyone that tests aren't perfect and sometimes *do* show things they shouldn't. All this I shoved to a corner of my mind and made a point of thinking about other things. But of course that only meant I was free to return to Mr. White and his extraordinary, confounding gift.

When I got to the Garden it seemed odd that things looked exactly the same. It also seemed odd that though I usually told Liz a lot, about what went on in my life, to the extent that anything did, I had no intention of telling her this. I was conscious she'd draw wrong conclusions, as I certainly would have, in her place. Well? Were such conclusions wrong? And what was the right conclusion? Mr. White would surely expect something for his money, wouldn't he?

I found out soon enough. Right on the stroke of five, here came Mr. White, and there was Jake, with his tonic, and there was I, pouring it for him at his table, quite as though nothing had happened. He sipped it, leaned back, wiped his lips with the napkin. "Well!" I said. "I'm still reeling, Mr. White. And I'm still not too terribly sure it isn't a dream. How can I possibly thank you?"

"…The thanks I prefer that we skip."

"But I have to thank you."

"Please!…Please."

He was very quiet, and held up a hand as though to cut me off. I said: "Very well, then—I can't help it, though, if I feel deep gratitude."

"O.K., but let's change the subject."

"…That's a beautiful place you have."

"You like it? I built it myself." He warmed to the topic, and even more to the change of topic. "I had the architect model it after the Harbor House in Annapolis—except, of course, for the octagonal wings. They strike me as wrong, but the rest of it, the proportions, the general layout, and the size, I had him follow quite close. I think it comes off pretty well."

I didn't care about any octagonal wings, but it wouldn't have been polite to say so. I let him go on in this vein for a while. When he paused, a response from me seemed called for, so I said: "It almost seems to float, rather than stand."

"I think the white door casing and window sills are the reason for that—they match the oyster shell drive. That glittering dead white effect comes from the lime. It lightens the whole prospect, and gives that impression you speak of, of floating, rather than standing. You're quite observant, Joan, to notice it."

"I notice all sorts of things."

I sounded waspish in spite of myself, and knew that my chronic weakness, a temper that wouldn't stay put, was going to make me trouble, as usual. I heard myself say, not wanting to: "If invited to look, of course. Of course, today, I wasn't. Wasn't allowed to get out of the car."

"Joan, there was a reason."

"Why don't you say what the reason is?"

It popped out of my mouth like a firecracker, I trying to shut myself up, not with much success. He said: "It would upset me no end to say what the reason was. Joan, you must know by now I'm quite mad about you, and—"

"Then why don't you act like it?"

"I thought I did. Today."

I swallowed, I did everything I could think of to make myself shut up, but no soap. I went right on. I said, glancing around and grateful to find us with no one in earshot: "So O.K., you gave me fifty thousand dollars, and I've said how grateful I am. But when I really try to say it, you cut me off. So what do I do now? O.K., I'd like to know, what do I do?"

"Not what you think, Joan."

"How do you know what I think?"

"Then Joan, what do you think? Tell me."

"If you mean, what I think of what you want me to do for my fifty thousand bucks, I don't know, but I'm human, and I won't be too proud, whatever it is that you want. For fifty thousand dollars I could swallow my pride. But if you want to know what I think in general, what I think you should do to prove it, how insanely you feel for me, there's just one way, Mr. White—that I'm supposed to be too modest to speak of. Well, I'm not. If you wanted a woman for a night, you could have one for a lot less money than you just gave me—perhaps one of the other girls who work here, as I'm sure you know. If you like me enough to give me the amount you gave—why, there's a way for a man to share that much of what he has with a woman he likes, and only one way I know that's got any legitimacy to it." I saw pain flit across his features again, as it had that time before, but mixed, I thought, with a sort of longing, and though I knew it wasn't the way to go about it, I couldn't stop myself and plunged right in. "You could ask me to marry you, that's how—well, goddam it, why don't you ask me?"

"I'd give anything to," he whispered.

"Spit it out, then. Why don't you?"

His face fell, and his next words were so quiet I could barely make them out.

"I have angina, Joan."

I had to rummage around in my head to remember angina, what it was, and finally placed it was some kind of heart trouble, and after getting connected up I said: "I don't get the point, Mr. White. What's angina got to do with it?"

"With angina, marriage is out. To you or anyone. As my doctor has warned me repeatedly, I can't…be with a woman. He's quite certain, my heart wouldn't stand up to the strain. Or in other words, marriage, with you, for me, would be a sentence of death. That's the fantastic torment I live in: I've never met a woman I've wanted more, I think about you to the point of distraction, of insanity we could say, but if I do about it what any normal man wants to do, I die."

I stood there, not really believing him, thinking it was just an excuse, something he had cooked up as an out, a reason for keeping me from hoping for more from Earl K. White III than a mere cocktail waitress should—and then, suddenly, knowing it had to be true—and I don't know what told me. His expression, perhaps: I'd never seen a man so downcast and frustrated and ashamed. And of course he'd already given me more than I had any right to hope for, and asked for nothing in return, in fact refused what little I'd offered. And I remembered the episode where the touch of my body had left him red-faced and out of breath, and I suddenly felt compassion. I mean, a surge of pity swept over me, so I went over and touched him, putting my hand on his back and giving him a pat. "I'm sorry," I said. "I take back what I said. I didn't realize."

"I told you there was a reason."

"You did, and I accept it. It explains everything."

He sat there and I stood there, and for a moment things were awkward, as when two people are so overwhelmed by emotion they can't think of things to say. But then my mouth got in it again, with just one last peep over what had bothered me earlier. "Just the same," I banged at him, in a somewhat peevish way, "you could have asked me into your house. It's a simply beautiful house, and the least you could do was let me look at it, just once."

"There was a reason for that, too."

"I'm a little fed up on reasons."

"Casanova, somewhere in his memoirs, says a woman knows only one way of expressing gratitude. If that way had occurred to you, the consequences could have been catastrophic."

"Casanova?"

"He, of all men, ought to know."

"You think I might have taken that way?"

"If invited in, you might have."

"And you couldn't have resisted?"

"No, Joan, I'm not at all sure I could. And it would have been fatal."

He waited a moment, to let that soak in, and went on: "You'd have been left with a corpse in your arms, and a check no bank would honor—not till my estate was probated, and your chances then would have been slim, extremely slim, considering the characters of my stepchildren. And I know how badly you need the money, Joan. I wanted you to have it. So I had you sit in the car, I took no chances."

"I see."

"It's a fiendish sentence to live under. I realize we haven't known each other for very long, but there is no mistaking how you make me feel, and I know how rare it is, and if it weren't for this thing I'd give my eyes to marry you, to be with you morning, noon, and night—all the time. But it can't be."

"You make me want to cry."

"While you're about it, cry for me."

12

It took me a week to adjust, to catch up with this change that had come in my life, this tremendous, incredible change. Each afternoon I'd sit and look out the window, checking over things I could do with the money I had come into. It was a problem. I had the wherewithal now to get my son back for sure—but no way to explain how I got it, not and be believed, either by Ethel herself or the members of the court she'd hint to about the immoral things I must have done to get a man to pay me so much. Things that in the court's eyes would make me unfit to be put in charge of a child's welfare, and not just for now but permanently. I could hear her voice: *Where would you have gotten such a quantity of money, Joan? I won't use the word for what you are, but you and I both know the only thing you have to sell.*

At the same time, doing nothing with the money was hardly sensible, not when I had it and needed it so dearly. I had to find something that could get me out of this bind eventually. And then one day, as I stared at that house across the street, I woke up. I had often admired it: a two-and-a-half-story brick cottage, painted white, with nicely mown lawn and cedar trees each side of the drive. But what woke me up was the sign on the front lawn: FOR SALE, with a realtor's name on it, his address, and phone number. Suddenly I got up, went to the phone, and dialed. Then I hung up before anyone answered. In the Yellow Pages I looked up another real estate man, Ross P. Linden, with offices in Hyattsville just a few blocks away. I rang, made an appointment, and next day went in to see him. He agreed to take over the job of buying, and at the end of the week closed my deal. He had beat the price down from $35,000 asking to $28,000 offered and accepted. He charged me $1,000 for his work, which I thought reasonable enough considering what he did. Then I went out and bought furnishings for it. I bought them at auction sales, which for things of that kind are usually held at night. That meant taking time off from my job, first telling Bianca. "Telling her," I said, not "asking her"—and of course she put up a squawk. But, if she wanted me to stay on, there was nothing to say but yes, so she said it, swallowing hard. At the end of two weeks, for $1,200, I had the house very well furnished, with living room and dining room suites downstairs, bedroom things upstairs, and very nice rugs all around. On top of the $1,200 in regular furnishings, I put out $495 for a color TV, a beautiful cabinet-size thing that I splurged on deliberately. Because, I was getting this place ready to rent, rent furnished to the kind of people who might be in Washington only a short time, but needed a place to live in, a nice place they could have for themselves, their family, and friends—and a color TV, I thought, would act as very nice bait, something that might well tip the beam, make them decide between my place and some other place, if they liked to watch Steve Allen or Perry Como or Dinah Shore, all of whom were now broadcasting in color, or Howdy Doody if they had a little one. And within a week of the purchase going through I had the house rented, for $450 a month, to a couple from Akron, Ohio, who had jobs of some sort with HUD. When the husband and wife both work, they don't have to count costs too closely, and can afford a very nice rental. They didn't have any children and their name was Schroeder.

So, I had spent $31,000 of my $50,000, but still had things to do. On the mortgage, just under $5,000 dangled, and I went to the bank and paid it. I can't say what a relief that was, what a blessed load off my back, as well as an albatross from around my neck. It still left me with $14,000 of my $50,000, and I went out and bought a car. I didn't buy a new car, but one off a used-car lot, from a man I knew fairly well, from his coming in to the Garden and sitting with me quite often. He had a very nice Ford, a sedan, nicely polished, two years old but with not too much mileage on it, for $1,100. It was green, to blend with my hair, and when I drove it around the block, purred nicely, as though in good condition. The only thing was, it still had its original tires, and they were beginning to get worn. But I had Mr. Goss put five new whitewalls on it, for just over $100, and lo and behold, I had practically a brand-new car for the price of half of one.

So, I had one house free and clear, with no monthly $110 due, and except for taxes and upkeep, no expense at all, and another house free and clear, paying me $450 a month, subject to taxes and upkeep. Or in other words, with the $19.15 tip I still got every night, or nearly $115 a week, and the $150 a week over that that I made in tips at the Garden, I had about $1,500 a month before taxes, and over $10,000 in savings, making me $50 a month, about. Considering that just a few months before I was practically on relief, I knew I wasn't doing too badly. I also hadn't heard a peep from Private Church since the day he'd come to my house, leaving me to conclude that neither my recent transactions, if noticed at all, nor Ron's exhumation had raised any matter of concern to the police. So I was feeling pleasantly up, quite happy with myself, when I drove out to the Lucases' Sunday, for my weekly visit with Tad. I played it straight with Ethel, making no explanations at all of the car except to say that I had it, and all she could do was stare, first at it, then at me, and say: "I see, I see, I see." What she saw I didn't quite know, or to be frank about it, care. I'd been working long enough to afford a used car, on what I was making now; it wasn't like suddenly appearing with $50,000 out of nowhere.

Tad was all excitement, as I had hoped he would be, and I loaded him in for a ride I had in mind, to the university at College Park, where they had a dairy building, as part of their farm complex, where you can get ice cream of various kinds, experimental kinds, most of them wonderful, not at all like what they sell in "parlors" as they're called. They brought a book for Tad to sit on, but I held him on my lap, and ordered something made with diced dates for myself and plain strawberry for him, as being pink, pretty, and tasty.

He loved it. He ate it spoonful by spoonful, in the slow careful way a child has for something like that, and I loved watching him. When he was almost to the end he suddenly stopped, closed his eyes, and said: "M'm! M'm!" like he'd heard them sing on the Campbell's soup advertisements. It made my heart beat up, the most beautiful sound in the world, of my own little baby being happy. He didn't even complain when I hugged him tight, forgetting about his shoulder, so I knew he'd finally healed. I let him taste to the last spoonful, then ordered two quart cartons, one of strawberry, one of vanilla with chocolate chip, to take home to the Lucases. When we got back Jack was out on the curb waiting. It seemed odd, as previously he had shown me no special respect, and in fact took me quite for granted, in a way I didn't much like. But now he was deference itself, opening the door, helping me out with Tad, being so helpful I was crossed up, assuming at first it was respect for the new car, or something of the sort. However, it turned out that wasn't the reason. "Will you go up to Ethel?" he whispered. "She's in a state up there—went to bed, believe it or not. You were gone so long she thought you'd flown the coop. She thought you'd taken Tad back. So—*you aren't taking him, are you?*"

"He is my son, Jack."

"I know he is, and you are entitled to have him for the day any time you want. But Ethel feared—"

"I know what she feared, and she should fear it, because someday soon I hope to make it happen. I am the boy's mother and he should be with me."

"I thought you weren't ready yet, that you still couldn't take care of him, all by yourself—"

I swallowed what I wanted so badly to tell him, to tell Ethel, for I was still afraid of how she would turn it against me. "I'm not. But soon I hope to be."

"She's scared to death up there."

And then, as he walked me into the house, holding my arm, as I held Tad by the hand: "She's nuts about him, Joan, just nuts. Don't take him, please—not yet. He's what she lives for."

"What I live for, too."

"Yeah, we know about that. But—"

"I'll talk to her about it."

So I did, coming in on her as she lay on their double bed, staring at me with puffy cheeks and red eyes, and giving a little cry when Tad came toddling in, having let go my hand at the head of the stairs, to pull up his sock or something. She jumped out of bed, swept him into her arms, and listened close as he told her: " 'Tawberry! 'Tawberry! 'Tawberry!"

"Ethel," I told her, very calm. "I brought him back—this time. But I'm in better shape now, financially I mean, than I have been—the job has worked out very well, and I *could* afford a woman, one to come in and stay with Tad while I work. I mean to say I've been thinking about it, and though I haven't done it yet, you should prepare yourself for it."

She looked up at me from where she was cradling my son by the foot of her bed and wrapped one hand around the back of his head, as if to protect him. To protect him from me, his mother. "You may do that, Joan, when you're settled proper and have a situation suitable to the mother of a young boy. Not working nights for tips, from men who pay to drink and see your bosom, and if it's only to see it and not to touch it, and much more besides, I'd be surprised." She spoke this all in a syrupy sweet voice, as though the tone could hide from my little son what venom the words contained. "I know Luke Goss, and so does my Jack, and he bragged just two nights back about that car he sold you, saying he expected he'd have you in its back seat some night soon if the way you pet him on the arm and give him glimpses inside your blouse at the Garden is any indication of how you feel about him. Now Luke Goss does well enough with that yard of his and I'm not telling you he couldn't make a tolerable husband for some woman, so if you've decided to make a play for him, so be it. But I have to warn you, Joan, you might find marriage proposals aren't what you get put to you in the back seat of a used car."

I was frozen, my temper held in check only by the look of distress I saw had crept into Tad's eyes. He may not have understood all the words but he wasn't taken in about their meaning, and could tell that there was something like hatred between us. "Luke Goss is a liar," I said, "a salesman who will say anything to anyone to make himself shine in their eyes. I serve him drinks and that is all, and there never will be more, and if I ever touched his arm it was only to keep him from falling over in his seat from too many Manhattans. I will not be kept from my son by lies, not his, nor yours, nor anyone's, and if you try you'll wish you hadn't."

"…Wish I hadn't? What are you saying, Joan? That I might have an accident like Ron's someday?"

"I wouldn't know, that depends on whether you drink as much as he did."

She stood. "I'm sorry, Joan, but I don't think it is appropriate for us to continue this conversation in front of the boy. If you would kindly leave, Jack will see you out."

I bent to kiss my son, and he saw the tears I was holding back, because he flung his arms around my neck and clung, until finally I had to take his little hands and gently lift them off me and force myself to step away from him. "Mommy will be back," I told him. "Next Sunday. And the Sunday after. And more than that, soon, much more, I promise."

"More," he said, but his voice quavered as though uncertain. And I knew then I couldn't give up on Mr. White, however impossible it might seem.

13

All that time, I hadn't said anything, to Liz, Bianca, or anyone there at the Garden, about what had happened to me.

And I said nothing to Mr. White as to what I'd done with his money, not that I minded his knowing, but I feared he wouldn't approve, and shied off from letting him veto. I also said nothing to Tom, who came in as he had before—not every night, but two or three times a week, always sitting at Mr. White's table, always taking seltzer, and always staying completely sober, but it must be said leaving me feeling a little tipsy in turn. He kept trying to date me, for an evening, or early morning actually, after I got through work, saying he knew a place where we could go "and not be bothered," whatever that meant. And I kept putting him off, saying, "Soon, I hope—I'll take another rain-check," but it was harder each time. In spite of the way we'd begun, I'd come to like him. Or perhaps 'like' is the wrong word, but I was drawn to him, and I was coming to understand better what Liz had told me that first night, about the undeniable appeal of being asked, especially when it's an attractive man doing the asking.

Then one night he came in earlier than usual and didn't bring up the subject. He seemed in a very low mood, as though something was on his mind. I asked: "What is it, Tom? Did I pour gravy on your ice cream? What's on your mind anyway?"

"Plenty. I have a friend that's in trouble."

"Someone I know?"

"Jim Lacey."

"...Oh? The one whose son you spelled the day of the funeral?"

"The one. You may have seen him in the paper. He's been in-dicted."

"Indicted? For what?"

For answer, he dug into his briefcase and tossed a newspaper down on the table between us. The story was on the bottom of page one. James E. Lacey, senior municipal engineer with the county, had been indicted in a matter involving taking bribes to recommend sewer connections for some new development area. It was one of those cases they have all the time in Prince George's County, where millions are made overnight on the basis of re-zoning decisions, the award of sewer connections, of water connections, of paving connections. "Well, I'm sorry," I said, as pleasantly as I could. "It always hurts when a friend gets in some trouble."

"What hurts is, I'm not able to help."

Not knowing what help was called for, I said nothing, but in a moment he explained: "He's an idiot, a gambler, up to his ears in debt. No one would lend him a dime, and his trouble is, he can't make bail. It's been set at $12,000, and will cost over $1,000 for a bond, and he just doesn't have it. Can you imagine, a man with his power and connections, sitting in a jail cell because he can't raise a thousand dollars? If I had it I'd stand the bond myself—but it's out of the question for me."

"...You haven't got a thousand dollars either?"

He smiled at me as if to say, What care I about money? But what it said was, No, I haven't got a thousand dollars either.

"Once some of the things I'm working on ripen, I'll have that much many times over—but at the moment I'm strapped, at least for that kind of money, so I have to deal myself out."

Bail was something I knew nothing whatever about. I had heard of bail bondsmen, but just who they were and how they worked was completely out of my world. He waited some more, sipping his seltzer a bit, and then went on: "I have a house, of course. My father left me the place, and I still live there. And it's worth double the bail, which is what they require. Unfortunately, I borrowed some money on it—so that's out. I could sign a property bond otherwise, and I'd be only too glad to. But what you can't do, you can't. That's what's getting me. He knows about the house but not about the mortgage, and wonders why I don't sign his bond. And for some reason I hate to tell him the truth. It sounds as though I just cooked up an excuse."

"Start over. Explain about the house."

He did, in words of one syllable, telling how the bail bondsmen use one house over and over, to sign a dozen bonds, each one for a nice charge, "but the house must be free and clear. If it's mortgaged it can't be pledged."

"And it bothers you, not to be able to help?"

"Well? Wouldn't it bother you?"

He opened up a little bit then, saying how Mr. Lacey was more than a friend. "He's someone I badly need, for something I'm shooting for. I have an eye on a position in the administration—I want to run the Department of Natural Resources, and his cousin down in Annapolis could put it over for me. I'm pretty sure she could. She's close to the governor, and takes an interest in it." I drew a blank on that, and he said: "I'd give anything to have charge of Chesapeake Bay, on account of an idea I have." And he came out with the very idea Liz had mentioned, that if he worked things around he might be able to get the bay clear of the nettles. "Chesapeake Bay," he explained, almost as though making a speech, "is the garden spot of the world, of this part of the world anyway, the garden spot of the U.S.A.— perfect for yachting, swimming, wading, or what-have-you, all except for one thing, the goddam nettles. With them out there it's no good for anything. It seems to me we could get rid of those goddam things. And it seems to me, that those atomic plants might help. The whole population's against them, scared to death of what they might do. But suppose I can figure a way, to use those plants somehow? To use the water they spill? That hot water they sluice with their pumps? If all it takes is temperature, a slight change in how hot the bay is, to kill all those nettles we have, then that would do it, and not cost the state a dime. Then, 'stead of opposing those plants, the people would welcome them in—and we got a tremendous problem solved— the nettles, the atomic plants, the energy that we need, all at one fell swoop."

He got so excited talking about it, and it was all I could do to keep the expression on my face from breaking out in a grin like we both knew he was pulling my leg—because it was pretty clear he believed in what he was selling and didn't see it as leg pulling at all. It made me feel a little bittersweet, actually, as it put him in a new light, like seeing a beautiful home by day after only previously seeing it in the moonlight, only to realize that the shutters need painting and the roof's in a terrible state. Tom thought he had the prettiest little house in town and had no idea how rickety it was. Apart from the radiation, I wanted to ask him, wouldn't the hot water kill off all the fish…? But those were only two of a thousand arguments against his plan, and I didn't raise them. I just watched him deliver his pitch with all his heart behind it, and in a strange way the very hopelessness of it made me warm to him—not to it, but to him, this handsome young man with a mortgaged house and not a thousand dollars to his name and a castle in the air he'd never be able to sell anyone on but a couple of women at a Hyattsville bar who'd known him as a teenager and were fond of him.

And not even them, necessarily, as halfway through his speech Bianca was there at my shoulder, whispering to me: "He's a bit gone on the subject. Don't pay too much attention."

Then Liz was there, telling me: "Give him a drink."

They drifted away, but he kept going. I saw in his eyes, behind the unwavering conviction, a sort of desperation I recognized, and my heart went out to him. I saw the chance to do for someone, in a smaller way, what Mr. White had done for me—and perhaps also felt a bit of the same impulse that had led me to promise toys to all the children in Ethel's yard. I said: "You need someone, is that it? With a house that's free and clear? Suppose I had that house?"

He stared at me, then said: "Joan, it's a serious thing. Don't try to be funny—not on this subject, anyway."

"Who says I'm being funny?"

I snapped it, the least little bit, and suddenly he knew I was serious. "...You? Could sign that bond?"

"If that's what it takes, a house."

"I didn't realize."

"I'd have to be asked, nicely."

"I wouldn't ask you. I don't have the right."

"...O.K. Then for you I volunteer."

After a long time, still staring at me, he asked: "You'd do that for me, Joan?"

"And why not? It's just for a time, right? Once he shows up at the trial, the bond is cancelled?"

"Of course. But there's risk."

"There's always risk. If you'd trust him with your house..."

"I would if I could."

"Then why can't I?"

"Is it all right, then? That I call his lawyer and get him in? Because, as I understand it, Jim could be out tonight—they do it that quick, I've heard. *If,* as and when—"

"You have a house free and clear. Well, I have."

❖

He went into the alcove and phoned, then was back, taking a flash at his watch. Half an hour later a bald-headed man came in, dropped down at the table with him, took out a paper, and whispered something to him. Tom beckoned to me, and the bald-headed man, who introduced himself as Mr. Lackman, asked me about my house. Did I have one free of any mortgages, leases, tenancies or other encumbrances? I told him I had one, and he wanted to know where. So, on my scratch pad there on the bar, I wrote the address of my home, the one I'd got upon Ron's death and now owned free and clear, and laid it down in front of him. He copied it onto his paper, held the ballpoint to his teeth, then motioned me to sit down, make myself comfort-able, but I told him it wasn't allowed. He said he had to make a telephone call to someone in the courthouse or the hall of records, I don't remember which, to confirm that my name was on the deed for the property and that there were no outstanding liens or claims, and I told him I'd be surprised if anyone would be working so late at night. He replied: "You're working, aren't you? You think the justice system closes down at ten o'clock?"

He was on the phone for nearly twenty minutes, then he came back, sat down, and called me over again. He had another paper in his hand, a legal document, and he read it to me. It was a declaration that I owned the property at the address given below and was hereby offering it in pledge as security for the release of the named prisoner, or something of that kind. When he finished reading he told me to sign. So I did, and he waved it around in the air as if to dry it, then jumped up and scooted.

It took the better part of two more hours, maybe three, to the point where I thought we might close up before he made it back. But then there he was, diving back to the table, with another man by his side, a chunky red-faced man in a rumpled suit, unshaven, who shook hands with Tom and sat. When Tom motioned toward me, he got up, came over, shook my hand, and said he was Jim Lacey and how grateful he was that I had helped him out. He said: "You'll never regret it, I promise you." And then: "Now, Mrs. Medford, how about joining us? Tom, Mel, and me, for a little drink to celebrate? Celebrate my release?"

"Mr. Lacey, I don't drink. But thanks."

"Take seltzer, like Tom."

"It's also against the rules."

"Not tonight it's not."

He called to Bianca, to know if it was all right if I sat down with him at the table, and added: "It better be, Bianca, you know what's good for you." Bianca told him: "For you, Jim, we make an exception of course."

So I sat down at the table, and he ordered champagne, with Liz serving the order. I told her: "Ginger ale for me," and she nodded, but stared, all crossed up. It went on I suppose a half hour, I feeling very self-conscious, but then Mr. Lacey proclaimed: "Got to be going now—come on, Mel, time we both shoved off. We'll leave these other two here."

So, in a minute they were gone, and I jumped up to become a waitress again, but there were only two other tables occupied this late, and Liz had already seen to them. I stood by Tom's chair and looked down at him. He eyed me with an odd expression, and I guess I enjoyed his reaction. He said: "I wouldn't know how to thank you. You did a great thing for Jim—and for me, you helped me more than I can say."

"Well," I said, "there's a couple of ways, if you really want to thank me."

"Just say what they are, Joanie."

"To begin with you could apologize, at long last."

"For what?"

I didn't answer him, just stood my ground and waited for him to work it through. I thought perhaps he'd blush when he finally got there, but I suppose some men aren't made for blushes, and what came out in the end was a smile, and not a trace of shame behind it. "You mean that first night, here at the Garden? For what I did?"

"Now he's thinking."

"I do apologize, Joan, if you want me to, for being drunk and giving in to temptation, but I won't apologize for the temptation itself, since I'm just as tempted now, maybe more so."

It was not the apology I'd been waiting for, but it set my blood racing as that apology never would have.

I said: "Maybe I am as well, now—but that's after I've gotten to know you. And more to the point, there's a difference between temptation and action, and you know well enough to keep on the right side of that line."

"I apologize, then, for straying over the line."

"Thank you."

"Or for doing it too soon, if that's what you mean. So, what's the other way?"

"The other way…?"

"To thank you."

"Oh. Well, all this talk about taking me out, day after day. Now that I know you're so strapped I wouldn't expect anywhere fancy, but you could still—"

"You mean you'll go?"

"I don't know why not. We could celebrate too."

"You're amazing, Joan. I was starting to think you weren't—" He stopped and waved away whatever he was going to say. "Never mind what I was starting to think, I was obviously wrong. I'd love to take you out. I'd just love it."

He said we could go to a place called The Wigwam, which I'd never heard of, but that didn't mean anything, as what chance had I ever had to learn about the area's nightspots? I explained about the car, how I'd drive there myself, with him following along, so he'd have to give me the address, then meet me beside my car, so he could take me in. He wrote the address down on my scratch pad and when closing time came followed me out, put me in the car, and stood back to see me off. The car startled him too, because actually it was quite nice, a small sedan, but nicely shined up and smart. I drove off, following his directions, and at an address on New Hampshire Avenue spotted The Wigwam in due time. Then he was pulling in beside me and walking me to the door. I didn't appear to be in my Rose Garden costume, as over it was my coat, my nice little light spring coat, which came down to my knees and made it look as though I was dressed in usual clothes.

The Wigwam looked normal enough on the outside, just a double door with a sign over it, which Tom pushed open as though he'd been there before. But inside, it seemed different from any club I'd been in, though of course I hadn't been in too many. Instead of the bright, somewhat noisy atmosphere you would expect, it was twilight dark, a large room with a tall leather wigwam at one end and booths all around, with heavy curtains drawn close, shutting them off. And the girls were oddly dressed, if you could call them dressed at all. The hostess, a girl Tom called Rhoda, had on a buckskin coat with fringed bottom, which of course was decent enough, but the waitresses, who Rhoda spoke of as "Pocahontases," were practically naked—they were topless, and except for a skimpy swimsuit bottom in the French bikini style, bottomless too. Each of them also wore a feather, caught in a lock on top, and lopped down over one ear in a coquettish way. By looking at them, I knew those girls were for sale, and I guess I didn't mind much, as I knew that such things went on and, from talking with Liz, that women I might like and respect could do them; and yet I began to feel nervous, and sick at the stomach somehow— or if not exactly sick, a bit queasy, as they say. I felt I had my foot in something. But I didn't want to show it—I wanted to come off as a woman of the world, not a waitress. So I maintained an unruffled demeanor, smiled though my narrowed lips, and tightened my grip on Tom's arm.

Rhoda called us a Pocahontas, then took us to a booth, pulling the curtain open and sliding the table out, so we could slip in behind. But the table didn't have seats on three sides, as crosswise booth tables have, but rather just one seat on the far side, and a very long seat at that. It must have been six feet long, with an upholstered pad on it, and a pillow at one end. I slipped in, and Rhoda asked: "Can I take your coat?"

I hesitated for a moment before giving it to her, and she nodded appraisingly when she saw my uniform beneath it. I found myself feeling grateful for the darkness of the room. She put my coat on a hanger that was there, on the rail the curtain ran on. Then she asked what we wanted to drink, and Tom said seltzer, somewhat to my relief, and I said ginger ale. Rhoda didn't seem much surprised, and as she left us, said: "Amy will be by to serve you in a minute."

Then she left, and we sat there, very self-conscious, not saying much. Somewhere, a recorded orchestra played *Three O'Clock in the Morning*, and Tom said it was one of the great waltzes of all time. It never had hit me that way, but I said: "Yes, isn't it?" as though I really loved it. Then one of the girls came with our drinks. She put them down, and said: "Now, when I go I'll close your curtain, and won't bother you after that—fact of the matter, nobody will. You want your candle out just blow it, and there's matches, to light it again, you want to. You want me, I mean you want service, like more drinks or something, there's your light, that button there." She showed us a fixture on the table, beside the candle. "Just press it, it puts on the light in front, and pretty soon, I'll come. Or if not me, some girl. Like, with me, I could be tied up, you know what I mean? I might be more or less busy, but if I am, one of the girls will come, just give her a minute or two. What I mean, don't get antsy too quick. Take it easy, and one of the girls will come."

"…You could be busy, you say?" asked Tom. "Doing what, like?"

"Well the customer, he can get lonely."

"And you keep him company?"

"Something along that line."

I didn't much care for her, and couldn't resist the temptation to ask her: "Still wearing that bikini bottom? Or do you take it off?"

"It all depends."

Then, looking me straight in the eye: "Like, for a guy with a girlfriend that don't put out and he wants some help of me, I take it off—it unhooks easy as pie. See?" She unhooked it, to give Tom a glimpse of fuzz, and then, continuing to me: "So, if you want me to help you out, put your light on, just press the button once, and I'll do what I can. Something else you want to know?"

"No—beat it."

That was Tom, and she said: "On my way," and left.

"Well," I said, "that was making it plain."

"Drumming up trade, I'd say."

"Though, I have to admit she's pretty."

"I didn't notice."

He was quite solemn as he said it, and I guess I made a face. He didn't say anything, but suddenly blew out the candle. Once more, we could hear the waltz going. Pretty soon, in the half dark, he said: "…Well? Where were we?"

"I wouldn't know," I said. "Were we anywhere?"

"Yeah, we were somewhere. I recall your making me apologize for it. Maybe we can begin where we left off." And with that, first putting his arm around me, he slid his other hand right where he'd put it that night, and I locked my legs, in exactly the selfsame way. But he kept sliding his hand higher, up, up, up, stroking with his index finger as he went—until his hand was inside my hot pants, and then working its way across. And then, almost before I knew it, it was in a woman's most intimate spot, and I was turning to water. Instead of clamping tight to resist, I was quite limp, and have to admit, enchanted his hand was there. It had been a time, not just since Ron's death but for nearly a year before, and I forgot how much I missed it. Sitting there with Tom's strong hands on me, I felt like my ribs might crack from the force of my heart's pounding behind them. Then he suddenly took his hand away, and began unbuttoning my pants, at the placket on one side, and I was wriggling to help, to shuffle them off. My blouse came next, and his shirt, and then he was pushing me back, back against the pillow, his weight pressing down on me, his bare chest against mine.

Then, then at last, I thought of Mr. White, and how important the plans were that I'd made for him, and how it could all go in the soup if I let this thing happen with Tom. And I thought of Ethel, and her charge that I was doing with my customers exactly what I was about to do; and of Private Church, who'd been blessedly silent for weeks, but might not remain so if he got wind of this, a lover after all, even if it wasn't Joe Pennington. I thought of all of them, and fighting every instinct I had I got my hands clear and pushed, pushed Tom up and away. He fought me, playfully, and I fought him, to mean it, and at last bit him on the cheek. He began to growl, and I pushed some more, until I could sit up. My pushing reached the table, and suddenly it toppled over into the curtain. I jumped up, banging him in the face accidentally with my knee, got clear, slipped around, grabbed my coat, and raced through the nightclub, out the door, and over the lot to my car. I'd left my pants and blouse in the booth; I ran in just my panties, clutching my coat haphazardly in front of my breasts. Then I remembered my bag—and found it under my arm, how it got there I don't know, I don't remember grabbing it. Then into my car, snapping the safety catch down and winding the window up. In the bag I found my car key, but by that time Tom was there, shirt hanging loose, belt unbuckled, banging on the window and grunting: "Goddam it, Joan, open that door!"

I didn't open. I turned the key, stepped on the pedal, and when the motor spoke went into gear and backed. But to get off the lot, I had to turn and go forward. He raced to block me off, standing in front of the car and holding his hands up, like some kind of traffic cop. I ran straight at him, so he jumped up on the bumper and sprawled on the hood as I kept right on. Then I suddenly stopped so he toppled off. I swerved to miss driving over him and then kept right on, going straight home, the coat fallen into my lap, my body exposed by each passing streetlight so that anyone looking in might have seen. But I didn't stop so I could put the coat on; I didn't even slow down. I just said a silent prayer that no one would see me, and as far as I could tell, no one did.

When I turned in my drive, the dash clock said three o'clock in the morning. "One of the great waltzes," I thought, climbing out, unlocking the door, and going in.

14

In bed, I lay there terrified, for fear the doorbell would ring, and that if Tom was there, I would let him in. It didn't, and at last I slept. Next day, I was able to put on my uniform, as I had the extra pair of hot pants Liz had bought me and my own substitute blouse, and so I was able to go down to work as usual. It was Liz's week on the set-ups, so I got in just before five, and when I came out, after putting my coat and bag in my locker, there was Mr. White, at his regular place. I went over and asked: "The usual?"—but instead of the friendly nod he always gave me, he didn't look at me. He just sat there, his face in a scowl, so I knew something was wrong. However, I went to the bar, where Jake had his order all ready, took it over and served it. "Will there be something else?" I asked, taking no notice how he was acting.

"…No—nothing," he said.

"Nice weather we're having," I remarked, on purpose trying to sound idiotic, and all too well succeeding.

Then at last he looked up. "How could you do that to me?" he asked, his voice half choked. "How could you? How could you?"

"Do what, Mr. White? Why don't you explain yourself?"

"You know what I mean, don't stand there pretending you don't. How could you go to that place? That—Wigwam? *That whorehouse?*"

"How do you know where I went?"

"Don't try to tell me you didn't. You were seen, going into it with a man, at two o'clock in the morning."

"Was I seen coming out?"

"Answer me! I asked how could you?"

"Answer me, Mr. White. Apparently, you had a spy following me, a CIA man maybe, or someone in your pay. Well you should dock him for not sticking around, because if he had stuck around, for no more than fifteen minutes, he'd have seen me come out, and he couldn't have stuck around, because if he'd seen me he'd have remembered it. I came out running, I'll have you know, holding a coat in front of me to cover what was bare—which is to say everything, or nearly so, since I had a struggle inside with a fellow who thought he could have me if only he got my clothes off. But he couldn't—I assure you I got out of there with everything else intact, what we might laughingly call my honor. I agree it's kind of a whorehouse, but I didn't know that until after I went in, I thought I was being taken to a place to have a quiet drink. Now I do know what it is, it's a place I'll stay away from. Is there something else you want to know?"

"…Are you telling me the truth?"

"Your man didn't report my exit?"

"…No."

"Well then he must have walked away or he would have—I'm supposed to be quite an eyeful with no clothes on, if my departed husband can be believed, and your man surely would have told you about it if he'd seen the sight. Perhaps even shown you pictures. And now, if you'll excuse me—?"

I caught Liz's eye and motioned her over. "This is Miss Baumgarten," I told him, "Liz to her many friends. She'll bring you whatever you want."

I went back to the locker room and stretched myself out on the bench. In a couple of minutes Liz was there. "He wants to see you," she said.

"I'm kind of busy just at the moment."

"Joanie, the guy's nuts about you—the whole place knows it, been knowing it all summer, even if you don't. And as much as

I'd like to say I prefer Tom for you—you don't brush something like that."

"Who says I'm brushing him? Please just tell him what I said."

"...Just right now you're busy?"

"That's it. Tell him so."

I don't quite know why I played it that way. For a moment there, serving his order, I had had a horrible hunch I had lost Mr. White, had broken beyond repair what we'd had, based as it was, at least in part, on his sense that I was a 'lady,' or at least more ladylike than Liz. But then, there seemed to be something squashy in the way he was acting toward me, and I could feel it somehow that if I played it right I still might call him mine. But the last thing in the world, I knew, would be for me to lead to him. It had to be him to me, or he'd look down on me. So I let Liz go with her message, and didn't move off the bench. In a minute or two she was back. "He's gone," she whispered. "And he didn't like it much, you not coming out. At least to tell him goodbye."

"He's not supposed to like it."

"Joanie, with a fish like that on the hook—"

"You play him, you keep the line tight."

"I wouldn't play him that way, but—"

"He's not your fish."

What I would say to Tom, I hadn't the faintest idea. What I had thought I would say, as I rehearsed it during the night, was that I expected to be getting married, and couldn't risk an involvement with him. But now that I'd been caught by surprise, now that Mr. White knew what I'd done, or almost done at any rate, and had acted as any man would, I didn't know where I was at, and for that reason hated to face it, the scene I would play with Tom. But anticlimax, he didn't come. As his time approached I grew nervous, knowing "There was a reason" was no reason at all, and expecting a miserable mess, but when closing time came, he still hadn't showed and there I was, not only with nothing to say but no one to say it to. And it went on for some little time— I not only didn't see him, but didn't hear where he was, or anything about him. He simply stopped coming, and no one had any news.

With Mr. White, however, things were different, and little by little, and then much by much, the situation changed. He was in the next afternoon, after the one I've just told about, still grim, but with no repetition of his hysterical outbreak. He ordered, then sat looking straight ahead, saying nothing at all. However, I wasn't too bashful to speak. "In the first place," I told him, beginning right in the middle without any small talk at all, "you can get rid of that snoop, that spy."

"I don't have any snoop."

"I'm sorry, Mr. White, you have one."

"You doubt my word?"

"You want a straight answer to that?"

"I demand a straight answer to it."

"I not only doubt your word, I call you a goddam liar. You do have a snoop, and if you want to know how I know I go by that look in your eye. So spit it out, Mr. White. You do have a snoop, don't you?"

"I have a man, O.K. But not to *spy* on you, for heaven's sake."

"A snoop is a snoop is a snoop."

"This was a man that works for me, a man from down in the office, that I asked to keep an eye on you—not to spy, that's the truth, simply to see that nothing happened to you after leaving here at night. That was all, I swear it was."

I let him stew a bit before I relented: "Then O.K. I believe you."

Because I knew he was telling the truth, or at least thought he was. I went on: "But in return for taking your word, taking your word on him, I must have your word it's the end, that he won't stake me out anymore, that you take him off my neck. What do you say to that?"

"...Joan, if you insist, I say O.K., of course. But—"

"I don't need protection. Thanks to your great generosity, I have my own car now. I don't ride with Liz anymore, I go straight home, let myself in with my key, and if I need the police can call them. Do I have your word you're taking that tail off my back?"

"Joan, I've already said it."

"Then O.K., let's get on to the next matter."

He looked up in surprise, and I went right on, boring in: "About you and I, getting married. On that, you said you asked nothing better, and would go through with it gladly, except that your doctor forbade it, as a sure sentence of death. O.K., Mr. White, but whose life is it? Your doctor's?"

"...What do you mean, Joan? That it's up to me to die to prove how I feel about you?"

"No, Mr. White, it's not. *But*, there is a way out."

"What do you mean, a way out?"

"Way in, perhaps I should say. Mr. White, sex isn't everything. There's no reason at all that you couldn't marry me, stay in your bedroom, and let me stay in mine. That way, you'd have me with you always, if I mean what you say I do to you, and I'd have you with me always, and I do confess that would mean quite a lot. In addition to which, I could quit this job serving drinks, which has been a godsend to me, but which I confess I could do without. And most important of all to me, I could have my son back, and give him the growing up a boy dreams of, in that beautiful house, playing on that beautiful grass, and rolling his tricycle on that beautiful drive. What use is all that house and those grounds with just you living there by yourself? You've told me how lonely you are, how much more you like it here where we can talk and be together. For god's sake, Earl, why should a man like you have to come to a bar for companionship? Or in other words, once again to make plain what I mean: Who's running your life?"

"I'd love to have you helping me run it."

"O.K., then. What do you say to what I just now said?"

"I say I'll think it over."

"It's what I want you to do."

It was two or three weeks after that, I would say in mid-September, so it was coming on for fall, before he came up with his answer—if you could call it that. He came in, ordered, and then, in the most casual way, said: "I think I'm going to say yes—but I must go to New York first."

"New York? You mean, now?"

"I thought to leave tomorrow."

"For how long?"

"Oh—better part of a month. Maybe more."

There was something peculiar about it, and I asked: "What's in New York? Why must you go up there?"

"Lawyer. He's spending some time up there, working on a business deal for me, an important one."

"And what does he have to do with you and me?"

"About such a marriage as ours, such a marriage as ours would be, there are quite a few legal angles. I'm not sure I know what they are, except in a general way. I think I should talk to him. And I need to be there to see to the deal as well."

"I see. I see."

"You could talk to a lawyer too."

"That might be a good idea."

I left him, did one or two things at the bar, and thought over what he had said. Then I went back and told him: "It's really the best way, I agree. You go now, have your month in New York, and if you forget me, O.K. I have other chances, don't worry."

"...*Stop talking like that!*"

"I told you go—then we'll know where we stand."

15

So he went, and for a time, things were very humdrum, we could even say a bit flat. I missed him coming to the bar each night; at least I missed his nineteen-dollar tips. Things went on I suppose for two or three weeks, into the early fall. It was the tail end of September by then, and I'd switched back from my summer hot pants to the velveteen trunks and pantyhose, which I'd just gotten on one afternoon when the bell rang, and when I opened the door it was Tom. I hadn't seen him since that night, and no doubt acted cool. "…Oh?" I said. "Tom? What can I do for you?"

"Joan," he half stammered, "I have to talk to you."

"What about?"

"I think you know, and I won't enjoy it, I promise you. Just the same, I won't talk on your doorstep."

"Then—come in, please."

I brought him into the living room, and asked him: "How would I know what you've come about?"

"You haven't seen this?"

I noticed for the first time he had a paper under his arm, which he unrolled and waved around. "I don't take the afternoon paper," I told him. "What's in it to concern me? What is this anyway?"

He handed it over, and on page one, not the main story but big enough to make it onto the front page, was one about Mr. Lacey, the man whose bail bond I'd signed. It said:

LACEY CASE CALLED:
NO LACEY

—or something like that. The story simply said that when the case of James Lacey, indicted municipal engineer, was called for trial that morning, "Mr. Lacey didn't make the required appearance." It then went on to say that "Melvin T. Lackman, Mr. Lacey's attorney, told the court Mr. Lacey hadn't arrived at his office as scheduled to accompany him to the trial, and that he had no information on where Mr. Lacey was. The court, in the person of Judge T. D. Enos, ordered a bench warrant issued for Mr. Lacey's arrest." That was all, except for a picture of Mr. Lacey, looking as I remembered him, only younger and not so fat. My stomach began telling me this was bad news, but I still wasn't quite caught up. I asked: "Well? Where do I come in?"

"Joan, you signed his bail bond, that's where."

"You mean, I lose my house? It gets taken and sold to pay the bond?"

"On that, I don't know yet—I'm as caught by surprise as you are, and know as little about it. Where I do know what I mean, is to stand by you one hundred percent—you did this thing for me, and I'm not letting you take the fall for it alone."

"That's a lovely sentiment, Tom, but I don't see what you can do, unless some of those projects of yours have ripened and you now have not one but twelve thousand dollars to spare."

"I think I don't need it, and neither do you. If we can find that son of a bitch and bring him back for trial, we can let a court take it from there. But that's what I *think*, and what I know is nothing. As of now, the first thing is to get a lawyer."

"…I don't know any lawyer."

"So happens, I do."

He mentioned one I'd heard of, at the time of my real estate deal, with offices over in Marlboro, Dwight Eckert was his name, and Tom offered to drive me to see him. I thought to put in a call first, to find out if he'd be in, and it turned out he would be, after four o'clock. It was then going on for three, which just gave me time to change from my waitress clothes, and put on a suit I'd bought, which would do nicely, as the air by now had a nip in it. I excused myself, went back to the bedroom and started to change, when there he was, in the door. I asked: "Who invited you back here?"

He leaned against the doorpost and crossed his arms. "Figured we could continue talking. Not like it's the first time I've seen you undressed, brief though the last time was."

I was wearing no more than I'd been the last time, just my panties. I turned to him and held out my hand, palm up. "That'll be twenty-five dollars, please."

"...What did you say?"

"I said, pay. From being taken to visit a whorehouse, I learned some tricks of the trade. Now, you want to watch me undress, you pay to watch me undress. Twenty-five dollars, I said—payable now."

He stood there, stared, and then took out his wallet. He counted out two tens and a five, and tossed them on the bed. I snatched them up and threw them at him. "Tom," I said, in a way that really meant business, "you get out. You get the hell out, do you hear?" He picked up the money, took out his wallet once more, and put it back in. At the bedroom door he turned back.

"I don't understand you. Starting with the night at the Wigwam. If you'd pushed me away as soon as we walked through the door, all right. But you didn't. You can't tell me you didn't want me. Or you can tell me, but I know better—you were hot wet, and let *me* tell *you*, a wet—"

"Tom!"

"All right, let's say a woman's body, then—a woman's body doesn't lie."

"At that moment, Tom, I wanted you with every fiber of my being. So much so that I didn't even mind you taking me to that rotten place so long as it made possible what we both wanted. But Tom, there's something I wanted more, and I can't have both."

"And that's what?"

"Another man, one who will marry me—"

"Who said I wouldn't marry you?"

"—and provide for me, and what's more important, for my son, in a way you never could. I'm sorry, Tom, but it's so. You never could, not if all your projects succeeded, every one of them."

He nodded, said no more, and walked out the bedroom door, shutting it quietly behind him. I finished changing my clothes, then went back to the living room. He was sitting there waiting, and got up, very formal, when he saw me. I said: "Are we ready?" Then I remembered and called Bianca, to tell her I wouldn't be in. I could have just come late, the meeting with the lawyer wouldn't run more than an hour I was sure, but with what I had on my mind, an evening of serving drinks was more than I could face. She was upset, but had to say O.K.

Not much was said on the drive over to Marlboro, except for his answers to some of my questions as to who Mr. Eckert was and what I needed to ask him—all I could think of was, would I lose my house, but Tom reminded me that other things had to be asked, like how much time did we have, and actually what would be done, on a "play-by-play basis," as he put it. "I would think the sheriff figures in it," he told me, in a hesitant, guarded way, "and we ought to find out first how he goes about it, what-ever it is that he does. Could be we have to cooperate—or something."

I had a sudden vision of walking into a police station and finding Private Church there, suspicious as always and ready to jump on me at the least little sign of anything askew. I took some comfort from the distance between Hyattsville and Marlboro, but not as much as I would have if there had been a county line separating them. I almost said we should turn around and I'd take my chances, losing the house if need be, but by the time I'd reached that point we'd arrived.

Mr. Eckert turned out to be a youngish guy in lounge coat and gray slack pants, who shook hands, looked at me quite sharp, and came around the desk to seat me in a chair beside him. When he'd motioned Tom to a chair facing him, he sat down, and read what it said in the paper, which Tom still had in his hand. "Yes," he told us, nodding. "I heard about it and heard about the young girl who had no more sense than to go Jim Lacey's bail—which nobody else would do, considering the guy he was. Jim's wild, that's all that can be said—and the kindest thing, I guess, is to leave it at that and get on. Now hold everything while I check on how things stand."

He picked up his phone and called, then asked: "Sheriff's office? Dwight Eckert calling—about the Lacey case. Will you put somebody on that's familiar with it?" Apparently someone came on, a deputy from what Mr. Eckert said, and for a time it was nothing but all sorts of questions, the date of the warrant, what was being done to serve it, the officer in charge of the case, and: "So, what do we think, where is he?"

Then: "Oh, you have no idea at all? But don't you fellows know Lacey well enough…?"

Pretty soon he hung up, and reported: "They're on the case, they've been given the bench warrant to serve, the one the judge signed this morning, for Lacey's arrest, and they'll bring him in when they know where he is. But that's the catch: They *don't* know where he is, and being 'short-handed,' as that deputy said, they have no one detailed to find him. Now I'll leave you to decide if that's really the reason or if the fact that Lacey was the engineer who worked on building their new station house has anything to do with it. He hung around the station plenty, glad-handing and ingratiating himself as best he could. They all knew him."

"You don't mean they'd let him get away?"

Eckert shrugged. "Who knows? Maybe not; maybe they didn't even like him. Most people who got to know him didn't. But if they did, and if they're short-handed anyway, it could be they just wouldn't choose to put the few men they do have on his case. No one could fault them—you have to remember, it's not a regular criminal case. Still…" He looked me over in a way that made me feel like I was wearing my work uniform rather than my gray wool suit. "…it wouldn't surprise me, if a good-looking lady were to go over and talk to whoever's in charge over there and explain what she had at stake, that might light a fire under them. They're human too, after all."

"Thank you, Mr. Eckert. How much am I going to owe you?"

"…For our chat today, nothing. If you want me to stay on the case, put it on my calendar—oh, shall we say two-fifty?"

"Two-fifty's fine. Thank you."

I wrote him a check for $250, thanked him again, and led the way out, Tom following. "Which way is this new station house your friend built, if you know?" I asked him.

"Across the street from the courthouse."

"Then we can walk."

The sheriff's office was in a big room off the street, but shutting it off when you went in was an elbow-high counter with desks on the far side, girls seated at some, uniformed men at the others. We leaned on the counter, and Tom rapped with his knuckles. A girl came, and when she heard what case it was, called a deputy in the back of the room. He came, and remembering what

Mr. Eckert had said, I put on a bit of an act, playing the poor, upset little girl who'd gotten charmed into putting her property at risk—which wasn't so far from the truth, of course. "I went bail for a man who has skipped," I said with my friendliest smile, "and I've come to find out what I can do, what the Sheriff can help me to do, to bring him back so I don't lose my house."

"...On that," he said, eyeing me close, "I'd take it very serious."

"I do take it serious," I assured him. "If it was your house at risk, I think you'd take it serious too. But you seem to mean more than you've said. Give. What's your name?"

"Harrison."

"Deputy Harrison, I'm listening."

"Mrs. Medford, it's so rare for bail actually to be forfeited that I can't remember its happening. But most bail is signed for by bondsmen, professional bondsmen, who have tremendous political clout. They're not supposed to have it, but do. In the case of a woman who signed the bond as a friend, who has no particular clout—or do you have?"

"Not the slightest."

I aimed that at Tom, and saw him wince. "In that case," Deputy Harrison went on, "I'd say you could be in trouble. You could be the human sacrifice offered up, to prove the law takes its course —without fear, favor, or finagling of any kind."

"...And is that so, that the law takes its course without favor?"

"What do you mean?"

"I'm told Jim Lacey was well known around here, built this building for you."

At that, he snorted. "Oh, yes. He was known. Sheriff had to tell him three times to stop trying to give the men bottles 'for after hours.' Don't worry that he's got friends here, Mrs. Medford, for he hasn't."

"O.K."

"But that's not entirely the good thing you might think it is."

"Oh?"

"If he did have friends here, they might know where to find him. Now, we'll do all we can, but it's not a case with men detailed to search—we just haven't got the men. What that means, in practice, is you'll have to find him yourself. The good news is, you might be able to where we couldn't. After all, I'm sure he does have a few friends somewhere, who wouldn't help us, but who might shoot off their mouths to you. You see what I'm saying? If you can get them to tell you anything, we'll be on it right away, if you give us the barest hint. To help a young girl like you, who made a mistake and now is in a jam, we'll act and act quick—but we have to have something to act on."

"Well, then we're at a dead end, because I don't have the barest hint to give you."

"But why?" He looked genuinely baffled. "Why wouldn't you know where to find this guy, or at least his friends?"

"...Me? Why would I?"

"You went his bail, didn't you?"

I stood there, utterly crossed up, and then at last saw what he meant. I asked him: "You mean there was something personal, as you think, between me and Mr. Lacey?"

"Well it's what you would think, isn't it?"

"Lacey's *my* friend," Tom cut in.

"All right, then *you* must know—?"

"I don't."

Deputy Harrison looked at Tom in a very peculiar way, and the way Tom looked away, I suddenly felt that he did know something, at least more than he was telling us. I knew also, if I wanted to find out, I had to get him out of there. So I thanked Deputy Harrison, shaking his hand with both of mine. He smiled, nodded, and squeezed my hand extra, as if to communicate that he really wanted to help. Then I drove home with Tom, and asked: "What was *that* all about? What are you keeping from me?"

"I thought of someone, that's all. Jim has a girl. On the side, apart from his wife. I saw her once, leaving his office when I came to pick him up."

"And Deputy Harrison thought I was she?"

"I don't know that he knows about her. Probably not, and I wasn't going to be the one to tell him. But I guess he thought you might be something like that to Jim. He gave his reason for thinking it, and you can't say it didn't make sense—until you were explained, that is. Your connection with the case, through me."

"So who is this girl?"

"That's the problem. I don't know—not her name, not where she lives, nothing."

"What do I do now?"

"Joan, if I knew I'd certainly say."

I asked him in and he began making calls, or rather the same call, over and over, to at least a dozen people: "Jack?"—or whatever the name would be—"Where's Jim? I have a reason for wanting to know… O.K., but if you hear something, will you ring me at this number? Oh, and do you have any idea how I might reach his girl? No, not his wife. You know who I mean…" About the fifteenth call I went out in the hall to put my hand on the receiver, so he couldn't lift it again. "I'm sorry," I said. "I've had about all I can take."

"It's all I know to do. These people are his friends, and one of them might know something useful—if they'd want to tell me."

"O.K., but one more call and I'll scream."

"I'm doing this for you, let's remember." He shoved my hand aside and lifted the receiver.

I didn't scream, but I began slapping at him again as he sat
there at the telephone table, the way I'd slapped him that night
at the Garden. He got up, put his arms around me, wrapped me
up, and held me until I calmed down. "I'm sorry," I said, still
trembling. "—I have a temper, as perhaps you've found out."

"Well, you'd better get it under control, Joan, at least where
I'm concerned. It's not my fault Jim skipped."

That was enough to set me off again. "Not your fault? Not
your fault?"

I then recited it at him, the whole book, beginning with the
first night, what he did to me and what I did to him; then my
signing the bond for his friend Mr. Lacey, and then the thanks I
got, being taken to a so-called nightclub that was really a hot-
sheets motel in flimsiest disguise—I really screamed it at him,
until I was hoarse and could hardly talk. When I collapsed into
a chair and started to cry, he took his handkerchief out, wiped
my nose, and asked: "Are you done?"

"I guess so. Please, will you go home?"

"Not just yet I won't. First off, Joan, on this litany you keep
hurling at me. When a woman is really sore, when she hates a
man for what he's done, she doesn't entertain his offers night
after night, she tells him so and cuts him cold."

"Not if he's a long-standing customer and she's a waitress
who needs her job."

"O.K.—maybe. But at least, the one night he makes no invitation, she doesn't proffer one of her own, I think you'll agree
with that?"

I said nothing.

"So then we come to Jim Lacey, and why you signed his bail.
Well why did you, Joan? Why?"

"Because you asked me to."

"I didn't at all; I never asked you to."

"O.K., maybe it was so you'd know I wasn't a pauper, so you would stop treating me like some kind of cocktail girl—"

"You *are* a cocktail girl!"

"O.K., I'm a cocktail girl, and to thank this poor waif for helping your friend, you take her to a whorehouse."

"I had a reason for that too."

"Explain it, please."

"I had the impression that you liked me, that you might want more of my company than you could have just chatting at the Garden. But I wanted to take you somewhere special for it—somewhere where the lights would be dim and the music low, where people would be having a good time. A place where we could be with each other and not be bothered, but with a touch of excitement, too. You may not have cared for the Wigwam, but the fact is, it's an exclusive club—they've hosted some of the most famous and influential people in this town, perhaps even a president or two."

"That doesn't mean a thing to me."

"I thought at least it would be nicer than promoting an invite here, or suggesting you come back to my house. That felt too much like—well, like what Liz does, where it's for money, not because two people want each other so badly they can't stand it."

"You think I wanted you that badly?"

"I know you did. You admitted you did."

"In that moment! I lost my head for a moment. But I woke up quick enough, and when I did I ran out of that place practically naked, just to get away."

"It was more than a moment. When I was unbuttoning your pants, who was it helping me? Who pulled your blouse off? And who was it unbuttoned my cuffs? Unless there was a third person in there with us that I didn't notice, it was you, Joan."

Step by step, he took me back over what I had done, from the day of Ron's funeral on. "You want me to say it plain?"

"All right, all right, all right—I wanted you, I admit it. I'm human, and the way you touched me I couldn't help it. I—"

"O.K., O.K., O.K., now we're getting somewhere. So the question is why did you run? Why didn't you hold still for what you wanted, what I wanted, what we both wanted? I'll put it in three little words: Earl, K, White. I'll add a fourth and fifth if you like—"

"...The Third."

"The Third. A worn-out, washed-out scarecrow, old enough to be your father and then some, ugly to look at and I bet worse still to touch—but, he's got money."

He stopped then and waited for me to say something. And finally I did. "Don't knock money. I need it. You need it. Show me the person who doesn't need it."

"I wouldn't sleep with an old man to get it."

"Yes you would. If he'd have you. If he knew the governor and could get you that contract for the goddam nettles. You know you would."

A half hour must have gone by, with him at the window, just standing there, looking out. The phone didn't ring once.

Then suddenly he said: "I was going to suggest we get some dinner, but as I feel now, I don't want to. If you need me, let me know. I'm in the book."

And he left.

16

Around seven, I went over to the Royal Arms, had something to eat, then drove back and went to bed. I spent an utterly miserable night, still worried sick over the situation, still up in the air about Lacey, and in pieces at what Tom and I had said to each other. I woke at three and then again at six, at which point there was no sense trying to fall asleep again, so I sat in the living room looking out at the street until the sun came up.

Tom had tried phoning everyone he could think of the day before, except for one person, leaving her out for an excellent reason—but as nothing had come of any of his calls, it was the only thread left to pull. I had myself some breakfast, put on a dark suit, combed my hair back and pinned it up, then pulled the White Pages from the cabinet and flipped through until I reached the L's. I was afraid they might not be in the book, what with his being something of a public figure, but there they were. I copied out the address, got into my car, and just thirty minutes later was pulling up in front of their house, a modern split-level home with tile roof and towering shrubs framing the porch.

The door opened before I even shut off the ignition. The woman standing behind it was thickset and middle-aged, I would say perhaps fifty, with gray hair, and light-blue eyes that sized me up as I approached. I said: "Good morning. Mrs. Lacey?"

"…Yes, I'm Pearl Lacey."

"I'm Joan Medford, Mrs. Lacey. Your husband and I have—"

I'd been about to say *a friend in common*, but she didn't let me get that far. "Medford! My god. I never expected you to show up here. Well, you surely don't have to tell me what you and my husband have—I can imagine well enough."

"You can't, as it's not anything like—"

"I've heard it before, dear, and from ones that looked prettier than you. What happened, he's not taking you with him? Is it your fragile constitution, you just can't bear the tropical heat? Or tell me, did he cheat on us both...?"

I was taken by surprise, not so much by her anger, as I'd prepared myself for her drawing the same conclusion Deputy Harrison had, as by her recognizing my name. But her next remark explained it: "You poor thing—standing his bail and then nothing to show for it but the brush. And after all those evenings you two must have spent together when I thought he was working on his sewer projects. Well, I suppose in a way he was."

"Mrs. Lacey, I'll have you know there were no evenings together, or nights, or days. I only met your husband once, and the only thing that passed between us that time was a handshake."

"There's no need to lie anymore, dear, certainly not to protect him."

"I'm not." Something in my voice stopped her, made her look at me differently.

"...But you went my husband's bail!"

"Yes I did, Mrs. Lacey."

"Why would you go his bail if you weren't...?"

As I've said, my temper's my greatest weakness, and I wanted to tell her it was none of her business why, but I made myself remember the one great object today was to find out all that I could, and that to do it I'd have to be friendly, even to this woman. Especially to this woman, as she seemed to know something about where Lacey was, judging from her remark about tropical heat.

"I did it to please a friend," I told her, after swallowing one or two times.

"What friend?"

"It's what I was about to tell you when you cut me off before. Your husband and I have a friend in common, Mr. Thomas Barclay."

"Tom? You know him?"

"I've said: I count him a friend." At least, until last night, I thought; but I didn't say this to her.

She stepped back a bit, not enough to let me inside, but enough so that it no longer felt like she was trying to use her rigid body to block the doorway. "Jim thought Tom would sign his bond himself. Why didn't he?"

"He couldn't."

"He could have put up his house, as I gather you did."

"It's mortgaged."

"I never heard that before."

"It's what he told me."

"And you signed just to please him?"

"…Perhaps—I had other reasons."

"You mean you're sleeping with him?"

"*No, I'm not!*"

On that, I flashed hot, and at once I saw her take note. Then: "O.K., then you're sleeping with Jim. It's the only other reason you could have."

"It's not my other reason!"

I was having a battle with myself by now, to keep from going over and letting her have it, as I'd let Tom have it twice now. I stood there blinking at her, so she had to repeat once or twice before I heard what she asked: "What was your other reason?"

"I wanted to do something, something nice if I could, for Tom. Because…I'm marrying somebody else—or at least I think I am."

"Who is this somebody else?"

"That's where your business ends, I'm afraid. I've told you all you need to know: your husband and I were nothing to each other, not friends, not even acquaintances; I helped him to help a friend, and now it's backfired and I stand to lose something I can't easily bear to lose, unless you can help me get on your husband's trail—as I'd think you'd be glad to do, if you know where he is or where he's going."

"It's not so simple. If he's not going with you, he's going with another—" The word she'd been about to use would not have been complimentary and she saw, I think, that I was at my limit already. "...With another woman. And if he were caught and it came out..." She grimaced. "I can bear the shame of being thought the wife of a criminal, even of a fugitive. But to have it written in the papers that he left me for some girl our son's age—"

"O.K. I understand."

She looked at me closely, staring into my eyes in a way that made me uncomfortable. "...You do, don't you?"

"I know something about men, I'm sorry to say. I may be younger than you, but I've lived some. I have a child too, and no father for him, though in my case I couldn't be happier that he's gone."

"...Another woman?"

"A culvert wall, at seventy miles per hour."

She nodded slowly.

"Mrs. Medford, I'm sorry—I saw you and thought you were something worse than you are."

"Then, I'm sorry too, for getting upset. I have quite a lot on my mind."

"It sounds like we've both had men in our lives who are, to put it bluntly, sons of bitches."

"To put it truthfully."

"Well, you're right that I want my son of a bitch caught and brought back to face the music. And now that I see you're not sleeping with him but chasing him down, I'd love to give you some help—provided you agree to do something for me. Two things."

"Yes?"

"Keep the woman out of it—out of the story, I mean. Make sure the news photographers snap him alone, not her by his side. I don't care how you do it, just that you do. And—keep me out of it, too, as far as the police go." She saw that I was puzzled. Looking around the block, at the rush-hour foot traffic going past—wholly uninterested, but within range to hear—she stepped back further, allowing me inside at last. She shut the door behind us and, even so, kept her voice low when she spoke. "There were things I couldn't tell the police, when they came and questioned me about Jim's disappearance. Had I known what he was planning? Had I seen any signs…? I said no. What woman ever knows that her husband is about to leave her?"

"But you had seen something?"

"When he was in the shower Tuesday evening, the night before he was due in court. I found two tickets in his briefcase—two plane tickets issued under phony names, Mr. and Mrs. James Barnaby, leaving for Nassau at twelve o'clock Friday—tomorrow, in other words. When I shook them in his face, he said they were for us. We'd fly away together. Well, it was half the truth. In the morning, he was gone—and both tickets with him. But how could I tell the police this? That I knew about the tickets and let him hold onto them because I thought I would be taken along?"

I said: "You would have left everything behind? Your house, your son, your life…?"

"My son has been charting his own course for years now, since he turned sixteen, pretty much. My life, in this neighborhood at least, is over and has been over since the day Jim was arrested—I can barely show my face, even among people who were our friends once. As for my house and the other things we have, well…the tickets weren't the only thing I found in his bag." She held my gaze firm. "I didn't count it, Joan, but I worked in a bank before marrying, and I can still estimate by eye. He's got at least fifty grand in that briefcase, to go down to Nassau with, and lay in the sun for a while. And maybe more."

"But—if he had that much money—he could have made bail anytime he wanted!"

"Sure, and had less to live on when he got to the islands. Why should he, if he could persuade someone else to put up the money for him?"

"And where did all this money in his briefcase come from?"

A flush of red rose along her cheeks, and I remembered the newspaper articles about the bribes he was supposed to have taken. "I don't care to speculate. All I can tell you is, here was all this money, and a pair of plane tickets, with the alternative being no money, just a public trial and its aftermath, and I said to myself, sometimes you just have to jump."

"But then, he jumped without you."

"Now you've got it. And you can see why I couldn't share this with the police."

"No, of course," I said, seeing it perfectly. An officer like Young might have bent the rules for her, but a Church would have had her hunting up bail of her own in no time. "Well, they don't have to know I heard about the tickets from you. Tom made a pile of calls yesterday, to all your husband's friends. One of them might have known and told him."

"Mrs. Medford—Joan—if you can handle it that way you'll have my blessing and my thanks. All you have to do is look for Mr. and Mrs. Barnaby in the United Airlines terminal tomorrow before noon, and you should find him."

I stood there blinking at her, trying to realize she had made it possible for me to keep from losing my house. I wanted to thank her, but nothing I could think of to say seemed to cover it. So I just said, "I will," and turned to go.

As I opened the door, she said: "If you see Tom, give him my love. He's a good one, if a bit pie-eyed sometimes."

"Glad to."

"He ever tell you that idea he has for the Chesapeake Bay— some idea he can work the atomic plants to get the nettles out, use one against the other? If that's not screwy, I don't know what is."

"Yes, he's told me."

Next thing I knew, I was in Tom's car, and we were headed for Upper Marlboro, with this tremendous piece of information Mrs. Lacey had given me. I must have called him but don't remember doing it. We talked, very excited, about what our next move would be, with no backwash to last night and the sour note we had broken on. Then we were at Upper Marlboro, parked back of the courthouse, and then in the Sheriff's office again. Deputy Harrison came out to see me, and was really friendly about it. "Then O.K.," he said. "That cooks his goose, that does it. We'll be there, with our warrant to serve on him. We'll take it over—you've nothing to worry about."

"Feel better now?" asked Tom as we headed home.

"A little relieved perhaps. Once he's back in jail, then I'll feel better."

17

We got to my house, and I asked him in, of course. He dropped into the chair I usually sat in, staring out the window, the way I so often did. "…Something wrong?" I asked, after a while.

"No, not a thing."

But then, five minutes later: "I think."

And then: "Joan, I'm worried, and don't even know about what. But suddenly, it's all become too damned easy."

"…Well?" I asked after a moment or two. "The whole trouble was, they didn't know where to find him. Now they do. It takes care of everything."

After a long time, he said: "Jim Lacey's nobody's saint, but he's nobody's fool either. Being crooked does not also mean being stupid. So Jim Lacey knows his wife saw the tickets and knows what he's up to. So he knows she could do her best to louse him. So what does he do about it?"

"…You asking me?"

"Myself. I just don't happen to know."

But pretty soon he began snapping his fingers. "What I would do about it would be to go out to that airport, bringing the girl-friend along, and then separate from her, so as not to be spotted as a couple. Then I'd put myself somewhere, maybe topside in the lunchroom, where I could keep an eye on that waiting room, to see everyone that comes in. So here come the Maryland offi-cers—in uniform, perhaps, but even if not, I know them per-sonally from when I built the station."

"…O.K.? What then?"

"I don't know. Do you?"

"No, but I don't feel relieved anymore."

"Well, I certainly don't. O.K., I see them come in, and right away, I slip out. I slip out into a cab, and beat it to the bus station. There I wait for the girl—who may have slipped out too, and be waiting at the cab stand. So we go by bus to Miami, where I take the same flight the next day. So I forfeit the price of two tickets. So? It's better than going to prison."

"I don't feel relieved *at all.*"

"I'm sorry if I upset you."

"But what do we do?"

"You say we in that tone of voice, I have to think of something."

"What do you mean by *that*?"

"You know what I mean. Don't you?"

I felt weak and queer and smothered, and am not at all sure that I answered.

By now he was tramping around, showing every sign of excitement, and then suddenly snapped his fingers again, telling me very excitedly: "I've got it, I've got it, I've got it!" I waited, and he went on, kneeling beside my chair: "We need a hand, from someone else with the power to arrest and an interest in doing so, someone he won't recognize. We can't use the Airport Police, on account that they're Federal and take no part in local bail jumps. However, I think we have an alternative. He's skipping with fifty grand, and it's fairly certain he hasn't paid any tax on the money, which means IRS will move in, if we just give them the tip. *They* can claim help from the Airport Police, as they're Federal too. Come on, we're going to Wheaton."

We used his car again, and once more were in one of those

offices with counters in front, desks in back, and girls in short skirts chewing gum. I pictured all three being ordered in bulk from something like the Sears Catalog. At one of the desks was a man, who came and asked what we wanted. Tom let me talk and I did, being as brief as I could, yet at the same time explaining myself, who I was, and how I'd gone Lacey's bond. Then I said: "Where you come in is: He's skipping with fifty grand, fifty thousand dollars, or so I'm reliably informed, and if he's skipping to Nassau, we can bet he hasn't paid any tax, and could be he doesn't intend to. Sir, does that possibility interest the IRS?"

"Lady, are you being funny?"

"You mean IRS doesn't care?"

"I mean it does—and how."

"Then what does it do about it? And what do I do about it?"

"Hold everything—got to consult."

He went to his desk, picked up the phone and pressed buttons. Pretty soon another man was there. They whispered a minute, then spoke to a girl, who got up and went through a door. In a bit she came out with a card, which the men took from her and studied. Then they both came to the counter. "O.K.," the first man said. "This is Mr. Schwartz, who will act with me in this matter. My name is Christopher, and we've looked Mr. Lacey up—he filed a return last year, but paid so small a tax we checked him out. We didn't turn up a great deal—there's nothing now pending against him. But skipping to Nassau, with fifty grand in his pocket, sets up a risk for us that we simply can't ignore."

"Yes, Mr. Christopher, but what—?"

"I'm coming to it, Mrs. Medford. We collar him at the airport, count the cash he has on him, figure his tax from the tables, and impound it."

"In the waiting room, or where?"

"In the Airport Police office. It's downstairs from the main waiting room."

"And after you've taken the money?"

"That's all, we're done. We give a receipt, of course. If he doesn't like it he sues us in court."

"You mean he's free to go?"

"We have no objection, none at all."

"But what I'm interested in is the Maryland Police—having him held long enough for them to come in and get him."

"I see your point, but we can't help you directly. However, if the Maryland Police got there while we're working him over, if they knew where to come, to the Airport Police office—"

"You mean I should call them about it?"

"If we're all in sync, we don't actually work together, but the result will be the same."

"I see. I see. Then—thank you."

"Wait a minute, not so fast."

He and Mr. Schwartz whispered, and then Mr. Schwartz asked: "You know this man, Mrs. Medford?"

"I met him once, yes."

"You know his lady friend?"

"Not even by name, no. But Tom here, he's seen her. And he knows Lacey as well, much better than I do."

"All right, then." To Tom: "You can finger him for us, and her. She's important, because the possibility that we would be there must have occurred to him, and letting her handle the briefcase would be a simple way out—if we get him, she can slip away."

"He'd have to trust her for that," Tom said.

"Not at all," said Mr. Schwartz, grinning, but the way a cat grins at a mouse. "He just has to hand her the bag and tell her to take it onto the plane for him. He doesn't have to say what's in it."

"That's why we need you there," Mr. Christopher insisted. "If he doesn't have the case we can grab *her*, and impound the tax that way."

I said: "But then you'll let the girl go? I made a promise to the person who told us where to find him, that we'd keep the girl out of it."

"Why not? All we want is the money."

Then, we began "setting it up," as Mr. Christopher called it, how we would do the next day. They were concerned that if he saw Tom, Jim Lacey I'm talking about, he'd do what Tom had said, blow, but fast, and take the girl and the money with him. I was for Tom's wearing dark glasses, but he smacked it out at once. "You're practically advertising you don't want to be recognized, if you dress like that indoors. It's all Jim would need to take a second look." It was Christopher who came up with the idea of making Tom older, by having him put on a gray wig and darken the lines on his face with pencil and wear a jacket one size larger than he normally took. We had a look in the yellow book, and found a wig place right there in Wheaton that served men as well as women. Then he and I drove over there, though Mr. Schwartz cautioned us: "Be sure and check in again, so I know, so the both of us know, what you're going to look like."

The wig place was called Helga of Sweden, and the salesman was awfully nice. I was jolted the least little bit that a simple gray wig that looked as we wanted it to would cost thirty dollars, but Tom insisted he couldn't pull off what he was supposed to without it, and I put up the money. I had eye-liner in my bag, and I used it to put some wrinkles across Tom's forehead and deepen the creases on either side of his mouth. Suddenly he was sixty years old—"except for your walk," said the salesman, laughing. "You still walk like a young man."

"He means put some lead in your tail," I said.

"This way?" he asked, making a stab at middle-age sag.

"That's it."

Passing me close, he whispered, "Maybe I should have done this sooner, it seems to be the age of man you prefer," and I pretended not to have heard. It was the only word he'd spoken all day that hailed back to our standoff the night before, but it showed his feelings were still on a boil, even if he'd put a lid over the pot.

On the way back to the IRS office, I shelled out another twenty dollars for a loose-fitting jacket and five more for a pair of eyeglasses with plain glass in the frames. I let Tom go in first, alone, and at least from across the room Mr. Christopher didn't know him. "Yes, sir?" he asked, very polite, coming to the counter. "What can we do for you?"

"All we want is the money," Tom told him, and Mr. Christopher's eyes opened wide. Then he called Mr. Schwartz over, and though Schwartz saw through it, he nodded seriously and pronounced the disguise "good enough." We lined it out then, what we would do the next morning at the airport—how Tom would take a seat in front of United Airlines, open a magazine, start to read, and peep over the top. They would take positions at either side of the room, and the moment Tom saw either Mr. Lacey or the girl, he'd get up, walk past, and close the magazine as he went by. If Lacey was with the woman it would all be very simple. If not, it might get complicated. I, meanwhile, would be in the back of the room watching from a distance, dark glasses having been deemed sufficient cover for me, as first of all they are less unusual on women indoors than men and second of all, as Tom put it, "he only saw you once, for half an hour, at midnight in a bar after being let out of jail, and he spent most of the time looking at the gap in your blouse anyway, not your face." And the girl, of course, had never seen me at all.

With this all set, Tom and I started to go, but Mr. Schwartz reminded me I'd better call Marlboro and let Deputy Harrison know how things stood, so he could come to the Airport Police office at once when he arrived, and not search the waiting room with his men and possibly get spotted by "the quarry," as they termed Lacey.

18

We got home a bit after four, and took stock of what we should do. Tom sat by the window again, and pretty soon began to talk: "First thing, Joan, at least as I see it, is that we get where the action is—to a motel somewhere near National Airport, so we're not fighting traffic tomorrow morning and maybe we arrive too late. So—hold everything." He got the Yellow Pages, looked, and found a big motel that might not want to be named, on account of what happened next day, so I don't say which motel it was. He went on: "O.K., we go there—but not together. We go in separate cars, arriving at different times. I take a single with bath. You take a suite."

"...Suite?" I asked. "Why?"

"So we can see each other without being seen. Suppose Jim's staying there too? If he sees us in the lobby or some other public area like that—?"

"But why a suite? What does that have to do with it?"

"In a suite, you can have anyone up that you choose, male, female or neuter. They assume that with a sitting room it wouldn't occur to you to do things you might be tempted to do, if all you had was a bedroom."

"Are you sure that's the rule?"

"Well? Call them, why don't you? And ask."

"...That's O.K. I trust your superior knowledge of motels."

He went in his car to pack his things, and after I threw a bag together, I drove on down to the motel, a big one in three sections. At the registration desk I asked the price of a suite, "bedroom, living room, and bath." The clerk didn't seem at all surprised by a woman registering alone, and said: "We have them from thirty-seven fifty up."

"Is thirty-seven fifty outside?"

"All our suites are outside. The thirty-seven fifty tier looks out on the airport. For forty-five seventy-five, you can look out on the river."

"Airport's fine."

He gave me a key and told me how to go. I took my bag to the elevator, went up, followed his directions down a hall, unlocked a door, and suddenly was in my suite, feeling guilty and excited and a little dry in the throat. I went through the rooms—they were done in pale green, with darker green furniture to blend, and everything so recently cleaned you could smell it. I tried not to look at the beds, of which there were two, "though of course," the clerk had explained, "for two persons the charge is forty-two fifty."

After I put my things in the bureau drawer, such few things as I had, I went back to the sitting room. Out the window, I could see planes landing and taking off, but they were far enough away that I couldn't hear them. On one table was a telephone, and I used it to dial the Garden.

"Bianca please, Sue. Thank you." When Bianca picked up, I said: "I'm going to be out again tonight—and maybe tomorrow, I don't know."

There was silence on the line.

"I can't help it, Bianca. It's something personal and important."

"You sick in bed? On death's door?"

"...No. Not like that."

"Then you're not leaving me short-handed two nights in a row, never mind three. You get down here right now, Joan."

"I can't."

After some more silence: "You want to explain to me why I shouldn't fire you this time? Tom's not around to talk me out of it again."

"No he's not," I said. "He's here with me."

"…Oh!"

"He and I have something that can't wait. One way or another, it'll be done tomorrow, and then I'll be in again like always. But tonight—"

"I heard you, you can't. I hope you know what you're doing, Joan."

"This time, I do."

Still sounding upset: "…I'll go tell Liz."

As soon as I put down the receiver, the phone was ringing, and then Tom's voice was in my ear: "Just checked in. Feel like going over it again, maybe?"

"No maybe about it."

"On my way up."

Once he arrived, I called Room Service and had them read me the dinner menu, repeating each item to him. Maybe because of the day we had ahead of us, we were both hungry—we took salad with French dressing, chicken fricassee, baked potato, peas, ice cream, and coffee. Presently, a man rolled our order in on a metal table, served us and left, telling us: "When you're done, put the table out in the hall—I'll come for it later." When we finished the meal I poured the coffee, taking mine black, while Tom took two lumps and cream. "This feels awfully domestic," he said. "Like playing man and wife." He was right, it did—friendly, warm and comfortable. But his putting it that way suddenly got me nervous.

"…Let's get on to tomorrow," I told him.

We went through it all one more time. I'd help him put on his face in the morning, and the wig, then we'd drive to the airport separately. We discussed where he'd sit and where I would, what he'd do if he saw them together and what he'd do if he saw one of them alone. We ran through it all twice.

"What if the Airport Police ask you what you're doing there?" he asked.

"Why would they?"

"If they do."

"I'm waiting for a friend who's bringing our tickets."

"O.K. Fine."

"And what if they ask you?"

"Same, I guess. Or maybe I can whisper to them I'm there to help grab a rat who jumped his bail."

"Maybe—but don't."

"No."

"…Tom? You realize, don't you, that this will be the end of any chance you might have with Lacey for that help you wanted, with his cousin. All that work you put into him, getting close to him, doing errands for him—like covering for his son that day."

"Well, I'm glad I did that one, for other reasons entirely."

We both smiled. But I said, "I'm serious."

"Yes I do realize it."

"And you don't mind?"

"Yes I mind. But he can't get away with what he's trying here. If my house hadn't been in hock to a bank, it would be me he was doing this to, and I'd be on the street. The only reason it's you is because you know me and wanted to do me a kindness. So—if I lose him, I lose him. There are always other ways to a goal, and I'll find one."

"*If* you lose him? Tom, how could you not?"

"I am going to be wearing that wig you got me, and the glasses. Who knows, maybe he won't tip to who it was turned him in."

I saw then why he'd been so insistent on the wig. But I thought back to how quick Mr. Schwartz had seen through it, and didn't have the heart to be too encouraging on the point.

"Well—I thank you," I said.

After a moment in which neither of us seemed to know what to say, Tom set down his coffee cup and stood. "...So, I guess that covers that," he said. "Time we were getting to bed."

My stomach clutched—but he simply blew me a kiss and left.

Next morning I took great care with his face, putting three fine lines, like crow's feet, at the corner of each eye, and one heavier slanting line on each cheek beside his mouth, doing it careful so they followed actual grooves in the skin and didn't look like makeup even seen from close up. I did the same with the lines on his forehead. I kept telling myself, "Don't overdo it," and didn't. I realized when I pulled the wig on that he *was* sixty years old at a distance of more than six feet, and the plan was for him to stay that far away from anyone. He slipped on the jacket and glasses we'd bought and blinked at me, then put on his old-man gait as he headed for the door to my suite. It was strange seeing him go, as I did have a flash, just for an instant, of what it would be like if I married Mr. White, seeing him off in the morning and welcoming him home each night. I shivered.

Once he was gone I dressed myself in a quiet and practical outfit like you might wear for a plane trip, and went down to breakfast, first buying a magazine, the *Ladies Home Journal*, at the newsstand. Tom was across the room, finishing his own breakfast, and let his eyes cross mine, but we didn't speak to each other. He left before my food came. I ate quickly, paid my check, and went at once to my car, which I had parked in sight of the door. When I got to the airport I parked on their lot, added a pair of dark glasses to my *ensemble*, and walked to the main building.

The waiting room was huge but I marched myself slowly down it, from the foot of the stairs to the restaurant, past the ticket offices of the various airlines, to the far end. I didn't see

Mr. Lacey, but did see Mr. Christopher, and then, on the bench facing him, Mr. Schwartz. I saw them each nod slightly when they spotted me, and Mr. Schwartz inclined his head in the direction of the corner of the room. I took a seat there, facing United Airlines, but also commanding a view of the entrance. I opened the magazine, holding it down by my lap in such way as to let me look over the top. The clock said 10:30, which meant it was getting up tight, as with the plane leaving at twelve o'clock, passengers were expected to show by eleven, and while Lacey might take a chance, and wait till the last minute, he ran the risk of being paged under the Barnaby name, and in that way calling attention to himself. But there was nothing to do but wait, and I did, getting more nervous by the minute.

At 10:55 a man bumped my legs going by and blocked my view of the entrance. I craned my neck to look around him. He was an old man, white haired and leaning on a cane, and he was slow going past. I cursed silently to myself—Lacey might be coming through right now and I would miss him, all because of this guy—

Then I took a closer look at the old man. He had his face turned away from me so all I caught was a portion of his profile, but I knew it at once. That angular nose, the jowls hanging down beneath his chin—it was Lacey! He'd had the same notion we had, only he'd gone us one better, shaving part of his skull bare to make himself bald on top, all except for a fringe around that he'd powdered white. Add a cane and a stoop and you had a harmless granddad that no one would think was Jim Lacey if they didn't look carefully, and then only if they were as near to him as I was sitting.

He hadn't noticed me, or hadn't recognized me, at least—that was to the good. But he'd passed me by now and was heading in his slow, measured way toward the gate at the end of the room, and I could see, looking around desperately, that none of Tom nor Mr. Christopher nor Mr. Schwartz had noticed or recognized him either. I wanted to get up and point, or shout, or do something—but then the game would be up, since Lacey had nothing on him but the cane in one hand and a light topcoat over his other arm. The money was surely with his girlfriend, and if I raised the alarm, she would bolt.

Where was she? Where—? I scanned the room left and right, looking for any female figure that looked out of place. But there was no reason, I knew, for her to look out of place. She'd be a woman, traveling alone, carrying a heavy case—but the room was packed, at the very height of the noon rush, and there must have been two dozen women traveling alone, every one of them with a heavy case in hand.

Then I looked over toward the gate. There were several women standing there, but one in particular caught my eye. She was holding a big dispatch case by her side and wearing dark glasses like mine. Neither of these facts was a guarantee of anything, of course. But as I watched, Lacey glanced at her and I saw her chin dip minutely in a nod.

Or had I imagined it? Had she been nodding at someone else? But no: he was heading straight for her, and though I couldn't see her eyes behind the shadowed lenses, she was facing him directly, her lips were drawn tight, and looking down I saw the toe of one of her feet tap impatiently.

I glanced over at Tom. Behind his raised magazine he was staring toward the entrance, the wrong direction entirely. And Mr. Christopher and Mr. Schwartz were looking at each other— I saw one glance at his wristwatch and shrug.

There was no time any longer for subtlety. In a minute he'd be at the gate and it would be too late. I got up and crossed quickly, my heels clattering loudly against the tile floor. I watched Lacey's back in front of me and prayed he wouldn't turn around at the sound.

He didn't. He just kept going, aimed like an arrow at the gate and the plane beyond, and the freedom they both represented.

A dozen hurried steps brought me to Mr. Schwartz's side and I bent to whisper in his ear: "That's him, the old man with the cane, the one who just went by. He did himself up like Tom did!"

He looked, and got up. Across the way, Mr. Christopher stood as well, seemingly casual—but not really so casual if you noticed how quickly he moved. They exchanged a glance, and I saw Mr. Christopher's eyes shoot along Lacey's path to his destination. And now at last Tom looked over too, following what was going on from where he sat.

Mr. Schwartz was at Lacey's side in an instant, one hand sliding in to grip his upper arm. Mr. Christopher, meanwhile, shot past, to the gate, and clamped his hand over the woman's on the handle of the dispatch case. I couldn't hear what she said, but saw a look of alarm on her face, and an attempt to pull away from him, until he flashed a badge that he held in his hand. At that point her shoulders fell.

They walked back past me toward a door marked PRIVATE — NO ADMITTANCE, all four of them, first Mr. Schwartz leading Lacey, who was no longer stooping or using the cane, and then Mr. Christopher leading the woman. I wondered what spectators might be thinking about the arthritic old man's miraculous recovery. "Come with us," Mr. Christopher said as he passed, and only after a moment did I realize he was addressing me. I shot a glance back toward where Tom sat, some distance off, and he hadn't budged; perhaps grateful that things had come to a head without his having to show his face at all. I was nearer in any event, and time was at a premium.

"Ma'am, please," said Mr. Christopher. I followed quickly in his wake.

He and the woman went through the door, then down a steep set of stairs, to a room marked AIRPORT OFFICE. Inside were some uniformed officers to whom Mr. Schwartz was showing his badge, and of course Lacey, looking frightened and combative. Mr. Christopher showed his badge as well, and then Mr. Schwartz got down to brass tacks: "We don't want any trouble, cause you to miss your plane or anything like that—but we hear you're carrying a large amount of money out of the country."

"Who said that? They're lying—"

Mr. Schwartz turned to me. "Is this the man?"

"Yes," I said.

"Who are you?" Lacey said, still not recognizing me. "What is this?"

"We're not the police," Mr. Schwartz said. "We're Internal Revenue. We don't care where the money came from or what you did to get it. We just care that Uncle Sam gets his fair share."

Mr. Christopher, meanwhile, had wrestled the case out of the woman's hand and as we watched he unpacked a top layer of clothes and toiletries and then turned the case over to dump packs of money out. I could see they were held by paper tapes with printing on them—apparently the denominations of the bills, and how many. I saw some fifties, some hundreds, and one stack of twenties.

The woman suddenly sat down heavily in a chair. I confess I felt sorry for her.

Mr. Schwartz leafed through one pack of bills and Mr. Christopher leafed through another. They didn't take off the tapes, but did each take out a card and write down an amount on it after checking a pack and putting it to one side. "O.K.," said Mr. Schwartz when they'd finished and compared cards. "We make it fifty-five thousand even, and the tax on that is twenty—which we'll impound, as taxes paid on account, giving you a receipt, and noting it's subject to repayment, in part or in whole, if, as, and when warranted by your timely filed federal income tax return."

Mr. Schwartz got a book out of his briefcase, a thing that looked like a checkbook, and wrote. It must have taken him just a few minutes to fill out the receipt, but it felt like ages as we all stood there in silence, glaring at one another. Then Mr. Schwartz tore out what he'd written, checked the carbons, of which there were two, and handed the original to Mr. Christopher. Mr. Christopher looked it over, handed it to Lacey, then put several packs of money into his briefcase, first letting Schwartz count each. I suddenly felt horror-stricken—they were almost done and still I didn't have Lacey. He was right there in front of me, but his plane would leave in ten minutes and there was no way I could stop him from taking it. "Are we done?" he asked Mr. Schwartz, suddenly.

"All done."

"Then, Flo—?"

But Flo didn't get up from the chair she'd dropped into. "Ah, for Christ's sake, Jim," she growled. "Wake up, this is it, you've had it."

"What's the matter, you scared?"

"I guess so, call it that."

"Well I'm not. I'm going."

He grabbed the dispatch case up and jammed the remaining money and the clothes back in any which way. He didn't even bother buckling it closed before heading for the door.

I wanted to scream from disappointment. "You're going to let him go?" I demanded.

"He's fully paid up now, Mrs. Medford," Mr. Christopher said. "We have no way to hold him."

At the mention of my name, I saw Lacey's face blanch. He bolted the rest of the way to the door and clutched at the knob. I leapt after him, but he got it open before I could lay a hand on him. I saw my last chance escaping.

Then he stopped dead, and so did I, my heart hammering.

"Hello," said Tom, blocking the way. He was still in his full regalia, but not for long. With one hand he took off the glasses and with the other he whipped off the wig. "Where do you think you're going?"

"Get out of my way!"

"Try and make me, Jim."

Lacey tried to push past him. But Tom pushed back, and it was no contest, Tom's strength against Lacey's, the younger man against the older. And then, then at last, came a flash of blue, as the Maryland officers appeared behind Tom in the doorway. "I'll take that," said Deputy Harrison, making a grab for the dispatch case and getting it. "You'll get it back, of course, any of it that's legal, but as of now we have to impound it. You're under arrest, Jim, for skipping bail. I'm sorry."

Lacey put his hands up. "O.K.," he answered. "O.K."

"That all you got to say?" This from the woman, Flo, still seated where she'd landed earlier.

"What else is there to say?"

"If this is the Mrs. Medford you told me about, the one who stood your bail, you could at least speak to her, and say how sorry you are."

Then Lacey faced me, quite solemnly. "Mrs. Medford," he began, "I assure you, I give you my word, I'd have seen to it that you wouldn't forfeit the bail you pledged for me. All I wanted was time to prepare my case, and once it was ready I'd have been back, long before you'd have been required to—"

"Jim, you're a goddam liar," Tom told him, coldly furious.

Deputy Harrison cut in: "You'll get your chance to settle it in court. Come on—let's go."

He jerked his head at two of his men, and they hustled Lacey out.

"What about me?" Flo asked.

"There a warrant out for your arrest?" Deputy Harrison asked.

"Not on your life."

"...You owe any income taxes?" Mr. Christopher said.

"I'd have to have income first."

"Well, then, you're free to go," Deputy Harrison said. "Might want to think over your choice in men next time, but that's free advice and worth as much as you paid for it."

She stood up, half nodded to me in a sort of sisterly solidarity, then walked out the door. I thought of my promise to Mrs. Lacey, to keep her out of the story, but figured I could trust Flo's sense of self-preservation to steer her away from any newspapermen with cameras that might have gotten tipped and be waiting upstairs.

"Thanks so much," I told the two IRS men, who returned their thanks. Then I let Tom take my arm and lead me out. I suddenly felt weak, and frightened of the stairs. He let me lean against the wall and then in a minute put his arm around me to help me. We took it six stairs at a time, with a little rest in between. Then we were up, walking out in the parking lot, and at last reached my car. "I'm O.K. now," I said, though my heart was still racing. "I think."

"O.K.'s not the word for what you are. You're a goddam wonder."

I looked in his eyes. "Give me a five-minute start, and then when you get to the motel, come on up to my room, without ringing or anything. That is, if you *want* to come up—?"

"What do you think?"

✿

My head was clear enough driving back, and when I parked and went up to the suite, I knew what I meant to do. I slipped into the bedroom and took off every last stitch. Then I pulled down the corners on one of the beds and folded them over to leave most of the undersheet clear. Then I went into the sitting room, sat down, and looked out. When the buzzer sounded I opened the peephole, and when I made sure it was Tom, opened. "So *pretty* out there," I said, waving at the windows with their view of the airport. "Or—would you rather we went in here?"

I led the way to the bedroom, lay down on the bed, and pulled the covers over me, but only to the waist. He stood looking down at me and I closed my eyes. When I opened them his clothes were on the chair. Then he was slipping in beside me and taking me in his arms.

19

When it was over I felt as though drugged, and lay limp, letting him hold me close. Then my head cleared a little, and I realized it wasn't only the sense of relief, that I wouldn't lose the house after finally getting it out from under its mortgage, or my feeling of gratitude to Tom, or, leave us face it, the ordinary pleasure of good, honest love, but also the months and months of deprivation. So it wasn't too terribly long before my mouth found his once more, and we had what he called a "retake," whispering as though it was a naughty word. It was almost the only talking we did. Then I lay close again, he whispered the word again, and found my mouth with his mouth. It went on all afternoon, till at last we had to get up and eat. For that we had to dress. Then we put the table out in the hall and went to bed again. But this time, whether from stomachs full of food, or plain, utter exhaustion, we were barely able to finish. When I opened my eyes a clock was striking three.

I could feel him warm beside me, but his breathing told me he was asleep, as I had been. I lay there, clear-headed for the first time since I left the airport. Then thoughts began to come, and the first one of all was: I wanted this man as I'd never wanted anything in my life but my little boy—wanted to lie beside him forever. But the next thought that came to me was of the grass in front of that mansion, so soft, so green, so smooth, and how my little darling would look, rolling and romping in it, and crowing from sheer joy. I lay there a long time, while the clock struck the half hour, and then struck four o'clock. Suddenly, not knowing I was going to, I slipped out of bed and began pawing around in the dark. I found the clothes I had taken off, put them on and eased open the bureau drawers. I found the nightie I'd worn the night before, my toilet set, and spare under-wear. I took my coat from the closet and took everything to the sitting room. There, with motel pen and on motel stationery, I wrote Tom a note, saying "Love, thanks, and goodbye." It seemed a little flat, but at least was what I had to say. I slipped out and the clerk looked up in surprise, from the book he was reading, but checked me out: seventy-five dollars for the suite, twenty-two dollars for food, forty cents for some phone call I couldn't remember making.

I picked up my suitcase, put on my coat, walked out to the car, and drove off into the dawn—of another life.

20

That night, I was back in the Garden of Roses, and five minutes after I got there, it was as though I'd never been away. Bianca at first acted insulted, but when I mentioned "money, Bianca—too much to lose just by turning my back," she eased off ever so little, and then life went on as before. Liz said: "Baby, have I missed you—but never mind that. The main thing is, you're back. And how's our Tom…?"

"He's fine," I told her, betraying not a hint of emotion. "He helped me quite well in a matter we were both concerned in."

"An overnight matter, as I understand it—some three nights running. I knew the boy had it in him! Now, spill, Joan, and don't leave anything out."

It was hard, as I would have loved to tell it all, but I answered, "Nothing to spill, I'm afraid, Liz. It was a legal matter, and it's done."

"A legal matter?"

"…And it's done."

An hour later, after business had got started, she was beside me saying sidelong: "Couple of big shots, Joan, here in the corner booth—they want to know if I have a pal, and would we like to see them later, after we close for the night. They already have rooms in a motel, and what they're flashing at me is hundred-dollar bills. So if it's true that you and Tom aren't an item…" I told her, "Another time, Liz—tonight I have to catch up on my sleep."

"O.K.," she said, "I'll take care of them both, I guess—it's what legs are for, one of the things anyhow."

"The main thing, maybe."

"We could even say that, yes." But then she blew out her lips and said, "Not an item...!"

The next night was nothing but one more night. The night after that Mr. White came in.

I saw him first and turned to the bar, where Jake had seen him too and was already fixing his drink. When it was ready to go he was at his table, the same one he'd always sat at. I served it without saying a word to him, and he asked: "Well? Aren't you speaking to me?"

"Are you speaking to me is the question. It's been quite a while, Mr. White. I wasn't sure you placed me."

"I place you."

"I don't take things for granted. It's been weeks, after all. Was your business successful?"

"Very much so. It should be signed shortly."

"And the other matter?"

"It's a tricky situation, but my lawyer says it can be done."

"...If you still wish to do it, of course. Let's not pretend you didn't go away for a month at least partly to try and forget me."

"I don't deny it, Joan," he said simply. "I did."

I opened my mouth to go on with it, trade some more blows back and forth, but looking at his expression I knew, the time had come to switch. I hadn't jumped in his lap, I hadn't yelped for joy on seeing him, had acted as though neglected, and not too pleased about it. But now I thought maybe it was best that I calm down, and remember the things that had been between us. So I said nothing until a minute at least had passed, and then, very quietly, asked, "So? Could you?" And then: "Did you?"

He let another minute pass, and then, barely whispering it, said: "…No."

"…Why don't you ask what I did while you were gone?"

"O.K. What?"

"Tried to forget you was all."

"So? Did you?"

I let him wait for a bit, then told him: "No."

And then he said it, what I'd left Tom's side to hear: "Joan, we have to get married."

"Your way?"

"It's not the way I'd want it—it's the way the doctors dictate, the way it has to be."

I stood there with my heart beating up, for I knew the way the doctors dictated was the only way for me—with him. I've asked myself, many times since that fateful night, if I was leading him on, pretending one state of mind while really being in another. The answer has to be yes. If I tell what I really felt, there on the floor that night, it was sure exultation, that I'd put it over at last, this gigantic plan I'd had, that would give my darling to me, on a lawn that he could play on, in a house we both could live in, as part of a world that we could be proud of. I'm trying to tell it as it was, not leaving anything out that matters, or putting anything in that isn't true. So, I was two-faced and now I admit it. But, if you're a woman, how about you, what would you have done? If you had exactly been in my shoes, with this opportunity offered you and that little boy to think of, I think you'd have done what I did. But not more than I did, not the things the newspapers later accused me of. And I swear on my life, on my blessed son's life, I didn't do them either.

"…When?" I asked.

"Not sooner than a week. My lawyer raised some questions

that have to be answered—or at any rate, gone into. I want you to be protected—fully protected, by law."

"On that, I trust you completely."

"I appreciate that, Joan—but with the best intentions in the world, I could leave you wide open for trouble in case of a certain eventuality."

"What eventuality, Mr. White?"

"I'd rather not talk about it."

"Then, if you mean what I think you mean, I'd rather not, either. I hereby withdraw my question."

"You sound like a lawyer, Joan."

"I grew up around the sound. My father is one."

"I've often wondered about him."

"...I'd rather not discuss him."

The bitterness I felt must have been in my voice, as he did something he very seldom did—reached out and patted me tenderly, on the side of my trunks. Suddenly he announced: "We'll be married, Joan, but actually, as we'll order our life, I'll be a father to you. That way we can be together. I can see you all the time, and fill what must be a void in your life."

I took his hand and held it, sealing the bargain.

During the night, it occurred to me that if he needed a lawyer, so did I, and once more I called Mr. Eckert in Marlboro, and around noon the next day I drove over to see him. He cut me off when I mentioned a retainer, saying the two-fifty I had already paid "still had some time to run, as I've done nothing to earn it—so, you're all paid up, and what's on your mind, Mrs. Medford?"

I told him.

When I was done he got up and started walking around. "I don't like it," he growled. And then: "I don't like it even a little bit."

I waited, and he went on: "You'll be married, but then if he changes his mind you won't be. I mean, suppose he seeks an annulment. No consummation, no marriage—you know about that, I assume? So, say you're willing to consummate, which you might think knocks his suit in the head. But not if non-consummation was part of the contract—a court would hold, I'm afraid, that you can't have it both ways. If you entered into a marriage that wasn't a marriage, that's the marriage the court has before it, not some marriage you're willing to make after the fact. And if I were a judge, I'd have to hold that a marriage that excluded consummation was never a marriage at all."

"...So? What do I do?"

"You mean, to get the money?"

"Do you have to put it that way?"

"If you want my legal advice I must know what you're aiming at."

"...Well—naturally I think about money. I imagine everyone does. It's not all I think about. Certainly not, Mr. Eckert." And more of the same for ten minutes. When at last I ran down, he said: "In other words, you want me to tell you how to get the money, and at the same time pretend it's not what you're thinking about?"

"...Then—yes."

"O.K., now we're getting somewhere."

I took another ten minutes on Tad, explaining where he came in, and he let me talk, but didn't seem to be listening. Then suddenly he cut in: "O.K., so you have a child, and you want grass for him to play on. So, what you do is go along—you get married this crazy way, and do your best to go through with it. But, Mrs. Medford, there's a possibility you don't seem to have thought about: He may want to consummate anyhow—take a chance the doctors could be wrong. My advice to you is: If he wants to consummate, consummate. Because the invitation could be only *his* way of entrapping you, of getting you to refuse, and in that way achieving an impregnable position in court."

"…Why would he do that?"

"He fell in love, didn't he? He could just as easy fall out—and just as quick."

"And what makes you think I'd refuse?"

"I don't say you would. I only said you shouldn't. If it were really the man's company you wanted, I'd advise differently—but I think, with you, it's the money."

I felt ashamed, and got up to go. He said: "I'm not quite done yet. Whatever you do, put nothing in writing, Mrs. Medford. Don't sign any marriage contract, or agreement, or anything that mentions this stipulation—except for the routine papers, such as the application for a license, don't sign *anything*. Then, when it happens, if it happens, the one thing that can win for you, there'll be nothing in this safety deposit box to louse you in Orphan's Court."

"What 'thing' are you talking about?"

"The same 'thing' you're thinking about."

"You certainly make it plain."

He stood there, looking down at me, and I stood looking up at him, and his gaze reminded me of Sergeant Young's, only without any of the kindness. After a moment he said: "If, after you're married, you want any help of any kind, legal or otherwise, I hope you'll let me know."

I asked: "Otherwise? What kind of help would that be?"

"Platonic marriage, to a dame as good-looking as you, might be a bit of a strain. If that's how it works for you, you might let me know—you might drop over some day and I'll take it from there. You're a goddam good-looking gold-digger, and I go for you, plenty."

He reached out with one finger and stroked it along the side of my face. I wanted to grab it and bend it backward, snap it clean through, but what I did was smile my prettiest smile and lift the digit off me ever so gently.

"If I want you, Mr. Eckert, I'll let you know."

I drove back to Hyattsville, with butterflies in my stomach, and a feeling that I might be playing with fire.

21

The week didn't pass, it flew. Then it was the day, and when I woke up I was panicky—I knew I was holding back, flinching from what I had to do. I found myself furious, frantic with rage at Tom, that he hadn't called, hadn't shown up at the bar, not once. He had to have known, the moment he woke, why I left him—I'd told him I meant to get married. And he had to know now when it would happen, since he was in touch with Liz, as she'd betrayed for two or three nights, by the questions she asked of me and the ones I asked of her, the ones she chose not to hear. So she'd told him about it, and why hadn't he come? To say goodbye, perhaps see me home one night, or something. But no, not even a kind look. He'd kept himself away from the Garden entirely.

I got up, dressed, had coffee and got in the car. Next thing I knew I was in Marlboro, and found myself driving past Eckert's place, asking myself what I was doing there. Was there more legal advice I wanted—or was I tempted by his other offer after all? I shuddered at the thought. And yet here I was. The prospect of shackling myself to Mr. White was clearly getting to me, though I'd been the engineer and architect of the plan and could hardly complain of the outcome. I turned the car around and headed for home.

At one o'clock I called Blue Bird, and asked them to send a cab to the Safety Garage, then drove my car there and left it. When the cab came I rode home, feeling queer. Before going in I rang Mrs. Stringer's bell, next door, and when she came gave her my spare key, and the $10 payment I'd offered, for looking in each day, making sure one light was lit, and taking in the mail. Then I went in, walked back to the bedroom and had a look around, as well as in my bag, to make sure I had everything. It was a big one I'd had from Pittsburgh, and the only one I was taking, as that was one thing I'd learned from my father, one of the few memories of him I respected: "Take one bag and one bag only—it'll hold what you need, if you use the facilities available where you go—the laundry, the cleaner, the bootblack, the barber, the beauty parlor—let them freshen you up. Don't try to take the whole clothes-closet with you." I checked my cash, $500 in twenties that I'd drawn and $2,000 in traveler's checks.

At two o'clock Mr. White's car stopped out front and I let Jasper get out and ring my bell, so I could have him take the bag and I wouldn't have to do it.

Mr. White was waiting on the brick platform in front of the mansion's door, with what looked like the whole household staff lined up behind him. I hadn't realized there were so many— three women, two in maid outfits and one in a cook's apron, and beside them three men in workclothes that might have made them gardeners or mechanics or what-have-you. They all looked warmly at me, but to see them arrayed there before me, almost as though for my inspection, gave the screw inside me another clockwise twist. Jasper jumped out of the car, snatched up Mr. White's two suitcases and loaded them into the trunk. Mr. White gave a little speech to his staff, how he was leaving solo but would return as one half of husband-and-wife, and he trusted they would each welcome me to my new role as mistress of the house. There was much nodding, and I had all I could do to nod back and smile with gratitude rather than bolt down the oyster-shell drive.

I followed him back into the car, and a moment later the door closed firmly and then the car began to roll.

"Hello, Joan," he said.

I said "Hello" back, but knew something more was called for; from the look on his face, he expected it. So I pulled his face down and kissed him. In a moment he kissed me back, whispering, "Our first." Then: "Joan, your lips are like ice—is something wrong?"

"I'm just the least little bit frightened—I guess your lips know without being told, what your heart is feeling."

I made myself sound wan, timid, and friendly, and he gathered me into his arms. They were narrow and I could feel the bones through the flesh. I started to cry silently. Then: "Frightened?" he asked. "Of what?"

"Just on general principles. After all, this isn't something I do every day."

"But not at something *I've* done?"

"Of course not."

I gave him a pat, and wiped away the tears that had made it out before I regained control over myself. But on account of my lips, I didn't venture another kiss. We rode along, I making myself lean toward him, though I didn't at all want to.

We bypassed Annapolis, then were out on the bridge over the Bay. Then we were on the Eastern Shore, which is flat, so a car eats up miles, without even going fast. Then we were in Delaware, and in a matter of minutes we were entering Dover. He said something to Jasper, who said, "Yes sir, I know," and pulled in shortly at quite a handsome motel. Jasper got out and opened the door for us, then followed us inside, carrying the bags. Mr. White told the clerk: "Three of us—we're reserved, Earl K. White, Mrs. Ronald Medford, and Jasper Wilson." The clerk eyed us, then offered the pen to Mr. White, who gave it to me.

I took it and filled out the card the clerk gave me, having a sudden panicky feeling at the realization it was the last time I'd write 'Joan Medford.' Motels don't have bellboys, so it was Jasper who took up the bags. In a moment I was alone upstairs with mine and a feeling of utter panic.

We had agreed to meet in the lobby, and he was waiting when I got down. So was Jasper, and we went out and got in the car. When I asked where we were headed he said: "Lab—we have to have blood tests. If they take their samples now we can get the report in the morning and get our license at once without waiting around." I said: "Oh," and Jasper stopped at an office building. The receptionist seemed to know what we wanted without being told, and was so coy it made me uncomfortable. The doctor was smiling too, and made quick work of us both, having us sit with our dab of cotton, holding it to our arms, and then telling us: "Just ask the girl in the morning—she'll have your certificates ready." Back in the motel, we went at once to the dining room, and all during dinner he talked of how happy he was, just to be with me at last, without having to get up and go, "or seeing that bartender eye me as though I were some kind of thief for occupying a table without ordering something pricier." I told him Jake didn't mean any harm, and that he'd been very nice to me from the first day, but it didn't do any good, as Jake, something I had not known, was obviously his pet aversion. After the dinner we went back to the lobby to talk over cups of tea in a little sitting area they had. Around nine I said I was tired and would like to turn in, and he took me to my room. For one horrible moment there in the hall I wondered what I would do if he tried to come in, but he didn't. He stood there, though, as if expecting something, and as I had in the car I knew what it was. I raised my mouth and he kissed me. "Good night, Earl," I whispered and ducked inside, too jittered to ask if my lips were warmer than they had been, or to care.

I'll remember that night as long as I live, for its gray, dry taste-lessness, and endless length. And yet not once, at least to re-member it, did I tell myself I could still back out, or have any impulse to. I would like to make that clear. I could have backed out, packed my bag, turned my key in to the desk, taken a cab to the bus station, and gone home—no new thing for me, as that's what I'd done with Tom. But, frightened though I was, and jittered, and numb, it didn't enter my mind. So far as I was concerned, I had what I wanted, and never once doubted I wanted it.

In the morning I dressed for my wedding, putting on the suit I had bought, a simple sharkskin thing, in the dark green I always liked, with a beige blouse and dark tan shoes, with gloves and hat to match. I didn't want a hat, but felt I should have one, out of respect for him. So I wore a tiny velvet one, that took up no space in my bag but gave me a formal look. He got the idea at once, telling me: "I was hoping you'd put on a hat—you have beautiful hair, but it's kind of a special occasion. Oh well, I might have known you would. You don't have to be Social Register to know what's what and what's not."

"But I *am* Social Register."

"...You're—what did you say, Joan?"

By his reaction I knew he thought I was kidding him, and also that for all his and his father's and his grandfather's wealth he was not Social Register himself. But I was, one of the only lega-cies remaining from my parents—that, and the bag I'd packed for this trip, and worth just about as much in my eyes, or less. But I saw what it meant to him that his new wife, best known to him until this moment for serving him tonic water with her breasts half revealed, was higher on the social ladder than he, and just for a moment I let this thing that meant nothing to me give him his moment of torture.

"Oh—I'm in, in Pittsburgh, of course. My father and mother are, and I'm listed as one of their children—or was. I guess I'm still in. Not that I very much care."

"I didn't know that."

All during breakfast he kept shooting glances at me, as though trying to readjust to something that to me was barely worth mentioning, but to him was apparently a staggering piece of news. At least it made a break in the talk, so I could eat my eggs in peace. Then, back to the lab to pick up our blood reports, and then to the courthouse for our license. When the woman saw Mr. White's name she was excited at once, telling him: "We got your letter, Mr. White, and the judge is ready when you are." Then a middle-aged man was there, shaking hands and congratulating us, and asking if we'd like two of the girls to be our witnesses. "Just one," answered Mr. White. "We brought one witness with us." He put his arm around Jasper, who seemed very pleased.

Then Mr. White, a girl, Jasper, and I all went in the judge's office. He was the least bit fussy telling us how to stand. Then he started the service and I suddenly felt suffocated, knowing what it meant. Then Mr. White was slipping a ring on my finger and repeating after the judge, "With this ring I thee wed," and I was promising to love, honor and cherish. Then Mr. White was kissing me, and I was hoping my lips weren't as cold to him as yesterday. To me, they felt colder.

Then we were out on the street, and Jasper was trotting off to bring up the car. I looked down, and pinned to my jacket were flowers, a beautiful corsage of orange blossoms—I hadn't the faintest idea, and haven't to this day, how it got there, or when. Then we were in the car, headed north, I didn't know where. Then I could see New York in the distance, and then, after tunnels, knew we must be headed for Idlewild Airport. By then I knew he had some surprise for me, but we were in front of the airline counter, and he was off to one side, whispering to Jasper and giving him money, before I was sure we were headed for London.

22

My seat was next to the window in a row of three, and his was in front of me, but he moved to the one beside me and I tried to act as though pleased, though on a plane I like to be left to myself, as the clouds and the sky and drone of the motor all make me feel dreamy, and dreams are a solo enterprise. However, his intentions were clearly friendly and I responded as well as I could. I suddenly realized, though, as he kept asking how I liked it, and if it made me nervous at all, that he assumed I'd never been on a plane before. So, once again, as when he brought up the Social Register, I had to cut him down to size. I said: "Oh no—I don't mind flying at all—never did. Even when I was little, and we flew to St. Louis each year, I loved it even in rough air, when the plane would go down and everyone was scared to death. Once I yelled 'Whee!' and my mother spanked me but quick. And then naturally my father had to make made out like he was really annoyed too."

"I find myself wondering about this father of yours. Who was he, Joan?"

"Lawyer. As I've told you."

"…He still living?"

"I don't really know—and don't care."

He took the hint and cut off the questions—for a while. But then after we'd been flying perhaps two hours he resumed, and I thought it best to cover the subject, of my parents and the falling out we'd had, once and for all, so once it was done, I'd not have to do it again. "I had a brawl with my mother," I explained, "over a boy she'd picked out for me, a rich boy from one of the steel families. But he bored me to tears, and when I refused even to consider marrying him, she put me out, and instead of standing up for me my father stood beside her. I've made my own way since, with what results you already know. If I don't seem as refined as a girl with my background should, it's being on my own from seventeen on, and not in the best of situations, that's done it." I shrugged away the sympathetic look he was giving me. "I wrote my mother when I got pregnant, but never heard from her—or him, as perhaps should go without saying. That was when I knew for sure I'd been cut off but good. Of course, no parent can be expected to respond with enthusiasm to the news that their unmarried daughter is pregnant. It's not as though anyone else was too excited either—Ron's enthusiasm for it wasn't visible to the naked eye, his parents' bordered on nausea, his sister's on galloping lockjaw. If that's why he drank I don't know, but it could have been, and eventually it was drinking that cost him his life, so you might say there were bad outcomes all around. But I did get one good thing out of it: my darling little Tad."

"You'll be pleased to know I've made arrangements for him, Joan—had a nursery fixed up, next to your suite, in the house."

It was the first moment since the ceremony—no, longer, since the day he'd returned from his business in New York and said he'd marry me—that I felt warmly toward him. I caught his hand, pressed it in both of mine, then lifted it and kissed it, and meant it.

We had left Idlewild at noon, so it was something like seven New York time when we got to Heathrow Airport, but late at night in London, on account of the time differential. We'd just had dinner on the plane, and in various ways it still seemed like early evening; however, I try to adjust to what comes up. Customs took only a few minutes, and then we were in a cab, headed for town. There wasn't much to see except streetlights, but after the snubs I'd dished out earlier when he'd tried to play mentor and guide, I thought best to act very pleased. "I just love it!" I kept saying. But it wasn't real until we came to the city itself and were suddenly on a bridge, rolling across the river. At that hour no boats were out there, or at any rate moving around, but the lights on the water reflected in a mysterious, beautiful way, and suddenly I was overwhelmed. "It's thrilling," I whispered. "It's just out of this world." He smiled happily, at having pleased me at last.

Our hotel was the Savoy, which is on a little inset, a half square with a theatre on one side, business places on the other, and the hotel in the middle—a quiet, elegant haven off the Strand, one of their busiest streets. A doorman got out our bags and took them in while Earl paid the driver in English money he'd bought in Washington, at the same time opening my bag and stuffing some in for me, notes as big as napkins. Then we were inside and I noticed Earl took off his hat, though in an American hotel lobby men leave their hats on. He registered, and when the clerk saw who this was he was all deference. "Yes, Mr. White," he exclaimed. "Your suite's ready as requested—sitting room, two bedrooms, two baths. We'll take you up in just a moment."

While we were waiting to be taken up, people were leaving the dining room, as it was coming on for one in the morning, and the theatre crowd was going home. They were all in evening clothes, and I felt the slightest bit self-conscious in my traveling suit, which was respectable but ordinary. He saw my expression and leaned in to me. "We'll get you a long dress tomorrow."

I couldn't help snapping, "I have one, thanks. It's just packed."

"Well then you'll have another," he whispered back, untroubled by my tone. Perhaps he'd been told to expect a new bride to be skittish; perhaps he remembered from the previous time he'd wed.

Just then an assistant manager came and took us up, standing around while we looked at the suite. "In the U.S.," said Earl, "you're given a room and you take it, if you know what's good for you. Here they let you see it, and if you don't like it, show you something else. Most people like it, I'm sure—but it's nice, having a vote."

To the assistant manager, he said: "Suite's fine—thanks."

When we were alone, Earl said, "Now I don't know about you, Joan, but after a wedding, a car ride, and a plane trip, I could do with a little bed rest."

"Oh, I'm quite tired too."

But once more the drawstring pulled in my stomach, as I still didn't quite know what to expect.

I found out soon enough.

Both our bedrooms opened onto the sitting room, and as he stepped into his, he half whispered, in a friendly confidential way: "I'll be getting my things off." It seemed to mean more to come, and when I went to my room, I couldn't make myself undress. I put my things away, then sat down to think, but managed only to feel numb. When there came a rap on the door I called: "Come." But I sounded muffled and strangled and queer. Then he was there in pajamas and slippers and robe. "So!" he exclaimed, very friendly. "Thanks for waiting. Now I can see the whole show."

I've spoken of my temper, and now I wrestled with it, trying to hold it back. I couldn't. "What show?" I heard myself say, sounding ugly.

"Why, as your husband, I'd like to watch you undress. Fact of the matter, I've been looking forward to it."

I wanted to do what I did to Tom, flatten his ears with slaps, but did nothing at first but sit there, swallowing, trying to get myself under control. Then: "Are you sure that's recommended?" I asked. "After all I'm anatomically normal, and might have an anatomically normal effect."

"So? I'm normal too. All God's children are normal. I can only go so far, but that far at least I mean to go—here, I'll take that coat."

He took it from me and hung it up in the closet. "Raise your arms, I'll lift off that dress."

I did, and quite expertly he slipped it off and let me take it. I hung it up, beside the coat, and rolled the closet door shut. That left me in bra and pantyhose, and I didn't know which to take off first. I stepped out of my shoes, rolled the closet open again, found my trees on the floor where I'd put them, pushed them in, and set the shoes under the dress, the toes pointing to the room. Then I took off the bra, and put it on the shelf above the hangers. But as I was still reaching up, his hands were cupping me in, raising my breasts, while breath blew on my neck. I wanted to cry out, to bite, to rear away. I had to think of my darling Tad, to remember what I'd been told by Mr. Eckert, that I must never withhold what a husband could legally claim.

I said: "You can't—your condition—"

He buried his face in the back of my neck, at the same time pulling me close, and kneading my breasts with his fingers. This time, I had to swallow hard to keep the plane dinner from spilling out on the floor. "I'd like to finish undressing," I told him after a moment. *If you don't mind.*"

"Be my guest."

He stepped back and I stepped from the closet back into the room. His face was flushed and he was breathing hard, but he had a smile on his face and his hands still outstretched toward me like little seeking mouths. I slipped off the pantyhose, tossing them up beside the bra, but had hardly done it before he was on me again, one hand over my heart, the other over the most private, sensitive, personal part of a woman's body, so I had to clamp my mouth shut for fear I'd scream. I knew I dared not fight him off, but also knew I had to end this somehow or I'd lose my mind. Presently, with one hand I slipped under his hand topside, and with the other under his hand below: "Please," I whispered. "I'm human too, and there's a limit to what I can take."

He eased off, and from the bureau I got out my nightie, a black one with lace yoke, and put it on. When I looked at him he was panting, with sweat standing out on his forehead, not a pretty sight. I said: "Now, if the doctor was right about you, if he knew what he was talking about, it's time you went to your room. It's time you went to bed."

"But Joan, tell me: You wanted me didn't you? You want me now—say it just once, so I know."

"I will *not* say it."

I made it sound very strict, schoolteacherish and cross. "If I ever said how I feel, God only knows what you'd do. You're a wonderful man, Earl K. White, but I don't trust you, even a little bit. And waking up here in London with a distinguished corpse in my arms, as you once put it, is not my idea of a honeymoon."

It was not, on the whole, unflattering, and in a moment he said: "O.K." And then, "O.K., O.K., O.K."

"You can kiss me now, goodnight. But just a kiss."

He kissed me, very quick, very dry, very proper.

"Now—" I said, stern.

He left me alone, stumbling out, almost in a state of collapse.

I got into bed, and could turn out the light at last. As I lay there, staring out at the London night, I knew I'd got myself into something.

23

If I slept I don't know. I must have, but I was awake at daybreak
and decided I had to get up. But when I put my foot out of bed
I did it softly, making no whisper of noise. I opened the bathroom door an inch at a time, so I could go in, wash my face,
comb, and put on my pantyhose. I went back in the bedroom,
walking on stocking feet and not putting my shoes on until
ready to go out. Then, a little bit at a time, I opened the sitting
room door to peep if he was there. He wasn't and I tiptoed
through, making the hall and closing the door silently. Then I
scooted for the stairs, not punching the elevator button for fear
it would keep me there, waiting in the hall. Our suite was on
the third floor, and I wound my way down and into the lobby. A
clerk was at the desk, working on some sort of paper, but I
simply said, "Good morning," as though it meant nothing at all
that a young bride should be up and out at six in the morning
after her wedding night. Then I was on the street, walking.

The sun hadn't come out yet, the whole place was veiled in
fog and completely deserted, in spite of which I began to feel
better. I walked to Trafalgar Square, which I knew from pictures I'd seen of it, to a statue of Queen Victoria, and on to a
big ugly building I didn't recognize. A police officer was there,
as well as a sentry, and when I asked them what it was, the sentry
said, "Buckingham Palace, ma'am." A slight chill went over
me. It was, I knew, the residence of the Queen, and if I'd ever
envied her I didn't anymore. Having to live in such a horrible
place, I thought, must certainly take the fun out of the rest.

I decided I'd come far enough and turned around to walk on back. Now people were out, most of them women, who I knew by their looks were servants of one kind or another. And I was suddenly upset, that to make a living they had to get out at such an hour—it was still not yet seven. When I got back to the hotel it came to me that in some ways I liked the country a lot, in other ways not at all.

When I got back to the hotel I stopped at the desk to send a cable to Ethel. By now, of course, I knew the papers must have had the marriage of Earl K. White, but courtesy called for a wire from me, so I wrote one that began, "Surprise, surprise," and then told her, and wound up, aiming for a friendly tone, with "Love, see you soon, Joan." I paid for it myself, without it being charged to the room. Then I went up to the suite, to face my lord and master.

He came out of his bedroom with a razor in one hand, his face all lathered up, and wanting to know, "Where've you been?"

I told him "Out," and then gave him a kiss like the one I'd allowed him the night before, a peck. He reacted so fast that it startled me, changing from annoyance to surprised affection, and pleading for "one more" as though it were something from heaven. I gave him one, realizing suddenly something I hadn't quite got through my head before: that his feeling for me, though so far as I was concerned repulsive, was real. Or in other words, if I chose, I could have this man utterly, wind him around my finger and make him do as I wished any time I chose. And I thought to myself, then *choose*. He has all that you want out of life, not only for you but your child. So get on with it, get on with *him*, so life can move forward.

Easier said than done.

✻

I spent the whole day trying to go through with my big idea, of being nice to him. There were three buttons on the table, each with a picture beside it, one of a waiter, one of a maid, and one of a bellboy. "A lot of their guests," he explained, "don't speak any English, so for them it's made plain." I punched the one for a waiter, and suddenly there he was, a napkin on one arm, a menu card in his hand. "I never take anything but rolls, butter-milk, and black coffee for breakfast," said Earl. Of course I wanted bacon, eggs, and toast, but I smiled and went along with his tonic water of a breakfast for myself as well. We ate it together in the sitting room, he still in pajamas, I in my walking clothes. When the food was gone, he dressed, not inviting me to watch, to my relief. Then started what would have been an interesting day, if it hadn't been for the finish I was dreading it would have.

We went to lunch at Simpson's, a place I'd heard about, which was just a few steps from the hotel. I ordered steak, being hungry still from breakfast, "a Delmonico steak, just a small one," but the waiter told me they didn't have one—"We're strictly a join-'ouse, ma'am." "Join-'ouse" seemed to mean a place that served roast meat only, so I ordered roast beef instead. When it came he carved and served me—one slice only, and I fear my face blanched, or perhaps my stomach rumbled. Earl passed over a coin, and the waiter, looking pleased and surprised, said "Oh, thank you, sir," and cut me another slice. "You'd think," said Earl when the waiter had gone, "that no one had had that idea before, of pitching in with an extra shilling—in point of fact it's a ritual. If I hadn't done it he'd have found some way to remind me. They're a funny bunch, the English. They always have to pretend."

I, meanwhile, was wolfing down the meat, which was tender and terrific. I wanted to know more about it, so when we had finished our lunch Earl disappeared for a minute, only to return with the manager, who showed me around the kitchen while my new husband took some more coffee at our table. I must say I was fascinated. The meat hangs on hooks at the end of chains, which turn slowly in front of a bank of live coals, roasting out in the open. To keep it from burning they wrap it in brown paper.

When I went back upstairs I felt I had learned something.

It was after three when we got back to the hotel, and he led the way up to the suite. "Time I took my nap," he said, "Doctor's orders—but everyone ought to do it, they'd feel better, and probably live longer. Why don't you take one, Joan?"

"Then O.K., why not?"

I didn't much care, one way or the other, but if it pleased him, was willing to give it a try. So we went up, he going to his room, I to mine. I slipped off my clothes, and was just reaching for my nightgown when there he was at the door. He stood there for a long moment staring at me. "…I hope you don't mind," he stammered. Then: "You're so beautiful I have to look."

"I don't like to be looked at," I answered. "At least in the day-time—it doesn't seem right, somehow."

"Day or night doesn't make much difference in how you look. You're the same girl, either way."

By now he was close to me, and I instinctively turned my back, but that turned out a mistake. When he put his arms around me, it put his hands over my breasts, and he did what he'd done the night before: cupped them and kneaded them with his fingers. I hated it, and began pushing him off, hooking my fingers in his, to pull them away from me and make him turn me loose. We began to wrestle, he making a game of it, laughing and gasping for breath. But I'm fairly strong, and pretty soon had his hands in mine, holding them clear, while I shoved him with my hip. Then suddenly he gasped, and when I looked was lying across the bed, his hands pressed to his chest. "Joan," he whispered, "will you get my pills for me—my nitro pills, from my bed in the other room? They're in a bottle, at the head of the bed. In a little vial—would you hurry, please?"

I hurried, not waiting even to throw something on, and there sure enough, on the shelf at the head of his bed, was the tiny bottle he spoke of, and I raced with it back to him, unscrewing the top as I went. "That's it," he gasped. "Give me one—so, in the palm of your hand."

He took the pill I gave him, popped it into his mouth and then poked it under his tongue with his finger. Then, in a moment: "Give me another one, Joan." I did, and he jammed that one under his tongue, too. Then he lay there, eyes closed, as though waiting. Slowly the strain on his features began to subside. Then: "I'm sorry, Joan—I can't help it. The pain is indescribable, and the pills help but it still goes on." Then: "If I die—"

"Earl!"

"If I die," he insisted, speaking still with some difficulty, "I want you to know what to do. Please have me cremated—it's important to me, Joan, please listen. Have me cremated and take my ashes to Maryland, for burial in our family plot, in the College Park Cemetery. My will is drawn, signed, and in my deposit box. You're the sole beneficiary, Joan, except for some remembrances to my staff. I had my lawyer see to it."

"Please don't talk like that."

"I try to face reality."

I didn't think he was going to die. I certainly didn't want him to, despite what he'd just told me about his will. All I could think of was that now at last I'd have a real excuse for holding him off, and not letting things get started in the way he seemed to want, when it came time for me to undress.

24

Unfortunately, it didn't last. He remembered the pain only as long as he felt it, clamping his chest in a vise. Once past, it was quickly forgotten, or if not forgotten then he chose to overlook it, and was back each evening despite all my reminders of the danger he faced. "I'll only watch," he would say, cajoling me. Except that he wouldn't only watch, as seeing me in the nude seemed to exert a magnetic pull on him, such that his hands invariably found their way to my body, at which point he'd say, "I only want to feel you in my arms"—but if I'd let him do that, I know it wouldn't have stopped there, either.

And to think he'd once waved Casanova in my face, as proof of women's weakness and inability to resist the physical act of love—or of their not knowing any other way, to be more precise. Well, he didn't seem to know any other way, and I had my hands full just keeping him off of me. Twice more he'd needed an application of his nitroglycerin, to the point that I began to worry his supply might run out. But he reassured me, when I raised this concern, that there was a British chemist on call to supply more if he needed it.

For a week or more, I bore up under the strain. During the days, I could relax and enjoy London, which I proceeded to do, in the morning mostly, slipping out as I had that first day, before he got up. I picked up a pal, a girl I ran into by accident in front of the National Gallery. I knew she was American by her clothes and we hit it off at once. Her name was Hilda Holiday.

She was from Texas, just a little bit older than me, and was staying, with *her* new husband—her first and only—at the Charing Cross, on the Strand, which was where I stopped by for her each day. She wouldn't come to the Savoy because, as she put it, "I wouldn't have the courage." I told her it didn't take courage to walk through those doors, only money, but she laughingly said, "I wouldn't have enough of that either."

Her husband was a stay-in-bed type, mornings at least, leaving her free to wander the city a bit, and we took to wandering together. We hit it off with one another, and did a lot of laughing, like at the sentries at Buckingham Palace, trying to make *them* laugh. We never succeeded, but once, by the way he cut his eyes in our direction, we knew one boy heard us. Then we laughed at the parking lots, which seemed to be everywhere in the most improbable places. We said, "They have more lots than cars," for by that time we'd both noted how little traffic there was, even in the rush hour—not a tenth of what New York has, or any American city. And then one day, piled alongside a lot, we noted a wall made of loose bricks, and of course started laughing about it, how "a little mortar might help." But the attendant chimed in, "Temporary, you know—" or "temp'ry," as he called it. "From the Blitz, that was all that was left from the bombing. Nothing to do with the space but rent it—it brings in a bit, and it helps."

So the parking lots were explained, and didn't seem quite so funny.

In the afternoons and evenings I lost Hilda's companionship and regained my husband's, and it became a pitched battle, or anticipation of one, until he finally fell asleep—and even so, I was never sure he might not wake in the middle of the night and be taken with the notion to join me in my bed. The bedroom doors did not have locks on them, but I took to placing a chair under the knob. I didn't know if it would keep him out, or how I would explain it to him if it did, but at least the sound of his trying to get in would wake me, so I'd have some warning.

One morning, coming into the lobby of the Charing Cross, I must have looked tired, or anyway anxious, and perhaps a bit haggard as well, with dark circles beneath my eyes that no amount of makeup could entirely hide, because Hilda pulled me aside before we stepped out and asked if everything was O.K. I said yes, of course, but opened up a little—her husband was older as well, though not as much older as mine, and she'd confessed to me earlier that she'd had some fear leading up to their wedding night. Of course, she had been a virgin; I didn't have her excuse. But fear was fear and she recognized the signs on me, so I admitted I was feeling some tension, and when pressed conceded, without explaining the actual situation, that the tension was connected to relations with my husband.

Reaching into her purse she pulled out a small pill case, one of those little metal ones with the appliqué flowers on the top, to make it look more feminine and less pharmaceutical. Inside, on a layer of tissue, were five broad tablets and she urged me to take one. When I took one out, she urged the rest on me as well and wouldn't hear no, saying she had more upstairs and could give those to me too if I needed. "It's a sedative my doctor gave me, before the wedding, when I told him how I was feeling about—well, you know. Thalidomide, it's called. He says it isn't bad for you, not like Miltown or those others you hear about."

I swallowed it dry and she insisted again that I take the rest with me, for later, "as I no longer need them, now that things are so good with Tom." I thanked her, already feeling better.

"You might as well have the whole bottle then, Joan—I'll bring it tomorrow. I like knowing they'll get some use. And you look so worn out."

✻

The timing was fortuitous, as the next day brought a new cause for anxiety that made all the prior incidents seem minor. Earl, writing some sort of bank draft in the sitting room, looked over from our desk and asked what the date was: "It's on the paper, will you look?" I looked, and it was October 22. He thanked me for it, and kept on writing. This would have counted as one of our less troubled conversations, you might think—but suddenly I was struck by the significance of the date. I felt it in my belly like I'd been punched. The day we caught Lacey, on the way back to my car afterward, I remembered passing the information counter with its giant clock and the date posted on the board beside it, and saying to Tom, "September 30 will be a date to remember the rest of my life." So, that was three weeks ago—three weeks and a day. *And how long before that was my period?* It came to me I was due, and that if I had passed the date I was pregnant. And suddenly a trip to London, something I'd always dreamed about, was transformed into a nightmare.

What to do? I was no innocent anymore, I knew how women dealt with these things—but I knew nothing of English laws, where one might go for an abortion, or even who to ask. Back home I could ask Liz, but surely none of the helpful doctors she might refer me to were on this side of the ocean.

There was only one answer: We had to get back to the other side of the ocean, and fast.

I went to Earl's side and stood over him where he was writing, then put one palm lightly on his shoulder. He started. "…What is it, Joan?" And then, in the same words Hilda had used: "Is everything O.K.?"

I might have thought the Thalidomide would have kept me from looking anxious, but clearly it wasn't up to the task. "No, Earl. I'm afraid not."

"What's the matter?"

He tried to take my hand, to stroke it, but I pulled it away from him. "I want to go back home. Earl...I'm going stir-crazy here."

"You don't like the hotel?"

"The hotel's lovely. The restaurants have been lovely, the country's lovely—but it's not home."

"I thought that's the point of a honeymoon, to get away from home. I thought you'd like it."

"Oh, I did, Earl, I did like it, and I appreciate it—you've been awfully generous. But enough's enough. I need to see people driving on the right side of the road again, and eat a proper American meal again, and hear good old American voices again..."

He stared at me curiously. "Is that it? Voices and meals? Or is it that you can't bear to share a suite with me any longer?"

"No! No. It's true I'm concerned for you—you run such terrible risks, and you promised me you wouldn't. But no, I don't mean we have to go home to Hyattsville, and on with our regular lives right away. We could stay on in New York a while, after we land—at a hotel there."

"I've made no arrangements."

"But you could! I'm sure there's one or another of the hotels there that has a pair of rooms going asking."

"What's in New York for you to see or do?"

"As much as in London," I said. "We could see a Broadway show. Or—or that one people are talking about, *The Fantasticks*, down in Greenwich Village."

"I didn't know you had any interest in theater."

"Two weeks ago, you didn't know I'd ever flown in a plane. There's plenty you don't know about me yet."

At that he eyed me again, and there was a challenge in his

look, but I could also see his resistance weakening. Perhaps he'd had enough of England too; after all, he always had business to do, which I was sure he could do better if he weren't living five hours later than everyone he worked with. Sure enough, he said: "All right. It'll give me an excuse to see Bill again—my lawyer. Maybe I can be of help getting this piece of business closed at last."

"What piece of business?" I asked

He waved away the question. "Just a sale, of a partnership interest in my company—there's a fellow who's been after us for a while, and I've decided to let him in. It'll provide some extra liquid assets, which I figured we might have a use for, what with the extra expenses—your son to raise, and all."

I took his hand again. "Thank you. Thanks for humoring me."

"All right. All right."

First chance I got, I called Liz, asking the operator to put me through to her at home, as it was too early there for her to be at the Garden yet.

"…But that's wonderful, Joan! Isn't it? Right out of the gate, and you've gotten it done. Must be some sort of a record."

"Some sort, if you count from our wedding night. Less so, if you count from the night I spent with Tom."

This brought a long silence from Liz, long enough that I became concerned the call might have been dropped. "Oh, Joanie," she said finally, "I'm sorry."

"I need your help. Or I may need it, that's the thing, I don't know."

"I can give you a name, of someone to see, but you can only go there once you know you need it."

"Why? Couldn't he tell me whether I need it too?"

"You can't trust him to tell you that—he'll say yes and scrape you just the same, whether you need it or not, just to be able to charge the full amount. No, you go to a laboratory, a perfectly regular one, and get yourself tested, and if they say it's yes, then and only then do you make the call to my guy."

Her 'guy' was a Dr. Ernst Fleischer with an office up in Yorkville, or in any event an address there—I didn't know if abortionists had offices, exactly. I took down his information and thanked her.

"Please, Joanie, let me know what happens. Call anytime, day or night."

"I promise."

The next day we were on a plane, and at Idlewild there was Jasper to meet us. Earl had made some calls from London and now, as we climbed into the back seat, he said: "The Waldorf Astoria, Jasper. You know where it is?"

"Yes sir."

We drove in over Long Island, crossed the river on one of the bridges, I don't know which, then pulled up in front of the hotel. It was three in the afternoon, and I knew I had things to do—look up a lab, get to it, have blood samples taken, or whichever samples they needed, and get back before Earl got to wondering what I was up to. I let Jasper hand me down, went in the lobby with Earl, and when he had registered, said: "And now, if you'll excuse me, I have some things to do—may I join you later?" He stood there startled, about to say something, but I walked away and out the door, but fast.

I had to get to a phone book, the one with yellow pages, or I was nowhere. I started down the avenue the hotel was on, Park as I know now, though I didn't then know what it was, and at 49th Street happened to look, and there just a block away saw a drugstore. I walked over, found the Yellow Pages in their red cover, turned to Laboratories, didn't find any, then discovered I had to look under "Medical Laboratories." I found one only two blocks away, on 50th Street, walked over to the office building it was in, and went up. The lady on the desk was quite friendly, gave me a receptacle and showed me into a room. I produced my specimen of urine, feeling horribly guilty about it, paid her in cash, and asked when I could get my report. "In the morning," she told me. "We open at nine o'clock."

I was back at the hotel by 4:30, trying to act casual. Earl greeted me with a small envelope in his hand. "The concierge was able to swing it." And when I didn't respond: "I have our tickets. If you still want to go?"

I took the envelope, looked inside, and there found two tickets to that evening's performance of *The Fantasticks*.

"Yes, yes, of course. I'm sorry. I do want to see it—or them, whatever you call it."

"Are you sure? You don't look well."

I nodded, and forced a smile onto my face.

So we went, to some box of a theatre on Sullivan Street. But what *The Fantasticks* were like, or who they were, or what clothes they had on, don't ask me, as I have no more idea than the man in the moon. I took another of Hilda's pills at intermission and it got me through the second act intact, as well as the cab ride uptown, during which Earl's hand never left my thigh.

Next morning, as I'd been doing in London, I sneaked out before he woke up. I wandered east to Lexington Avenue and sat over a cup of coffee at a luncheonette for an hour or more while the cook stood at his counter cutting bologna sandwiches. It was plenty of time for me to imagine what sort of a neighborhood Yorkville might be, as well as the rooms of Dr. Ernst Fleischer, whom I pictured in a white coat, only slightly frayed at the seams from too many washings, with a padded table whose dark leather surface had been worn shiny in places, with a pair of metal stirrups that creaked when adjusted, and a tray of clamps and devices I couldn't name but could see all too well in my mind's eye. He handed me up to the table kindly and patiently, did Dr. Fleisher in my imagination, but his hand shook, and when he reached out for the ether bottle, it tumbled to the floor and shattered…

Nine o'clock came, but slowly, slower than it ever had in all my life. The waiter, a heavy-featured Greek whose cheeks already bore a blue shadow even at this early hour, refilled my mug three times, joking the last time that he might have to charge me for another cup. The wall clock had a second hand that took an eternity to make its revolutions, and I found myself staring at it grimly. Once more, I urged it, and once more after that, and then I'll know, then I'll know.

I left the price of a second cup and didn't answer when the waiter called after me with thanks, just hurried out the door and down the block, the endless block, and rode the elevator to the top floor (of course it was the top, of course it was, and how the elevator crawled!). I was certain when I got there I'd find the door to the laboratory locked, the hallway dark, no sign of life. Or else my sample would have been lost, or contaminated, or the results unclear without further testing, or—

But no: the lights were on, the door unlocked, and the girl had my report in an envelope. My hand trembled as I opened it. It was only one word, in penscript:

Negative.

I must have shown how I felt, as she laughed. "I thought it would please you," she said.

On the way back to the hotel, I felt relief flood through me. And not just relief. I'd heard great stress could do it, could turn your flow off or on, but this was my first experience of it directly, and I rushed into our suite just in time. I let him see me get out my Kotex, then disappeared into the bathroom.

When I got out, I came over, kissed him on the forehead, and whispered: "Sorry to have been such a pest, but there was a reason—I never seem to remember the effect it has on me, this particular time of month. I hope you'll make allowance."

He acted as though shook, and said of course he understood.

25

We left New York at the end of that week, Jasper returning to pick us up. The drive back was smooth and swift and I spent it with my face turned toward the window, staring out at the highway rushing past. Earl let me alone, as he had since my announcement, being like most men mystified by and a little scared of the processes of a woman's body.

Then at last we arrived, and around five that afternoon, after swirling up the oyster-shell drive, getting out on the brick landing and going in by the front door, which was held open by one of the maids with the cook and the other maid beside her, I entered my new home for the first time.

I wasn't raised in a stable, and grew up with nice things, but I have to say that this place was five times as luxurious as anything I'd been accustomed to. The hall was wide, with a staircase leading up and curving over the balcony topside, on the second floor. Past the stairway was a door at the rear, which opened on what he called "the patio." At right and left were doors standing open, one to a big dining room, the other to a living room, or drawing room, I would call it. Beyond drawing room and dining room, through other open doors, I could glimpse what looked like corridors, but with windows in them. Those were the "hyphens," the passageways that connected the wings of the mansion to its center. Throughout, the furnishings, the glimpse I got of them, were fantastically luxurious: heavy mahogany chairs, tables, and settees, upholstered sofas, and rugs that looked to be Oriental. In the hall were heavy chests with upholstered pads on top, and along one wall a brass rail, "a feature," he explained to me later, "that I borrowed from Ireland. It's for drunks to hold on to, they'll tell you, as they're taking their leave at night—actually for wraps, much more practical than closets, racks, or the other things people have. Anyone can dump his things on the rail, pop his hat on top, and be ready to join the party."

That afternoon all I could do was stare. I kept on staring when one of the maids took me up to my room, my suite, actually, as I had a sitting room as well as a bedroom. And then my heart beat up when through the open door I could see the nursery beyond, with a cot that had two guard rails, a horse with electric motor, and walls with pictures of Peter Rabbit. In a minute or two, as soon as I could go tearing downstairs again, I said: "Earl, you've got me all excited, with that beautiful nursery you had fixed for Tad—and now I want him. I want him with me tonight. Is it asking too much that we—?"

"I've been assuming you'd want to go get him."

"I was hoping you'd say that."

He was very grave. It crossed my mind he was too grave; that he really did not want to go, but was agreeing nevertheless, as his way of going through on a bargain, one that hadn't been made, for we had never talked of this moment, but one that had been there, just the same, lurking under the surface.

I called Ethel and asked if I could bring my new husband "to call," and I suppose enjoyed for a moment the stunned way she took it. There was dead silence for some little time, and then: "I'll be here, of course—I can't speak for Jack, he isn't home yet, and it may be late when he comes. But—very well, I'll expect you." Then Earl and I were in the car, Jasper driving, on our way over. No one was out front when we pulled up, and we were out of the car when Ethel appeared at the front door, in Levis. They were her way of cutting us down to size, as she'd had plenty of time to go up and put on a dress, and when she hadn't paid us that courtesy, it showed what she thought of us. When I presented Earl, she nodded and exclaimed, "White—so that's what your name is. In Joan's wire that she sent from London they spelled it What, which we all thought must be a mistake, but of course we couldn't be sure. Why don't we go out back?"

Earl had smiled, but said nothing to her bitchy show of bad manners, and let her lead us past the house, by the walk that ran beside it, to the backyard, where my heart gave a jump, as there by the back fence, with two other children, playing on a slide, was Tad. He didn't seem to see me, which suited me just as well, as it gave me a chance to tell Ethel why we had come, which I proceeded to do: "Well, he looks fine, Ethel, and I'm eternally grateful to you, the wonderful way you've taken care of him—but I'm taking him now, if you don't mind. At last, I have a wonderful place for him, thanks to my new husband—so you won't have to bother with him anymore."

"...I thought I'd made clear by now—he's no bother, Joan— to me, anyhow."

"What's that supposed to mean?"

"Well, he seems to have been quite a bother to you, but if things are different now—"

"He was never a bother to me, as I think you know—"

I would have said more, no doubt, but Earl cut me off by raising his hand, and saying, most soothingly: "I'm sure he's never been a bother, to you, Mrs. Lucas, or anyone—and he won't be one to us. Tell me, how much do we owe you?"

It was the very way to cut her down, and I couldn't have been happier with Earl than in that moment. She protested that nothing was owed, but Earl already had a palmful of money out, carelessly extracted from his pocket, and he picked out bills to-taling a hundred-fifty dollars, then added twenty extra for good measure. "Here. Please accept it, it's nothing to us and I'm sure you can use it." Oh, the look on her face! But she took the money, of course.

And now I said: "I think it's time Mr. White made Tad's acquaintance."

"...Yes, of course."

So, while Ethel plopped herself down in a garden chair, I led him back to the swings. When Tad saw me at last he came over, not running or with much show of interest, but at least with a smile, as though he was glad to see me. I stooped down and kissed him, and then made a mistake. Instead of presenting him to Earl, quietly, with no explanation at first, and letting him get acquainted little by little, I was too excited to use good judgment, or quite to know what I was doing. I leaned down, kissed him, held him close, and said: "Yes, it's Mommy, it really is, and she's glad, so glad, to see you. Are you glad to see her?"

He nodded, his shyness wearing off, and held his mouth for another kiss. I gave him one, and then at last got to it: "And now for Mommy's big surprise, the wonderful surprise she has for you. Tad, this is Mr. White, Mommy's new husband, who's going to be your father from now on—and we're all three going now, in his big automobile, to the beautiful new home we're going to have, where we'll all live together and—"

With that I picked him up and held him out. But before any more could be said, he took one look at Earl, who was standing there, smiling at him, his hand held out, and let out a scream, not only of fear, but one of utter horror. Then he started to kick and twist and wriggle, so I had to put him down. Without the least hesitation he started for Ethel, where she'd got up from her chair. She gathered him in her arms and began kissing and patting and shushing him, until at last he was quiet. I had to stand

and watch it, and hadn't a word to say, as there was nothing else she could do. I don't take exception, even now, but there's a limit to what you can take.

Presently I mumbled: "Then, Ethel, if you can keep him a little bit longer—"

Her eyes danced, gloating at me over my son's head. "Yes, Joan. You needn't even ask."

"Just till we get straightened out a bit better, how we're going to do—"

"Joan, he's welcome the rest of his life, if that's how he wants it to be." She broke off, and then burst out again: "And how he wants it to be is something you might have thought of, when you had this grand inspiration."

"Ethel, I think we'd better be going."

"Perhaps you'd better, at that."

So next, we were walking around the house once more, Earl and I, and then were in the car, driving back.

I have to say he was very decent about it, and very understanding, patting my hand, and telling me: "Don't be upset—it was just one of those things that happen, we don't know why. I assure you I did nothing whatever, at least that I know of, to provoke it. I thought him a most attractive child, a wonderful little boy." I kept saying it wasn't his fault, but mine, mainly, "for not handling it right," but my mouth was taken over, so I hardly knew what it said. At the house, when we got out and went inside, I suddenly heard myself tell him: "Earl, I'm going up to my room. I want to be alone. I have to be alone."

"But of course, Joan. O.K."

So I went up, took off my things, lay down, and closed my eyes. Then at last I knew the truth: My beautiful dream, that I'd worked and schemed and plotted for, and then at last had made come true, in one ghastly, dreadful moment, had exploded in my face.

❋

For some time, there with myself alone, that was as far as I took it, or could take it. The effect it would have on the future, on Tad's future, on my future, on my future relations with Earl, I didn't get to at all—I was too shocked, too numb, even to try. When at last my head began to clear I began wondering what had caused it, this reaction of Tad's—what I had done, what Earl had done, what Ethel might have done to account for something that seemed to be automatic, completely instinctive. And for a time I blamed myself, for rushing things, introducing a new father and promising a new home all in one breath, as part of a wonderful surprise. If I'd just taken one thing at a time and let that soak in before going on to the next, things might have gone differently. Indeed, for some little time it seemed that I could start over, perhaps put Tad in the car, bring him over here, and then see the surprise Earl had bought him—a new tricycle perhaps, or a little car, or something. But then suddenly I sat up in bed and began staring out the window, as the truth dawned on me, why the child had been terrified of Earl.

If I was, why wouldn't he be?

I knew then, at last, that the thing that had happened was final, that nothing could be done. There popped into my mind the things I'd felt when he'd held me in the car before our wedding, and when we'd kissed, and the way I felt about him when he barged into my room, claiming the right to watch me undress. And my belly began to tell me how deep my fear was. And then at last I began to realize how terrible a thing it was, the dream that you make come true.

26

It was dark when a tap came on the door, and when I called, he came in. I turned on the light and he sat down in the chair beside me, where I still lay on the bed. "Feel better?" he whispered.

"I suppose so, a little," I told him. "At least I'm getting readjusted. Earl, I've lost my child."

"Perhaps not—all sorts of things can happen. But I'd like to say one thing. Joan, I'm as baffled as you are. I swear I did nothing to make him act that way—"

"Earl, I know you did nothing, know it without your telling me."

He was doing nothing now, and yet as I lay on the bed, I felt the same clutch of fear as Tad had betrayed with that scream. His eye moved to my legs, which were crossed in my pantyhose. I took no notice, but switched the talk to Ethel, saying: "It's what she's been hoping for—she lives for the day when she can claim Tad as her own."

He nodded. "I've detected something," he said, "whenever you speak of her. It's clear enough now—I mean, the reason for it is. The silver lining is, at least, if she's fond of the child, you know he'll be well taken care of."

At this, well-meant though it no doubt was, my heart stopped. It froze utterly and for good. For I thought I heard in his voice a thread of relief—as though he'd been prepared to take on the duty of raising my child but was happier still not to have to.

Briskly, he said: "Joan, are you ready to go down?"

"...Down?"

"To dinner?"

"Oh. I hadn't thought."

"Or would you rather go out?"

I had my duties as well, I realized. And I at least wouldn't leap at any chance to escape them. "...I imagine the servants would be hurt, after outdoing themselves to please the bride on her first night home, if she decided to eat dinner out. No, let's have dinner in. May I ask what their names are?"

He told me: "The maids are Myra and Leora—Myra is the shorter. The cook is Araminta, goes by Minnie. Jasper is her husband. The men you'll meet tomorrow—they won't be at dinner. Incidentally, when you pay them all the first of the month, they rate a small gift from you, in appreciation of—"

"Services well rendered—or in other words, a tip. I'd have given it anyway—I've worked for tips myself, as you well know. I've taken them from you."

"...They were the least that I could do."

"Yes, well—they lightened dark days for me," I said, leaving off the word that threatened to spring to my lips at the sentence's end: *temporarily*.

I got up, went in the bath and freshened my face, came out, combed while he watched, and then led the way downstairs. The maids were at the dining-room door, making me little bows, which I acknowledged by calling their names and shaking hands. Then I went out in the kitchen to greet the cook, whom I called by her full name, Araminta, pleasing her, as I thought it might. Jasper was there and I shook hands with him as well. When I came back and took my place at the head of the table, both maids seemed very friendly, and I detected surprise in their manner, and also in his. I don't know what they expected, but I'd been brought up to treat servants as human, and have never regretted doing it.

For dinner there was fruit cup, roast lamb, new potatoes, peas, salad, and ice cream. While Earl carved the lamb, Myra poured us drinks, tonic water for him and, unasked for, a glass of wine for me. I thought it surprising that he hadn't let her know I didn't drink, but this was no time to correct the error, so I simply smiled and pretended to have a sip. Even the taste of it on my lips made me slightly ill—I remembered it as the taste on Ron's lips many a night when he'd come home soused and pressed himself against me.

When we'd finished the meal and had our coffee, I went out and complimented Araminta on the beautiful dinner, and thanked the maids for the way they served it. Then I led the way to the drawing room, where I felt it was well to say: "I feel a bit better now." I didn't; if anything, I felt worse as anxiety began to possess me over what was going to happen when we went upstairs to bed. However, nothing did—he let me go to my room, making no move to follow, and saying goodnight at the door, with no more than a small token kiss, there in the hall outside.

It surprised me—but then he had seemed very preoccupied, as we sat for an hour after dinner in the drawing room, where I took a chair instead of a place on a sofa, and he took a chair on the other side of the room. After a time he'd said: "In a way perhaps we can be glad it happened."

"Glad?" I said, keeping my voice neutral, or trying to.

"It cleared the air, kind of."

"In what way, cleared the air?"

"From now on it's you and me. It puts ideas in my head."

"What kind of ideas, Earl?"

"You'll see—friendly ones, that's all I care to say till I know where I'm at. I think you're going to be pleased—we could even say excited. But—let's let it be my little surprise."

My big surprise for Tad had turned out quite a bust; how this little one for me would turn out I didn't know, but the way my stomach was jumping warned me. And though when we went up he didn't follow me into my room, or try to watch me undress, or in any way make the kind of pest of himself he'd been making before, just kissed me once and said goodnight, as he turned away he winked. So, I lay in the dark and tried to guess what *that* meant. I sat up after a while and stared out the window. For the thought had occurred to me: The way you guess what it meant is, you guess the worst possible thing you can think of, and with him, that has to be it.

The worst possible thing I could think of was that he meant to renege on our bargain, and consummate—or try to. I felt my mouth go dry, and wanted to echo Tad, with the scream he had given, of horror. I thought: That can't be it! The doctor has warned him—it's unthinkable. It turned out, though, that if you want something badly enough, it's not only thinkable, but doable.

I was asleep when the tap came on the door, but when I called he came in, kissed me good morning, and said he must go to work—"I've been away, and things have piled up." I said something, how proud I was of him, "that you carry on as you do, letting nothing interfere. It's the kind of thing I respect." And if I sound hypocritical, I wasn't, as I said what I felt, quite honestly. I do respect the person who works at his job, as barber or waitress or whatever, and I try to have manners, however I feel. "O.K., O.K.," he whispered. "Now you go back to sleep. But tonight, as I hope, I'll have something to report."

He went and I got up. When I came down to breakfast, I knew from the way they acted that I'd made a hit with the servants. Myra introduced me to the others, the men, whose names were Jackson, Coleman, and Boyd. Boyd, it turned out, was Myra's cousin, and spelled Jasper as driver when Jasper had a day off. Today was one such day, and he offered to take me anywhere I needed to go, but I told him I preferred to stay in and discover the place for myself.

There was a phone extension in the upstairs hall, and I put in two or three calls, one to Jake, at his home, one to Bianca, and of course one to Liz. I begged her to stop by that very day, and she wound up by coming to lunch. I was so glad to see her I cried, and especially at how she was dressed, so distinguished, and all in my honor, and in honor of who might be there. She had on a beige pantsuit, very smart and very becoming, with a red ribbon on her gray hair. After lunch I took her upstairs to my room, but had hardly closed the door when she led me to the bed, pushed me onto it, and pulled up a chair beside me. "Get to it, baby," she whispered. "What happened?" For I hadn't called her, in spite of my promise. I told her now, about the lab and the test results, and she said, "Thank god, Joan. I had all my fingers crossed for you. But you don't seem happy. What is it?"

"It's my little boy, Tad."

I told then, about the scream he'd let out, and what it had done to me. But then I couldn't stop. I went on and on about my marriage to Earl, and the deal that had been made. "But now," I said, "something tells me that deal is off—that our marriage is to be like any other. That he wants to—consummate, as the lawyer called it. That's what I'm up against now—what I think I'm up against."

"And you don't want to?"

"...Not even a little bit."

"So O.K. baby—it's something a girl runs into—I do myself, occasionally. But, one reason or another, you have to anyway. So, how you do, you close your eyes, and pretend it's Rock Hudson."

"I wish I could."

"Well what's stopping you?"

"All kinds of things."

"You mean, like Tom Barclay?"

I didn't answer her. I wanted to—I wanted to scoff and ask what he had to do with anything. But I realized, when she spoke his name and my heart leapt, that he did have something to do with it, a lot, in fact. And from my reaction she realized it too.

"Then, we call it that, we call it him. And you can't pretend your husband's him, on account you really wish it was, and it would be getting messy. So, I'd say you're in a spot—but, at least, Tom will be glad to hear it."

"…What makes you think so, Liz?"

"You'd like to know, wouldn't you?"

She lit a cigarette, inhaled, and went on without me answering: "O.K., then, I'll tell you. He comes in, Joan. He sits with me, and when he comes in he talks."

"About me, you mean?"

"About nothing else. He's bitter, baby. He feels you crossed him, that you did it for money, and that he doesn't respect."

"I didn't do it for the money!"

"…What did you do it for?"

She was suddenly sharp, and I felt, close as I was to her, that I didn't have her respect, either. "I did it for Tad."

"And where did that get you, I ask."

"For Christ's sake, shut up."

"Baby, you've got it coming."

"You say Tom comes in?"

"Every night, so far."

"Then you might mention to him, Liz, if you find occasion, that…I have been true to him—so far. And I'm goddam well going to be. But please, please, please, don't say I told you that."

"If I do, he might rush over a minute later."

"And he could get pushed out."

"I'm not sure of that," Liz said. "I'm not so sure."

"Please don't do it."

"I'll use my judgment what to tell him."

"I'm not ready for him yet."

She looked at me quite some time, then asked: "What do you mean by that?"

I guess I looked at her a while too. Then I told her: "Liz, I'm not sure I know."

"If you mean what I think you mean—?"

"I mean, Rome wasn't built in a day. I mean, first things first. And first of all, for me, I've got to make clear a deal is a deal is a deal. Once that's understood, life can go on, and we'll see where we take it from there."

"And Tom? What does he do?"

"One thing at a time, Liz—!"

"O.K., O.K., just asking."

I was suddenly half hysterical, and she reached out to calm me down. Then, looking at her watch: "Got to be running along, or Jake will have my skin. Bianca still hasn't found someone to replace you, so I'm back to doing double the work."

"I'm sorry, Liz."

"I'm not complaining, I'm just telling you how it is." She hesitated. "On Tom, I'll tell him keep his fingers crossed, there may be more to come. Tell him calm down, take it easy."

"Thank you."

"He may not take it well. He's not a patient boy."

"He'll have to take it, Liz. What's his other choice?"

27

She went, and I got up and dressed. Then I went down and sat in the drawing room, waiting for Earl to come home. But I didn't sit there long, for at 4:30 here came the car, and he bounded inside, bright and cheerful, "all ready for my walk to the Garden of Roses—except that this time, that woman Liz will serve me, instead of a beautiful girl I know." I patted his cheek and gave him the smile he was after. I admit I was surprised he intended to keep up his pattern of visiting the Garden, but there was no reason I should have been—he'd been going there long before I came into the picture, so why not keep going now? "But Joanie," he whispered, and took me in his arms, "when I get back, have I got a piece of news! I'm still pinching myself. I'll give you a little hint: From now on, we can lead a normal life, like other people."

He went up, changed to walking clothes, the rough shoes he had always worn, the double-weave trousers, flannel sport shirt, and coat. He patted me, kissed me, and headed for the door, waving at Boyd and tapping his watch. Then, quite briskly, he went marching off. He hadn't said anything about me, if I wished to go somewhere, and I thought: I'll fix that, right now. So I got a coat and went out to where Boyd was in the car, waiting to start down and bring Earl back. I got in the back seat and asked him to drive me to the garage where I'd left my car. He looked startled, but then said: "O.K., Mrs. White."

"I'd prefer you call me Joan."

"All right," Boyd said. "Joan."

At the garage, I paid the storage bill, $35, and then drove back. On the way I drove past my house, my out-of-date little bungalow, the only home I'd known since I bailed out of Pittsburgh. It looked exactly the same. I drove on. When I got to the White mansion—I can't make myself say "got home"—I drove around back to the garage and put my car in there. Three other cars were there, a station wagon, a pick-up truck, and a slightly battered sedan, the last probably belonging to one of the servants. I'm sure I could have found keys to one of the other two and used it, but I was happier having my own car on hand.

Just before six here came Earl, in the car with Boyd, and I met him in the hall, asking if he had a nice walk. "Very nice," he answered, "except for the stop at the Garden. Your former colleague, Liz, is a wholly objectionable person, cheap, familiar, and in all ways dreadful."

"I like her."

"Well, I don't."

"She's a close personal friend, almost the only friend I have here, and I'll be grateful if you speak no ill of her."

"…As you wish."

"Good, then we'll say no more about her."

I was a bit disagreeable, while trying not to be. Then, thinking it best to seem interested: "But, Earl, you said you have news. What is it?"

His frown disappeared, his face lit up, and he said: "The most beautiful news imaginable. Joan, today I saw a new doctor, and when I told him what Cord had said—that I have to live cautiously for the rest of my life, that there's nothing that can be done—he just laughed. He says that's all out of date. Maybe ten years ago it was true, but not today. He's begun me on a course of treatments that he says will instantly show results. Something called intravenous chelation—it's a new technique, where they flush some chemical through you and on its way out it takes whatever's causing the problem with it. I don't say I understand all the details, but that's the gist of it. That, and shots of Vitamin E twice daily."

"And he thinks that will cure your angina?"

"He's certain of it. He's done it for a dozen other patients—two dozen, maybe—and it's worked for all of them."

"And you tried it today? Is it painful?"

"Not bad, really. The injections are like any injection, and the chelation, well, you sit two or three hours with a bag slowly draining into your arm through a needle. There's a pinch when the needle goes in, but after that you forget it's even there."

"Until you get up and try to walk away."

"It's on a stand," he said. "It rolls."

"…Well, it's awfully exciting," I said, trying to make myself sound pleased. "And I guess worth a try. But how will you know if it's worked?"

A grin came over his face, like a young boy's. "We'll just have to give it a trial. He said tonight's not too soon, since it's had a few hours now to do its work."

"Earl, I'm not so sure…you'd be taking an awful chance…"

"Dr. Jameson assured me I'm not."

"Dr. Jameson is not the one who's at risk."

"His reputation is."

"Your *life* is!"

Earl looked frustrated. "Are you saying you won't?"

"Give me a minute to think."

"I'll give you ten seconds."

"Then, no. I'm too scared. Of a repeat of what happened in London, only worse."

"What happened in London was caused by all that wrestling you made me do. If you'll stop arguing about it, and cooperate instead, then—"

"*I won't cooperate.*"

I heard my mouth say it, cold and quiet, to mean it. His whole manner suddenly changed. Then, also quiet, to mean it, he said: "No, you won't, will you."

"I don't want you dropping dead beside me—"

"No, Joan. Don't lie." He stepped closer. "That isn't why. You sound quite noble, but there's one thing wrong with it, slightly. You won't cooperate because you don't want to cooperate. I feel like a fool."

"Earl—"

"You've been playing a game with me, haven't you? You've been pretending it's me you want, when actually it's my money— my fortune, this house, these servants, and the rest that I've given you. It's—"

"Earl, it's not, as I can prove."

"O.K., start proving."

"If it were what you've said, all I'd have to do is cooperate and lo and behold, a corpse would be holding me—and everything would fall in my hands. Instead of which, for your own good, I refuse to cooperate at the risk of your life. Now, does that prove it?"

"It might have, when I still was at risk. Now, it does not."

"Well, you might think this new treatment is a sure thing, but I call it wishful thinking, and possibly quackery, and if I'm right you could die from it. What else can I say?"

But he was shaking his head. "There's nothing you can say, because you're not telling the truth. You're lying to me, also to yourself."

"Oh, you know what I tell myself? I wish you'd tell me how."

"Be glad to. What your eyes say is not the same as what's coming out of your mouth. They have the same identical look as that boy of yours, when he screamed at me. You look exactly like him, Joan, and your eyes say the same thing. He hated me, and you do. I've been suspecting, since London, since you wouldn't let me touch you, since you insisted we fly home early. And now—"

I tried to take hold of his arm, but he shook me off, then at the top of his lungs he called: "Jasper! *Jasper!*"

From the kitchen, and then out the dining room door, along came Boyd, buttoning his coat as he ran. "Jasper's got the day off today, Mr. White, remember?" Earl didn't answer, just stormed out to the car and got in. Boyd followed, bent low beside the window, touched his cap at some word from inside, got in, and drove off.

I didn't feel like dinner, and went out to the kitchen to explain to Araminta, as well as to Myra, who was also on duty. I apologized for having no appetite, and they said that was O.K. They were quite nice about it, but I could tell by their manner they knew why.

I went upstairs and stewed—but then after a while felt hungry after all. Having passed up the dinner they'd already made, though, I couldn't change my mind and ask them to do it over. Then I knew where I would go to eat. Going out through the kitchen again, I surprised Araminta and Myra having their own dinner together, and told them: "If Mr. White comes in while I'm gone, will you tell him I'll be back around nine or ten? There's something I have to do. I'm using my car, tell him."

"Yes, Miss Joan. We will."

I drove to the Garden, parked, and went in the cocktail bar. It was jammed, with Bianca helping Liz cover. Bianca came over, shook hands, asked how I'd been, and then when I explained I'd come for dinner, brought me to a table, the same one Earl had sat at and that Tom had sat at, and asked what I was going to have. "What have you got?" I asked her. "I'm good and hungry."

"Roast beef, fried chicken, goulash."

"I'll have the goulash, Bianca."

The goulash was done to her own special recipe, and she was quite proud of it, so it was kind of a compliment to her that I said I'd have it. She went out in the kitchen to call it while I went over and shook hands with Jake, then put my arms around Liz, kissed her, and said "Surprise, surprise." Then, taking my starters to the table as I'd done for customers so many times— the napkin, knife, fork, spoon, bread, and butter that everyone got with dinner—I sat down. But I suddenly had an impulse: "Never mind serving me, Bianca," I told her. "I'll eat in my usual place."

So, carrying my starters back through the swinging door, I went out in the kitchen, shook hands with Mr. Bergie, as well as the dishwasher boy, who was new. Then I told Mr. Bergie: "I'm the goulash Bianca just called—and I'll have it here at my regular spot." I seated myself at the same folding table I'd sat at my first night, between the stove and the pantry door. I made myself comfortable and waited while Mr. Bergie put my plate together. Then I went and got it, used the cutlery I had in my hand, sat down and ate it. "Goulash is nice tonight," I told him, and he gave a little salute. I took some salad from the crisper, decided to skip dessert, and drew myself black coffee. Then I sat there and sipped it, feeling easy, relaxed, and as though I was with friends.

✻

When I went back to the bar, the dinner rush had eased off, and I sat down at my same table, to continue my talk with Liz. "Someone was in," she whispered.

"…Oh? When?"

"Today, right after we opened."

"…And?"

"I told him I'd seen you."

"O.K."

I tried to act unconcerned, but she did not let me get away with it. She just stood there and waited, and finally I couldn't take it any longer. "Well?" I burst out. "What did he say?"

"That he couldn't care less—or words to that effect."

"…So? He couldn't care less."

But she stood there some more, and then once again I burst out: "And what did you say?"

"Nothing I could repeat."

Then: "I told him stop handing me horseshit, that if he wanted to hear the rest, say so."

"And? Did he?"

"What do you think?"

"And what did you tell him then?"

"Baby, I don't know if I did right, but there's such a thing as heading a mess off—I mean, if he knew what you told me today, he could feel better already, and not go barging off to do something foolish. So, I took the liberty. I told him what you said—not all, but so he got the idea."

"What idea, Liz?"

"That you're hooked on him still and haven't slept with your new husband because of it."

"But—that's not true."

"Then I misunderstood you when you said you hadn't consummated. If I told it wrong, I'm sorry."

"You didn't misunderstand that—it's just as you told him it is. But not for that reason. I wish it was, but it's not."

"Baby, I'm getting dizzy."

"Liz, if it was as you said, that I have that kind of marriage on account of torching for Tom, I'd say so, I'd be only too glad, I wouldn't be too proud. But it's not that. If I could, I'd have gone through with it, Liz—the lawyer told me I had to. But it came to a head tonight, everything just as I feared it would. And I *couldn't* go through with it—not because of Tom, just because I couldn't stomach the thought of that old man climbing on top of me, and—and—"

"So, you're leaving him?"

"...I don't know yet."

"Joan, you're as bad as Tom. Suppose you stop handing me horseshit too. Why did you call me today? Why did you ask me to lunch? Way I saw it, I was to take a message. O.K., then, I took it. Now you've given him hope. So if you go back on the message, he's been made a fool of. And I'm warning you, he may not take it friendly."

"...O.K., Liz. Thanks."

All that took longer to talk out than it takes for me to tell it, and by then the place began to fill up again, this time with the late, after-the-picture-show bunch. As usual, they were younger than the dinner people, and as usual, they began running Liz ragged. In a minute I got up and began filling orders for her—a lot of people knew me, and began calling my name very friendly, not paying too much attention that I wasn't in uniform. And then all of a sudden in front of me there was Earl, his face trembling with rage. "Mrs. Earl K. White," he roared, "does not serve drinks in a bar!"

"Mrs. Earl K. White *the Third*," I told him. "Let's use the full thing if we're going to use it at all. And Mrs. Earl K. White the Third decides for herself where she serves drinks, whether she serves drinks or throws them in somebody's face that interferes—or tries to interfere."

I was at the bar, a tray of rickeys in my hand, and he stepped aside, but quick. However, I didn't walk past him—not yet. "I thought I told you," I went on, "to call off that snoop you had—*and I thought you promised to do it.*"

"Snoop? I didn't need any snoop! A dozen people have called to tell me you were here! That Earl K. White's wife was serving drinks—"

"The Third," I said, and walked past him with my tray. I set the rickeys in front of the guests and beckoned Liz to make out the check—I being strictly a bus girl helping out. Then I turned to Earl and told him: "I'm ready now if you are."

"…Ready for what, Joan?"

"To go home, what else? Having been left alone all evening, I decided to visit with friends—and when they needed help, to give it—being in the Social Register has obligations—noblesse oblige, it's called. But now, as you've arrived and made a scene—"

He snapped his fingers in the direction of the vestibule and I saw Boyd come forward. "We're going home," he announced. "Bring the car around."

"Yes, sir."

"Not for me, thanks," I said, "I'm using my own car. You may ride with me if you like, Earl, or take yours, as you prefer, but I'm taking mine."

He was steaming, and I expected him to storm off as he had earlier. Instead, he told Boyd to take the car back on his own, and waited for me to get my jacket. I suddenly realized it was not his humiliation he was here to make sure I knew of, or his embarrassment, or his shame, or any of the things he pretended, but a triumph of some sort, that he had to gloat over with me. There was something he wanted me to know, and he didn't want me out of his sight until he'd said it. But my realization was vague, as I wasn't caught up yet, as to what kind of evening he'd had. I just had an uneasy feeling there would be more.

I didn't know the half.

28

I led outside, opened the passenger door for him and put him in. Then I got in myself and drove home—his home, at least, and the place I had to call home, as I seemed to be living there. I drove around to the garage and put my car away, then walked back to the front door with him. All this time he was holding in whatever it was he wanted to say. As soon as we made it inside the drawing room, he burst out: "What was the idea? Disgracing me? Earl K. White's wife doesn't work in a cocktail bar!"

"Earl K. White's wife *did* work in a cocktail bar, as Earl K. White well knows—and Earl K. White's wife can do as she goddam well pleases, and it pleases her, when left alone for an evening, to spend it with friends, and if they need help in the work, to give it. Any more questions?"

"…Why don't you ask one?"

"Such as which one?"

"Why don't you ask where I spent the evening?"

"It's none of my business, that's why—but since you make it my business, O.K., where did you spend the evening?"

"Massage parlor."

"You mean, a junior whorehouse?"

"…O.K., call it that."

"I call it what it is—at least as I've heard, in such way as to believe it. And you enjoyed your little visit?"

"You bet I did."

"Then I'm glad."

"I thought you would be. You might be interested to know it proved you wrong, and Dr. Cord wrong. I had myself what we can call a massage, two of them, matter of fact—with no fatal results, as you see."

"That's wonderful, Earl, but it doesn't prove Dr. Cord wrong."

"It doesn't? I'd say it does."

"Not if by 'massage' you mean what I think you mean, namely a young woman working you over with her hands. All right, she took the towel off at the end and worked a little more than she's supposed to under the law—you might have died from that, and thank goodness you didn't. But there's a difference between that and what you were proposing we do, and if you don't know what the difference is I'm not going to be the one to tell you."

"I survived the one, and I would survive the other just the same."

"You might as well say, I can step off the curb so I can step out a window."

"You're saying you think the act with you would be that much more tremendous?"

"I'm saying you do, or you wouldn't be pursuing it so single-mindedly. Earl, I've seen what happens to you when you get excited. A woman you've never met and will never see again cannot excite you like your wife, and the touch of a woman's hand cannot excite you the way possessing her entire body would. You've learned something tonight about what your body can withstand, but you haven't learned enough to say you're ready for what you want. And the only way you could find that out is too dangerous."

"And you know that how? You're an impressive woman, Joan, I don't say you aren't—but I don't recall your having a medical degree. Let me show you something." He got up and pulled over a little stairway, a mahogany thing no more than eighteen inches high, with two steps on it, for use in front of the bookshelves, which on one side of the room were quite high. "Journal Dr. Jameson lent me—has an article in it, on angina."

"Won't change my mind, but all right, show me."

Fuming, holding onto the shelf with one hand for balance, he climbed up, stood on top, and reached for a narrow volume. Suddenly, instead of getting it, he clutched his chest and turned to face the room. I knew a seizure had hit him, and that if something wasn't done quickly he'd topple and fall. I got to the stair and wrapped my arms around his legs. Then, "Lean on me, Earl," I whispered. "Don't try to step down—lean on me and slide down."

He did, and then was down on the floor. I'm fairly strong, and was able to half carry him to a chair. Then: "Your pills are by your bed, the way they were in London?"

"Yes! *Yes!*" He whispered it, and then: "Joan, hurry! For Christ's sake, get them, *quick!*"

I hurried. I didn't even know for sure which room was his, but by opening doors I found it, then found the vial, in the corner at the head of his bed. I grabbed it and ran downstairs. He was still in the chair, in agony. I got him a pill and put it in his hand. He popped it into his mouth, and I could see him roll it under his tongue. He held out his hand for another one and I gave it to him. He popped it in and after a moment his breathing began to ease. Whispering hoarsely, he started in again, as he had in London, about what to do if he should die this time.

"Will you, goddam it, shut up?"

He exhaled hugely, his whole face red and tortured.

"You won't die this time. I'm here, and I'll see you don't."

"You don't want me to?"

"What do you think?"

"…Joan, you don't love me, not even a little bit, but I love you, I can't help it."

"Earl, I love you, but know no way of loving a corpse."

"O.K. O.K."

Little by little his seizure passed. "When it starts going away, that's the worst of all. Feels like a hand was there, squeezing the air out of your lungs—not your heart, your lungs, though of course your heart is the cause of it all."

"Take it easy."

"Joan, I'm trying to."

And then, all of a sudden, it was over, and he half lay in the chair, still in a state of collapse. When he was somewhat recovered, so he could sit up, I asked: "Now—can we talk?"

"…O.K. What is it, Joan?"

"About the massage parlor."

"…All right, but I want to add something to what I told you. It all happened as I said, except that it happened with you, not the massage girl at all."

"Oh?"

"I pretended, that's why. Pretended she was you. In my mind, in my heart, she *was* you—it's what I wanted to say. I'm trying to tell you, spite of everything, spite of how you feel toward me, I do love you. I do."

There, once more, was the thing Liz had suggested, to fix everything up by pretending. I suddenly realized I had, back in the early days of my marriage, when Ron and I were still trying, and I've since read it's something the whole human race does, at one time or another. But with Earl I just couldn't. No amount of pretending would help.

He waited, and then: "But I interrupted you, Joan. What was it you wanted to say?"

"About the massage parlor—please don't go there anymore."

"Will you give me a reason not to?"

"You can still ask me that, after what just happened?"

He didn't even look abashed. "It wasn't the parlor that did it," he said, "it was the argument with you, the strain of it—"

"It was both, Earl. It was the combination. And even without the argument it might have happened if what came before had brought you to a similar emotional peak. And if that happened with me, as a result of my allowing you what you've been begging for—I couldn't live with myself, knowing I'd been the cause of it. Do you get my full meaning, why I can't, won't let myself, say yes? Do you realize what that would mean?"

"But do *you* realize, Joan, what it would mean to me, to know I can be normal—live the life everyone leads—and forego it just because you are afraid? I cannot promise that, Joan. I can't."

"…Then, if you must have it, at least we can remove as much of the risk as possible."

"Meaning what?"

I said: "You liked her, that girl in the massage place?"

"Believe it or not she was very nice—kind, understanding, and sweet."

I couldn't help myself, and snapped: "I'm sure she was."

"It wasn't cheap, what I did."

"Who knows better than I that you couldn't be cheap, Earl? So O.K., do you know her name?"

"Bella."

"Do you know the name of the place?"

"Kitty-Cat, in Arlington."

"Then, if, as, and when, tomorrow night or whenever, you feel the urge coming on, and can't resist or don't want to, I want you to call them—I'll look up the number for you—and have Bella come here."

"Joan, that would be messy—"

"Nothing like as messy as what *could* happen, in the Kitty-Cat, if you had a seizure there. Earl, to them you'd be just a problem, something to be got rid of, to be put out in the street before the police could get there. We can't have that happen to you." I brushed a few strands of hair out of his eyes. "The same as you need to know how I feel, and accept it, it's up to me to know how *you* feel and accept that. And—I guess I do. I wish, for your sake, you didn't—but you can't hold back Niagara—and it seems to be that strong, this compulsion you have."

"You'd actually want me to…?"

"If you have to, I want you to do it that way. So that you're here, where we know what to do with you, and how to get hold of the doctor, in case he's needed."

"If you put it that way—"

"I do put it that way."

"You're remarkable, Joan."

Next day, he went in to the office, but came back almost at once, as I was finishing breakfast. He said, "Something occurred to me, driving in, that I want to get out of the way—that I've been intending to do, but realize I had better do now. Can you come with me now, to the bank?"

"But of course."

I took a coat, went out with him and got in the car while Jasper held open the door, and drove with him to the Suburban Trust in College Park. There the manager, Mr. Frost, came bouncing out of this office, to shake hands and be introduced to me, as of course the marriage had been in the paper. "Dick," Earl told him, "I want to change all four of my accounts, the checking, the Special No.1, Special No.2, and Savings, from single, in my name, to joints, in my name and Mrs. White's—so she's protected in event of my death."

"…Which seems highly unlikely, Mr. White, but if that's the arrangement you want—?"

"It's not only likely but certain—give God time, it's amazing what He can do."

"He always has his little joke," said Mr. Frost, smiling at me. "Oh, always."

He cut off with the small talk then, and took us into his office, a sizable one, enclosed in glass. We sat down, Mr. Frost called a girl, and then told her to bring certain forms, which ones I don't recollect. Then we signed—Earl, to O.K. me as joint holder on the accounts, I to give specimen signatures on four different cards. The Special accounts, it turned out, were for taxes, one for federal, the other for state. I was put on all four, and finally, Earl called for the balance showing on each. I was stunned. On the checking account it was over $600,000, on one Special $230,000, on the other $90,000, on the savings $65,000. I had known he was rich, but had had no idea how rich. When we were done, I shook hands with Mr. Frost and thanked him, and Earl gave him a nod. Then we were at the door, going out, but Mr. Frost took the nod as a dismissal, and didn't come with us. In the glass vestibule at the bank's entrance, Earl suddenly took my arm, and said: "Joan, I said some bitter things last night, as a man in love does, every so often. Make no mistake, Joan, I *am* a man in love. I love you insanely, and—"

"I love *you*, Earl."

I said it without a hitch in my voice this time, without hesitating, and without, I hoped, Tad's look of fear in my eyes.

"Maybe so," he said, "in your own way. At least I do know you don't wish me dead, as if you did you've had plenty of opportunity to let me die, last night included. But still and all—" He waved back in the direction of the bank. "...I'm glad to get this done. Now you have every bit as much with me alive as you'd have with me gone."

"Please don't talk like that."

"I just don't ever want it to be an issue, in your mind or anyone else's."

*

That night, he was as I wanted him to be, quiet, courteous, and not demanding, physically, I mean. We watched television, and when I, very nervous about it, said I wanted to go to bed, he patted me, kissed me, and took me upstairs, but made no attempt to follow me into my room, and didn't knock after I turned in. What a relief! At last I could sleep without fear sleeping with me. In the morning he came in and kissed me, I being still in bed, then drove off to work with Jasper. In the afternoon he came home, changed his clothes for his walk, set out for the Garden, and returned without incident.

That evening was another like the one before, and likewise the one after that. Next evening, however, things weren't the same, even a little bit. He took his walk as usual, came home, and kissed me, but in a queer, guilty way, and at once went upstairs, asking me to stay off the phone so he could make a call. Then when dinner was served he didn't come down. I went up, knocked on his door, and pushed it open, and found him sitting with his intravenous mechanism attached, the rubber tubing feeding his medicine from an elevated bottle into his arm. He started, looking embarrassed, almost as if he'd been caught at something, which was silly, since I knew he was taking the treatments and he knew I knew. I said nothing about it, just informed him that dinner was on the table, and he said he didn't want any—"not just yet anyway." It was an odd way of putting it, as though he was hungry but was putting off food for some reason. He didn't look at me, and I went down, had dinner myself, and tried to figure it out, with no success. I was in the drawing room later when the doorbell rang. No one was due that I knew of, and I had a sudden feeling about it. "I'll take it," I called to Myra, who had started for the door to answer it.

When I opened, a girl was there, in a sort of nurse's uniform, a coat over her shoulders, a cab in the drive behind her. She blinked, then said: "...If you're the housekeeper, I'm Bella, calling on Mr. White."

I confess I felt rocked down to my feet. She was here at my suggestion, no doubt about that, but actually to see her, with her cab waiting outside, set my head to spinning around. "Oh yes," I said, "I think Mr. White is expecting you—come in, please."

She did, and I got my bag from the drawing room, went out and paid off the cab—twelve dollars and something. I gave him fifteen, then went back inside. Running upstairs I knocked on Earl's door and called: "Earl? *Company!*"

I guess I did it with malice, at least a little bit, as someone had told me once that that's what a madam calls when a visitor comes—"Girls! Company!" Anyway, I beckoned her up, showed her the door to knock on, and went down. When I heard it open and close, I went to the kitchen and told Araminta, "Mr. White has a visitor. He's not to be disturbed, but if anything happens— if he has an attack—you can reach me at this number." I wrote the Garden number on her kitchen memo pad. To make sure she understood, I asked her: "You understand about his attacks?"

"You mean the pain he gets in the chest?"

"That's it. Let me know, *at once*. You can give him his pills if he needs them, but don't call anyone else, even the doctor, till I get here. It'll take me no more than ten minutes."

"Yes, Mrs. White. I got it."

She looked at me very oddly, but I felt warmth under the squint, and felt things would be under control. Then I put on my coat, got out my car and drove down to the Garden.

It was a Friday in early November, with the hatcheck open again, the first time in months, as of course in summer no hats are worn, or coats, or anything checkable, and October had still been warm. A new girl was on the booth that I didn't know, but it's where the phone was and I had to depend on her. I gave her a buck and when I told her my name she knew who I was, and was quite excited at meeting me. I guess I was known as the girl who'd made good. I told her: "I'm expecting a call, a very important call, and I'll be in the bar. Don't fail me please. I may be helping Liz, so if you don't see me, tell her."

"You can depend on me, Mrs. White."

"Joan."

Liz first seated me at the bar between two other customers, then moved me to my regular little table when it opened up. I didn't really expect any call, and was happily losing myself in helping her with her orders when something touched my arm, and when I turned it was the new hatcheck girl. "Call for you, Joan. Woman says it's important."

It was Araminta: "Get out here, Miss Joan—it's hit him. He's bad off this time—real bad."

I parked the car out front, and she had the door open by the time I jumped out. I went in and upstairs. Myra was there, in a chair by the bed, and Earl was there, under the covers with no clothes on, judging by the pile strewn on the floor, pants, shirt, underwear and all. Beside it was a dainty lace brassiere, left behind by its owner in her hurry to exit.

He was holding his chest and had his eyes tightly shut, but when he heard me enter he forced them open. "Thank God you're here, Joan," he groaned, each word coming at a great cost. "This is it—you win."

"Win? *Win?*"

"You were right, I'm trying to say."

I told Myra: "O.K.—you've done the right thing, all of you. Now—"

"Let me know if you need me, Miss Joan."

She went and I asked: "The girl left you like this?"

"…I told her, go. She was scared."

I saw the pill bottle lying on its side on the bed, empty. "The medicine didn't help?"

"Not this time. This time's the end, I can feel it. You—win."

"Will you please stop saying *I win*? If it turns out the way you say, I'm the biggest loser of all time."

"It *will* turn out that way. It's not only the pain this time—I can't get my breath—a new twist. It can't go on. If I'd only listened to you—"

"Stop it. Stop it." I had the phone in hand and looked up Dr. Cord's number in the book beside it. There were two numbers, one with an 'H' alongside, which I took to mean it was his home; when you're rich enough, and I suppose sick enough, I guess your doctor gives you his home number to call him day or night. Sure enough, Dr. Cord picked up at home, and before I got through a sentence of explanation he said he'd be over at once. When I returned to Earl's side, he looked worse, his jaw clenched against the pain. Through it he said: "I heard you— beat a guy up once—at the Garden."

"...I certainly did beat him up."

"For—trying something with you."

"Yes."

"If you'd only—beat me up. Just once. If you'd beat some sense in my head."

For a couple of minutes then he didn't say anything, and I didn't either, just watched him struggle to get air and held onto his hand. He let out a little whimper.

"It's my fault," I said. "This whole thing was my idea, I thought you'd be safer here—"

"No. Not—your idea."

"I was the one told you to call her."

"I had the idea—weeks—before you popped it out. It was so crazy —couldn't make myself say it. But I had it. Joan, listen— there's one thing still unsaid."

"Yes, Earl. What?"

He raised up on one elbow to say it, but what it was I didn't find out and don't know to this day. When he fell back he was gone, and at that moment a man walked in that I'd never seen, who I realized was Dr. Cord. I told him: "Thanks for coming, Doctor. However, I think you're too late."

He went over to Earl and felt for a pulse, and finding none let Earl's arm gently down. "He was long overdue, Mrs. White."

29

He began with the death certificate, then interrupted to call the police, "so there can't be any question," and then turned to me and said: "He probably didn't mention it, but I tried to tell him that marriage could well be fatal. I was upset when I saw the news in the paper, that he had wed—"

But I cut in to say: "He told me everything, especially what you said, and we got married anyhow. He knew the risk, I begged him to remember it, but he wanted a normal life."

Dr. Cord looked me over then, in a way that was all too familiar to me—Sergeant Young had done it, and the lawyer, Eckert; Tom had done it, and Lacey, and Luke Goss, and plenty of other customers at the bar; all sorts of men had, hundreds probably, since I turned twelve and first began developing a woman's figure. At the job I'd invited it, I suppose, what with my uniform putting my legs and my bust on display, but there was nothing inviting it here, in my husband's bedroom, with his body not ten feet away, and *my* body in nothing revealing or alluring at all. But Dr. Cord, perhaps used to dead bodies in his line of work and so not deterred by Earl's, looked me over all the same. I felt tears come then, if only tears of rage, of frustration.

"Earl was certainly entitled to a normal life," Dr. Cord said, "but I'm not so certain that's what he had." He gestured in the direction of the intravenous chelation equipment, still standing by the armchair in the corner, hypodermics for the vitamin injections lined up on the shelf behind. Then he bent and picked up the brassiere between the tips of his second and third fingers, like something unclean. "This is a lovely piece of lingerie, Mrs. White, but unless I'm mistaken, at least two sizes too small for you to be its owner." I snatched it from him and jammed it in the pocket of my jacket.

He went on: "The police will be here momentarily, but it needn't be anything but a routine matter for them. I'll let them know of Earl's medical history, his prior attacks. They won't even perform an autopsy if I do that. They won't see any reason to. Assuming…"

"Assuming?"

"Assuming I don't tell them about the article of clothing in your pocket." He walked over to the chair and lifted the empty bottle from its hook. "About medical treatments I didn't sanction. They might do an autopsy then. I really don't think I need to tell them, though. As a favor to Earl, rest his soul. He deserves better than to have his good name tarnished by a scandal in the papers. There isn't a man, alive or dead, who can't use a favor now and again."

I knew then what he thought me, what he thought I'd been to Earl—something like what Bella had been, only better paid.

"You go ahead and tell them," I snapped. "Tell them anything you want, everything you want. I have nothing to cover up. Nothing. "

"Mrs. White—"

"I don't want any favors. I don't offer them, either, not the sort you mean. Aren't you ashamed of yourself asking…?"

I heard footsteps in the hallway then, and the sound of the door opening behind me. Looking over my shoulder Dr. Cord stood up straighter, which told me it was the police. I didn't know how much of what we'd been saying they might have heard, but I, at least, hadn't been quiet. I only prayed that when I turned I'd see faces I'd never seen before.

Like so many of my prayers before it, this one went unanswered.

"If you could step aside, doctor, and put that bottle down," said Private Church, "we'd appreciate it."

They were neither of them in uniform, Church or Young, both looking as though they'd been rung up in the middle of an evening at home and had rushed over when they heard my name. It made me anxious—while once again I'd done nothing to answer for, it looked bad that here I was with a second dead husband on my hands.

Dr. Cord gave them the full report he'd threatened and I found myself having to explain the brassiere in my pocket, and the chelation, and pretty soon the whole story had come out. Only I didn't tell them that it had been my idea for Earl to call Bella, since after all he'd said he'd had the same idea himself, hadn't he? Nor did I know Bella's name, or the Kitty-Cat's, I was sorry to say. I'd simply received the call at the Garden and come running, much as they had, to find the room as they saw it and my husband on the verge of dying. It was the truth, with only a small lie attached, and not one of any consequence, merely one that spared me a measure of embarrassment.

"Why did you pick up the other woman's clothing?" asked Private Church, his voice neutral as ever, but his meaning much less so.

"The doctor picked it up, not me. He handed it to me. Said he wouldn't want Earl to suffer from a scandal."

The doctor had gone home by them, leaving behind the completed death certificate and a general air of having washed his hands of us all—Earl, me, the police, everyone. His patient was dead. His job was done.

"And who was she?"

I shrugged. "I gather there are women around this town, as

around any, that will take money for intimate acts. Men know where to find them, somehow."

Sergeant Young was looking at me with grave sympathy in his eyes, or so I thought. It was Church, however, junior partner or not, that was leading the grilling, and I saw that his zeal for pinning something on me had not ended with the exhumation of Ron's body, but had merely gone into hibernation, or what they call remission if you have had cancer. The danger never wholly goes away, it merely sleeps for a time.

"We're going to have to take some of these things back with us, have our laboratory men inspect them. And we *will* do an autopsy."

"…Do what you must."

"You could save us some time if you'd tell us now of anything we're going to find when we do."

"You'd have to talk to Dr. Jameson about that—he's the one set all this up, the treatment Earl was on, the chemicals."

"Then why did you call Dr. Cord when your husband needed help? Rather than Dr. Jameson?"

I waved a hand at the equipment. "Because I didn't trust it, any of this. I told Earl I didn't. Dr. Cord was the one warned him of the risk, the one who told him he might die of it. So he's the one I called."

Private Church nodded, as if he thought that very reasonable, and I breathed a little easier. He extended a hand and ushered me toward the door.

But before I stepped out, he spoke again: "I know I don't have to say this, but let me say it anyway. Don't leave Hyattsville, Mrs. White. O.K.?"

"Where would I go?" I said.

"Anywhere. But don't."

"Can you tell me what the reason is?"

"We might need you here, for the inquiry." That was all he said, but I could see in his eyes there was more he wasn't saying.

I went downstairs while Young and Church remained with the body. Araminta came in to the drawing room and I asked her to keep me company. Then Myra was there, and Leora, and we all four just sat there, not speaking. I started to talk, telling them I hadn't made any plans, so I couldn't speak of the future, but assured them that "whatever seems indicated," I would deal decently by them, and help them find other work. They were quite sweet and understanding. Then the bell rang, and Church came down to let them in. Two men were there with a stretcher. They asked for the death certificate, and Church handed it over to them. Then Earl was going out, of the house, of this world, of my life.

This time it was I, not Ethel, who was calling the undertaker, or funeral director, as they now seem to be known. I called the same one, and a girl was on night duty. She said she'd contact the police the next afternoon to inquire about releasing the body. She thought it would take that long for the autopsy to be completed.

It was, as I've said, Friday night, and no funerals are held Saturday or Sunday, so the service would have to wait until Monday. Plenty went on over the weekend, however. Both newspapers called on Saturday morning, the *Post* and the *Star*, on the basis of the death certificate, which it seems they get automatically. They asked me about the circumstances of the death, but they didn't seem to have heard too much yet, since they accepted my simplest answers and didn't press for more. They also asked about Earl's business, the one started by his grandfather and continued by his father—who would carry on now, they wanted to know. I hadn't the faintest idea, but realized, with butterflies in my stomach, that I might have to make the decision.

By the time the afternoon editions came out with the story in them, the lawyer had come, Bill Dennison, flying down from New York with the will, the one Earl had drawn just a short time before, which left everything to me, except for some small bequests to the household staff and some to the people in Earl's office—$2,500 to his secretary, and $1,000 each to the others, about a dozen in all. By the time I'd read all this and had some parts explained to me by Bill, I was getting dizzy. But more people kept coming, most of them strangers to me, but some of them friends, like Jake, Bianca, and at last Liz, who I craved to see most of all—not counting Tom, who did not show. I begged Liz to stay, to spend the night, to see me through what was getting to be an ordeal, but she couldn't, having to work. While she was there Mr. Garrick rang the bell. He was the undertaker, and of course had to go over such things as the casket, the number of limousines, and the time of the funeral. He seemed to know about the White funeral plot. So, I chose a mahogany casket, the urn, after cremation, to be placed inside it, and on his suggestion, set twelve noon on Monday as the time of the funeral. He suggested his chapel for the services, and the Rev. Archibald Fisher as the minister. "He was Mr. White's rector, and I think would be indicated." I accepted all his suggestions, ordered four limousines, "just in case," and then accepted his suggestion that he send one more car, just for me. "One of my men, of course, will take you over—and be at your disposal in case something comes up."

"It's on the air," said Araminta, coming in right after he left. "Mr. Wilcox, he act like it was his brother."

"You mean, the radio?"

"Yes'm."

As Ethel kept hers on all the time I knew she must have it by now—the death, I mean. I wondered what I would say when she called. I found it was one thing I did not have to worry about. She didn't call.

By nightfall Saturday I'd had it, and thought I would go insane if I didn't get some peace. Suddenly I told Araminta I was going out, not to bother with dinner for me. I picked up a coat, went out, got in the car and drove to the Garden. I got there before the dinner rush started, so I could grab my regular table, and Liz was terribly sweet. She kept company, standing near whenever she could, meaning whenever she had a minute. She wouldn't hear of my going out in the kitchen, but brought me my dinner right there, with knife, fork, spoon, and napkin. I had steak, and was surprised to find out I was hungry. Then I realized I hadn't eaten since breakfast.

Next day was Sunday, and when I answered the bell three people were there, a man and two women. I instinctively knew who they were, and as a matter of fact had been expecting them as soon as the story of Earl's death had made the papers. I asked them in, offered them tea, which they didn't take, and water, which the two women did. Then the man said: "Mrs. White, my name is Olson, and these ladies are my sisters, Mrs. Hines and Mrs. Wilson. Our mother was the first Mrs. Earl K. White, and we've come to find out if he did what he said he would do, make provision for us in his will, so we come into our proper inheritance, the money our mother left us, which he got from her by a trick, then told us he didn't mean to help during his lifetime, 'you'll have to wait till I die.' So, we had to wait. And what we've come to find out, Mrs. White, is whether he made provision for us, in his will. Have you seen it, Mrs. White?"

"Yes, so happens, I have."

"What does it say about us?"

"Nothing. It leaves everything to me."

He got up and took his hat. "O.K., Mrs. White," he told me, "you've been very pleasant to us, and perhaps don't know the details of how Mr. White cheated us. We do, however. We've been getting the proof together, so you can expect a lawsuit, to be filed against you tomorrow. That will is going to be contested."

"That I seriously doubt."

"It will be. That's a promise."

"Want to bet?"

"You being funny or what?"

I opened my bag which was on the sofa, took out a one dollar bill, pitched it down on the cocktail table, and said: "There's a buck that says no suit is going to be filed."

"This isn't a joking matter."

"Who's joking?"

Reaching into his pocket, he put a dollar beside my dollar.

"O.K.," I asked him, "how much did my husband owe you?"

"...Well that I couldn't say precisely without figuring up."

"Then figure."

"It would take me some little time."

"We have all day."

"Hey, wait a minute—"

"For heaven's sake, Vincent, she's asked you how much—so, *figure!*"

That was Mrs. Hines—so loud Araminta popped in, asking: "You need me, Miss Joan?"

"No, Araminta. Thanks just the same."

She left, and when I turned back to my visitors they were huddled around the table, using it as a desk to write on a half-sheet of paper Mr. Olson had fished out of his pocket, taking down information from several documents he'd laid out in a neat row. At last he turned to me, saying: "By the bank statements she left, she turned over cash to him, our mother I'm talking about, four different amounts, one of fifty-two thousand dollars, one of thirty, one of seventy-five, and one of one hundred ninety-seven—three hundred and fifty-four in all, that she meant to leave her children, to be divided equally between us."

"And when was this?"

"Our mother died six years ago."

"May I have the paper please?"

I took the paper, turned it over, borrowed the ballpoint, and wrote $354,000. Then I multiplied by .06, and got $21,240. I did that five more times after adding $21,240 to $354,000, so I was figuring compound interest. After six years, it came to $502,155.77 and I asked them to check my arithmetic. Then I got my checkbook, for the joint account Earl had arranged with me, and wrote three checks for $167,385.26 each. It was almost all the money in the main account, and I could understand why Earl hadn't done it sooner—the account probably hadn't had enough in it until he'd sold that new partnership interest in his company, and afterwards he'd wanted to hold onto the money to cover the expense of raising Tad. Well, I would still have that expense, and others besides—but paying the amounts these three were owed was the right thing to do. They had been on my mind since the day Earl first told me about them, and I wanted to square things up.

"You'll just need to sign this to make it all legal," I said, handing them, along with the three checks, a sheet of paper I'd asked Bill Dennison to prepare the day before. "I accept the amount presented herewith in settlement of all claims, past, current or future, against Joan White, the estate of Earl K. White, or any other," it began, and went on in similar vein for the rest of the page. At the bottom were three lines for their signatures. One by one, they bent over the table and signed.

On his way out, Mr. Olson all but kissed me, and both his sisters did. "Mrs. White," he said, "you're so decent, I don't know what to say." He turned back at the door. "You win your buck, of course."

"I said I wasn't joking," and smiled at him, the first honest smile I'd had since Earl's death—and the last I'd have for some time.

30

Not an hour later, the bell rang again. I opened, and Private Church was there, by himself this time. His expression wasn't neutral any longer. "May I come in?"

"...Of course."

He stepped inside and followed me to the drawing room. "Where's your partner?" I asked as we went.

"Not working today."

"But you are?"

"It's an important case."

"My husband's death? Why?" He stopped in the doorway and took a moment just looking at me. It almost made me long for the other sort of look, as this one had no affection in it at all. "It's important to me," I said, "but why is it to you? The man was sick, his doctor told him this might happen—"

"Were you pleased, Mrs. White, when it did?"

"How can you ask that?"

"Some women would be. If they were young and their husband old. If they were poor and their husband rich."

"How dare you—"

"We completed the autopsy on your husband's body," he went on. He strolled over to the bookshelves and pushed the little rolling stairway back and forth, the one on which Earl had been standing when he'd had his attack. "Do you know what we found?"

"How would I know what you found?"

"...Would you like to know?"

"Clearly you wish to tell me."

"Our chemists say they found a substance in his system called, hold on—" He took a card out of his jacket pocket and read from it. "—alpha—fatha—limido—gluta— I give up, Mrs. White. That's why they're chemists and I'm only a policeman. But they say they found this chemical in your husband's body."

"So…?"

"So, we called Dr. Jameson to ask him if he put it there, and he said no, not only didn't he, but he never would, not with an angina patient like your husband was, because it not only doesn't help angina, it makes angina worse. It can trigger attacks in some patients and makes the attacks more severe in almost all."

"Maybe he gave it by accident."

"That would be some accident, Mrs. White, like meaning to throw a drowning man a rope and throwing him a brick instead."

"Then my husband got it some other way. Maybe some other pill he took? One the other doctor prescribed?"

"We thought of that possibility, but no—first of all, Dr. Cord denies prescribing it, for exactly the same reason Dr. Jameson gave, and second of all, there was residue of this chemical on the inside of the intravenous bottle and of the tube that connected it to your husband's arm. It got in there somehow, and it wasn't his doctor who put it there."

I sat down, though he remained standing. "I don't know what you want me to say. I have no idea what was in those bottles. I didn't like them, I wish Earl had never used them, but he did and that's all I know."

"Maybe. Maybe so. But you have to admit it would have been convenient, if you had wanted your husband dead—"

"I didn't! Ask anyone. I *saved* his life, more than once, when he had attacks that might have killed him."

"—if, I say, *if* you wanted him dead, it would have been convenient to place this chemical in his medicine—"

"How? Will you tell me that? It was a sealed sterile bottle, a sealed tube."

"With a syringe, Mrs. White, like the row of syringes that were sitting behind his chair. You dissolve this chemical in a little water, draw it up with a syringe, put a tiny hole in the rubber seal of the bottle and presto, you've laced his medicine with what for a man in his condition was pure poison. Then you let him exert himself with another woman while you're conveniently away—"

"My husband *chose* to exert himself, as you put it, it wasn't a matter of me letting him. And as for the other—did you find the chemical in one of the syringes?"

"No," he conceded, "we did not. But of course we don't know how many syringes there should have been. The syringe in question might simply have been disposed of after being used in this way."

I fought to control my temper, to keep from shouting at him. "And how would a person get her hands on this chemical? How would she even know what it would do? A person like me, I mean. I'm no more a chemist than you are."

"No, of course not. Why would you be. But—" He waved an arm at the bookshelf, with its tall narrow volumes. The one lent to Earl by Dr. Jameson was still there, the one he'd been reaching for the day of the attack. "—your husband seems to have been a reader, and a man who suffers from a terrible condition might be expected to devote some of his reading to articles about what treatments might make it better or worse. You might have found the information in one of these journals."

"You haven't answered the first question. This alpha-fatha-ludo—I can't even say it, much less know where to get it."

"Well, it might get easier if you asked for it under its common name, its trade name, if you will."

"What's that?"

"Thalidomide."

He must have seen the blood rush from my face. "What is it, Mrs. White? Do you know that drug?"

"…I've heard of it."

"Heard of it, I see. Have you ever been prescribed it?"

"No."

"Ever known anyone else who was?"

I shook my head. "I don't think so."

"You're not sure?"

"How would I know?"

"If we asked your co-workers at that restaurant, do you think we'd find that one of them has a prescription?"

"I have no idea!"

"We'll just have to ask, then."

I exploded: "Ask all you want. You won't find anything. Even if one of them has a prescription, she never shared it with me." My brain, of course, was racing all the while, thinking of Hilda and the favor she'd done me, of this terrible coincidence and how it might put me in the electric chair. For of course I hadn't crushed any of her pills and injected them into Earl's intravenous solution—but if they found her somehow, in Texas, and she told them she'd given them to me—or if they found the remaining pills, which I'd kept in a cabinet upstairs—

I realized after a moment that Private Church was saying something and apparently had been for some time, had repeated himself with no answer from me. "Do you hear me, Mrs. White?"

"I'm sorry. I was just distracted a moment, thinking of all you've said."

"As you might be. Let me ask it again, then, now that I have your attention. I said, was your *first* husband on any medication?"

I stood up then. I did more than that, I stepped forward until my face was no more than an inch from his, though he was taller, and I had to tilt my head to look directly into his eyes. He took a step back and his hand found its way to his hip, where he wore his gun. "My first husband medicated himself with one thing only, and it came in something bigger than a pill bottle. He took it orally. You'll find it on the shelf of any liquor store or bar, and it comes without a prescription. Side effects include dizziness, inability to perform sexually, and a tendency to beat the tar out of those you love. You can see my son's x-rays if you think I'm making it up."

"We did see them, Mrs. White—a dislocated shoulder, if I remember correctly. Ample reason for you to leave your husband and to take your son with you. Or to go to the police and have him arrested for battery. But that's not what happened, is it?"

"You know what happened."

"I know he died. And I can't help wondering if perhaps he had some help. Maybe some medication that would have made him sleepy behind the wheel? Something crushed up and added to that beer you said he kept yelling for you to bring him...?"

"Get out of my house."

"Your house," he said. "That didn't take long, did it?"

I stormed past him to the front door, threw it open and waited with one hand on the knob and the other on my hip. My heart was hammering and I didn't trust myself to speak.

He came forward, set his hat on his head, pulled his uniform jacket tighter around himself against the cold. His voice was quiet, calm and emotionless when he spoke. "You and I both know you killed your first husband, Mrs. White. We dug him up too late to find any traces, but that doesn't mean you didn't do it. You served him a drink that killed him, and now you've done it again, and this time I'm going to prove it, and you're going to burn for it."

"Get out, you son of a bitch, get out!"

I heard Araminta behind me, rushing toward the door, and from the direction of the dining room I saw Myra coming as well.

Private Church tipped his hat. "Ma'am," he said.

31

I asked Myra to draw me a bath, as hot as she could stand it when she put her hand in, and I lay back in it, crying, until the water cooled.

Then I found myself dressed and standing at the front door, with no memory of having gotten myself there. I was in a fog and needed badly to clear my head. I didn't even take the car this time, just headed off on foot, following the path Earl had taken each night and arriving at the Garden around the same time he always had. Jake saw me first, as the hatcheck booth was standing empty when I entered, and he stepped out from behind the bar to put his arms around me, a sure sign of how bad I must have looked. I tipped my head onto his shoulder and wept. Liz came out of the kitchen then, carrying a plate. "Oh, Joanie," she said. "Let me serve this and then you and I can go back to the locker room for a good talk." She hurried off to a corner table, the small one at the far end of the room. But when I saw who was sitting there, I knew there would be no talk in the locker room for me, not now.

I came over when he raised a hand and beckoned, and took the seat across from him as I had done once before. There was a glass on the table, drained. The mint leaves in the bottom told me it had been another smash.

"I thought I might find you here, job or no. No one likes to be alone after a death."

Sergeant Young was in his civilian clothes and looked no more like a policeman at that moment than Jake did—yet following so close on the heels of my encounter with Private Church, I couldn't help feeling a moment of terror.

"I'd hoped to warn you you could expect a visit from my partner, but I see from your look it's too late. I hope he didn't frighten you too badly."

"Only if you find talk of the electric chair frightening."

"He didn't—"

"Oh yes he did. He made it very clear what his goal is."

"You have to understand, he's young and aggressive. That doesn't make him right."

"It doesn't matter if he's right, does it? All that matters is what he can get a judge to believe."

"I think what's right matters. Most judges do, too."

"Most. That's some comfort."

"I don't say don't take it serious. But if you're innocent, the storm will pass."

"Right now it just looks like it's gaining steam."

"Well, that's the other reason I'm here—another thing I thought you ought to know. You've got someone else working against you, not just Private Church."

"Who?"

"Same as last time," the sergeant answered. "We got a phone call from a woman, sounded like the same one that called before, though Private Church says she made an effort this time to disguise her voice. She wouldn't give her name, but had the same package of news."

"…Which was?"

"That it seems funny your first husband died, so you came into a house, and now this second one died, so you came into a fortune."

I felt like I'd never stop defending myself, for the rest of my life. It was a sensation like drowning. "My first husband died when he crashed a car, a car lent him by a friend, into a culvert wall," I said. "My second husband died of angina, which had been diagnosed before I met him."

"Yes, I know."

"He was under a doctor's care. Two doctors. Whatever chemicals might have been found, I didn't give them to him."

"I'm not saying I believe it. But others might. Did you hear Paul Pry today?"

"That man on the air?"

"The same. He dishes up dirt—that's all his program is, dirt collected around recent news. And you were today's news. He repeated, almost verbatim, what this woman told us on the phone—meaning, we're not the only ones she called. A campaign seems to have started. I just thought you should know."

"I can't thank you enough," I said. I almost wanted to ask him for help, but what could he do to help me, more than he already had? For all that he appeared to be a decent person, and concerned, he was still a police officer. Anyway Ethel was my problem to deal with; I'd known all along she would be.

I wished then that I'd brought the car, for her house was too far to walk. Instead, I headed for the hatcheck booth, drew shut the curtain, and took the telephone back as far as the cord would reach. Then I dialed the operator and had her connect me to Mrs. Jack Lucas. It rang eight times before Ethel finally answered.

"I'm sorry, Joan," she explained, "I was just giving Tad his bath."

"Good," I said. "He might as well be clean before he comes home to me."

"…Home to you?"

"I'm taking my son, Ethel. You know that. It's why you're trying so desperately to stop me, no matter how underhanded the method."

"Joan!"

"I know about the calls—to the police, to the radio show. I'm here to say it's going to stop, and stop now. You want to fight me, fight out in the open, not cowardly, from the shadows."

"I don't know what you're—"

"That's O.K., you deny it all you want," I said. "But you'll lose either way. A boy should be with his mother, and now that I have the resources to support him, no court will favor your claim over mine."

There was silence on the other end, for just a moment. Then: "...As long as you're not in jail, Joan. I'd focus on that if I were you." It was a threat, but her tone of voice made it clear that she was scared herself, as if she really believed the story she was peddling about me and thought me dangerous. Well, this was the one time it could work for me.

"Don't make another call," I said, keeping my voice low, "of the sort you've been making, or it might just be the last you ever make. Understand me?"

I could hear her breathing on the other end of the line.

"O.K.. then, you understand," I said, and hung up.

That night I returned to my other house first, the home I'd shared with Ron, to pick up clothes for the funeral. It seemed strange to be in it once more, with everything just as I'd left it, except for a smell that it had—a stuffy, close smell, no more than you'd naturally expect, but for some reason upsetting me. I picked up the same dark suit I'd worn to Ron's funeral, but not the same hat, as this was fall, and a satin one wouldn't do. Fortunately, a velvet one was there, and I took that. Also, just in case, I took the veil, folding it into my bag. Then I walked back to the Garden, and from there home.

✿

The limousines, one for me, two I'd ordered for the servants, and the two others, for Earl's relatives and friends who showed up and very courteously waited, were due at 11:30, and sure enough, right on the dot, here they came, up the drive, and parked out front. Through the window, I saw the drivers get out and stand by their cars, shoulders back, rear doors open. Someone else I couldn't see walked to the front door, oyster shells crunching underfoot, and rang the bell. Myra opened, and then she, Leora, Araminta, Jasper, Boyd and the others were there in the hall, ready to go, and they did. Then I picked up my own things and went out, closing the door behind me, and turning to the man who I knew was there to escort me. When I looked up it was Tom. "Surprised?" he asked.

It was the first I'd seen him since I'd left the note as he slept, in the motel by the airport, and I would be a liar if I said my heart didn't leap at the sight of him.

"I asked for the job—the undertaker remembered me from before. But if you want me to blow I can get a replacement…"

"I don't want you to blow."

He put me in the car and got in beside me, in back. The driver looked surprised, but then touched his cap, got in himself, and started.

"Is it true," Tom whispered to me as the road unfurled outside the tinted window, "what Liz told me one night, down there in the Garden, that you never…"

"That I never what?"

"Never consummated, with this husband of yours that you're burying."

"That's none of your goddam business," I told him, "what I did with my husband. Is that clear?"

He didn't answer. "Is it or isn't it?"

"…O.K."

Perhaps a hundred people were there in the chapel, and Dr. Fisher read the service. He gave a brief sermon, of no more than five minutes, about Earl's "exemplary, Christian character." Then once more I was at a graveside, listening to another service, seeing another man throw earth on a coffin. And once more I was thanking the minister, this time telling him myself, not waiting for Ethel to do it, that he would be getting his donation in the mail. Then I was back in the car with Tom. When we got to the house the servants were already there and opened for me to come in. I turned to Tom, held out my hand and said, "Thanks for coming, Tom."

"I thought you might want to be with me, Joan."

"I do—but I'm not asking you in. It wouldn't…it wouldn't be right. Or at least it wouldn't feel right to me, which amounts to the same thing." I was thinking, also, of how it would look to the staff—and to the police, if word got back.

"Then O.K.," he said. "I'm off."

Suddenly I felt weak, like I had after the incident with Lacey at the airport, and like I had then, I wanted him with me desperately. I said, "Tom, wait a minute. I *can't* have you in here. But—hold everything."

I went in and called to Myra that I was "going out for a little while." I hastily threw together a bag, then stepped out the front door again, told Tom to let the car go, and led around to the garage. I got my car out, moved over to the passenger seat so he could get in behind the wheel, and told him to drive.

"And where am I driving?"

I closed my eyes and put my head back against the cushion. "Anywhere you choose, Tom. Even take me to the Wigwam again, I won't mind. Just you decide."

The car pulled off onto the highway and we rode along in silence, I with no more sense of where we were than a child being driven by her parents. Once, Tom put his hand on my leg and I shivered beneath it, not from excitement but from relief. It was like a cool cloth on a burn.

He pulled to a stop and bade me open my eyes. We were outside a small house with shingled roof and a little patch of lawn—nothing lavish or breathtaking, but wholly respectable, and I followed him inside gratefully. He shut the door, and I turned to him. Closing my eyes again, I inhaled. He asked: "Joan? Are you all right?"

"…Tom, this smell."

"I'll open some windows—"

"No. I want to smell it. It's you."

Then I was in his arms, and then he was carrying me back, back to his bedroom, sliding my zippers, kissing my neck. And so, the day of my husband's funeral, I consummated with my lover for the second time.

32

Once again it went on until well into the evening, what with "retakes" and a brief break for food, eaten standing in Tom's kitchen without a stitch on, spooning scrambled eggs straight out of the pan. When we finally sank into sleep, it was not even in each other's arms, just lying any which way across the mattress.

I woke, hours later, to the ticking of his clock by my ear. I felt neither happy nor sad, not pleasant or troubled or anything, just empty, like I'd been drained of all the bad things that had been filling me up, but also all the good things; I felt like I could start over, and like I had to.

I got up quietly and crept out to the front room, where I slipped my dress over my head and my shoes onto my feet. I was afraid the sound of the door opening would wake him, but it didn't. I stepped outside as briefly as I could, the early morning air raising gooseflesh all over my arms as I retrieved my bag from the back seat of my car. I'd grabbed a change of clothes, a fistful of makeup, a comb and brush, a few other things, and I tucked myself in the half-bath in his front hall to put myself together. The space was cramped and I didn't dare turn on the light, but with the door half open I could see well enough in the mirror to get myself decent.

He still hadn't woken when I was finished, and I stood in the bedroom doorway watching him sleep. The faint light coming through his curtains fell glancingly across his naked torso, and I felt something for him that was a mixture of desire and gratitude. But I knew, too, that I wouldn't wake in this room with him again. I craved him still—I always would, and some night it might be with the same intensity, like life itself was nothing compared to the touch of his hands on my body and of his body in my hands. Perhaps tonight. Perhaps every night. But he was part of the life I was leaving behind, not the one I was beginning, and a girl has to grow up sometime. You learn, often the hard way, that satisfying a craving is no guarantee you end up satisfied in the long run.

I didn't leave a note this time. I just left.

I put my car away in the garage and came inside in my stocking feet, one shoe in each hand, and found my way upstairs without encountering any of the servants. In my bedroom I undressed and drew myself another bath, and once I'd washed and dried and put on a clean nightgown I lay down and didn't wake until noon, when Myra came knocking at the door to say I had visitors downstairs.

I saw them waiting by the couch with their backs to me, examining the bookshelves, and I almost walked the other way, toward the front door. But some sound from me must have alerted them, because they turned, and then I had no choice any longer. I walked into the drawing room to meet them.

Sergeant Young was in uniform again and wore an unhappy expression, while beside him Private Church looked neutral as ever. Church was the one who spoke: "Joan White...formerly Joan Medford...formerly Joan Woods...you are under arrest, for the crime of murder..."

After that I heard no more. His voice was just sound, wind howling, as I watched him walk toward me with both hands outstretched, and between them, linked by a short chain, a pair of gleaming metal cuffs.

33

Of the drive to the station in their squad car I remember nothing at all, except for the heavy metal grill that separated the front seat, where they were, from the rear, where they'd put me. Sergeant Young helped me out of the car when we arrived, assistance I needed because I couldn't use my hands, and then kindly stood between me and the flashbulbs exploding as we made our way into the building. Once inside, I was booked and stripped bare and issued a prison outfit of some heavy, uncomfortable fabric softened only slightly, and scented harshly, by a thousand rugged launderings. They didn't have a brassiere in my size, so I did without, a decision I swiftly regretted as my nipples were soon rubbed raw against the inside of the shirt.

They stuck me in a cell, and there I waited, alone, with nothing to see or to do, except for taking trips from the bunk that was attached to one wall to the sink that was attached to another. It wasn't cold, but I was shivering. I wrapped the thin blanket with which the bunk came supplied around my shoulders, and I sat, and I thought about what was in store for me.

I'd known Private Church was out for blood—he'd made that plain. But what he could possibly have found from Sunday to Tuesday that would have justified arresting me in connection with Earl's death, I couldn't imagine. I wished now that I'd used the car ride to ask them. Though probably they wouldn't have said, they might, and at least then I'd have been less completely in the dark.

But I hadn't. I'd been too shocked, too dumbfounded, even to speak in my own defense. I'd sat then as I sat now, staring straight ahead and wondering what my life would be from this point forward. I heard Ethel's cruel words echo in my head— *As long as you're not in jail, Joan. I'd focus on that if I were you*—and wondered whether I would ever see my son again.

Some time later a guard unlocked the cell door and walked me down a corridor to a gray-walled room. We didn't pass a window to the outside, so I couldn't have said if it was day or night. The room held three chairs and the guard guided me to one, where I sat.

Church and Young came through the door a few minutes later. They each took one of the remaining seats. Church was holding a sheaf of papers in a folder and he launched in without pre-amble: "Why'd you do it?"

"Do what?"

"Kill him."

"I already told you, I didn't touch his medicine—"

"Not your husband, Mrs. White. Tom Barclay."

I'd thought I knew what it was to be stunned, to be stag-gered—but this was one blow too many and I found myself reeling. "Tom? But Tom's not dead."

They exchanged a glance. "I'd say we know a dead body when we see one."

"…What happened?"

"Why don't you tell us? You were there this morning."

"How—"

Sergeant Young said: "Your car. It was seen outside his house. We have people going over both right now."

"Tom was alive when I left—asleep—"

"In the bath?" asked Private Church.

"No, in bed, naturally. Why, was he in the bath when—"

He got up from his chair and stepped closer to me. I knew somehow that I was supposed to stay seated, and I did, but looking up at him looming over me, clenched fist on one hip, put my heart into my throat—as no doubt it was meant to. "Yes. In the bath, with an empty bottle by him on the floor and both wrists cut." He turned a black-and-white photograph to face me. It was Tom, beautiful Tom, only not beautiful any longer. I bent double and vomited on the floor.

Sergeant Young handed me a folded handkerchief so I could wipe my mouth. I think I thanked him. I can't remember. I know I tried to say something to Private Church, something to push back against his accusations, but all that came out was, "I didn't— We didn't—"

"Mrs. White," he said, "you were seen together at your husband's funeral. You were seen driving off with him after. You spent the night with him."

"That's so, but—"

"In celebration of your husband's death, you started drinking."

"We didn't! Give me any test you want, you'll see. I don't drink. I never drink."

"Well, *he* drank, anyway, and not just whiskey." He waved another sheet of paper in front of me. "You want to read me what else his body was full of when he died?"

It was the coroner's report, and typed onto a line by his thumb I saw a long scientific term: *alphaphthalimidoglutarimide*. I shook my head.

"You put him in the tub—"

"He's six foot tall!"

"You're strong, you told us so yourself. You lifted your husband off that stairway to the chair, when he had one of his attacks."

"That was just ten feet away."

"And this was twenty-five, and you did it."

"You can't think—"

"You cut his wrists with one of his razor blades—sliced up the tips of his fingers a bit too, a nice touch—"

I let my eyes slide shut, let his voice wash over me.

"—and then you drove home and went to sleep like an innocent lamb. A three-time murderess, but do you have any of the deaths you caused on your conscience? Not Joan White, no. You're ready for number four!"

Then came Sergeant Young's voice: "Enough."

"No, it's not enough, she's still sitting there calm as anything—"

"It's enough."

Silence, for a time. Then, Private Church, in a cooler voice, said: "Take her back to her cell." And I felt a hand at my elbow, raising me from the chair.

I opened my eyes. Both men were staring at me intently. The guard who'd led me into the room was by my side, ready to lead me out again. Before he could, I spoke, more calmly than I thought myself capable of: "Yes we were together—Tom and I. Once before I married Earl, and then last night was the second time. In between we never saw each other. Not once. We never spoke. Not once. Ask Liz, where I worked. Ask Bianca. You know them both, Sergeant, they'll tell you the truth. I walked out on him the first time, to get married, and I meant it. He knew I meant it. As long as Earl was my husband, I'd have kept on meaning it, and he knew that too. The only thing that put me back in his arms was Earl's death, and the funeral, and you, Private Church, the way you were hounding me—it was too much to bear alone, and I needed to escape it, all of it, for just one night."

"Just one," Private Church said. "And then you killed him."

"No! No. Why in the world would I kill him? Especially when I knew you were watching me eagle-eyed and already suspected the worst—but forget that, why would I want to? I wasn't married to Tom, he had no claim on me. Leaving him was simple. I just walked out again, as I did the last time. Only difference was I didn't leave a note this time. But he'd have known what it meant." My voice caught. "That I wasn't coming back. That this was the end."

"And killed himself in despair?"

"Don't mock him," I snapped, some of my old temper coming back. "If he did as you say, then yes, I think we must assume he felt despair."

"Over losing you," Church muttered. "The poor fool, he should have celebrated."

Without thinking I raised my hand to slap him, but found it caught by the guard at my side, and thank goodness. I had enough laid at my feet already without adding a charge of assaulting an officer.

But he backed off a step or two, so I felt I'd accomplished something.

A knock came at the door then, and Sergeant Young went to answer it. He stood speaking to someone I couldn't see on the other side, and returned a moment later with a slip of paper in his hand. He spoke a few words into Private Church's ear and handed over the paper. As Church read it, I could see the muscles of his jaw tighten.

"Put her back in her goddam cell," he said.

I'd never seen him so rattled before. I asked: "What is it? Is it something about my case? Tell me—" All the while, being shepherded none-too-gently toward the door and on into the hall. "Please," I said, directing a last look at Sergeant Young. "Is it something—"

"Yes," he said, drawing an angry stare from his partner for answering me. "It's something, all right."

&

It took another 36 hours before I found out what.

In the cabinet beneath the sink in Tom's half-bath—the very place I had changed my clothes that morning, the very spot— the policemen searching his house had turned up a battered satchel containing, under a pair of paint-stained trousers and a leather tool belt, a used syringe, along with a small tin box. The box was empty except for some powder in the corners, but in the hands of the police chemists those grains of powder were enough to establish what it had once held.

And the syringe had traces of Thalidomide in it as well. How he'd gained access to our home I never learned. Private Church, of course, asserted that I'd let him in, but it isn't true. As far as I knew, Tom Barclay had never even set foot on the grounds before the day of Earl's funeral, much less inside the mansion itself. And yet, he must have—because how else could one of Earl's syringes have found its way into his possession? And how else could the drug have been introduced into Earl's intravenous bottle…?

Liz had warned me that Tom was not a patient boy—but I could never have imagined that his impatience would carry him this far, to craft a scheme of eliminating my husband to get me back. Armed with the information Liz had given him about the true nature of our marriage and the reasons for it, he'd hatched this elaborate plot to make one of Earl's attacks fatal. Of any other man I wouldn't have believed it—but Tom had been the one to hatch, and to believe in, a plan to irradiate the nettles in Chesapeake Bay to improve the swimming.

And then—

And then, having carried out his plan, having killed a man for me, and having had me again for a night, he'd woken without me there, without even a word of farewell. He must have been consumed with memories of my last parting from him, and of the utter silence that followed. Did he feel angry at me? Toyed with?

Despairing? I'll never know. But in the cold of dawn he'd gotten drunk again—hopelessly, terribly drunk—with what consequence you already know.

They meant to keep me locked up, but I called Bill Dennison in on it and he found me an outstanding courtroom man, a Mr. R. Harry Hoopes, Esquire, expensive as anything but worth every penny, Bill claimed. And watching him work on my behalf before the judge at my hearing gave me confidence, as clearly the man was competent, although he unfortunately reminded me strongly of my father, and so any good feelings were mitigated. And for all his promises of getting the case against me thrown out, he got to go home every night while night after night I returned to my cell.

But he made the case I needed him to make. He pointed out the many times I could have let Earl die, and chose to save him instead. He pointed out the fact that I'd given away most of Earl's money, when I didn't have to, to Earl's stepchildren. The argument was made that there was still a good deal left, by the standards of a woman who'd had no electricity, gas, or phone not so long ago, as well as an investment company still operating that would generate more, as I was now a part owner; but Mr. Hoopes, Esquire, countered with the joint accounts, which eliminated any need I might otherwise have had for my husband to die before I could get my hands on his money.

The other lawyer was no slouch himself, ingratiating himself with the judge and sounding oh so reasonable as he worked to tie the noose around my neck—yes, Your Honor, maybe it's so that she had access already to her husband's money, but faced with the choice between the money and an old, sick husband or the same money and a young, handsome one, what does Your Honor think a beautiful young woman like the accused would choose? To which my lawyer volleyed back, "...Then why would she kill him?" The reply being, "She'd conspired in a murder, sir, and knew the police were closing in, she needed to pin the crime on him so it would not get pinned on her." And back and forth it went.

The newspapers got hold of it, as I later learned, and ran story after story, with photographs of Earl from their files and of me from the day of my arrest, Sergeant Young's body only partly blocking me from view. They'd even got one somehow of me in my uniform from the Garden, how I don't know, and they ran it over and over, with black bars to cover up what they deemed indecent. Of course this made it appear more indecent than it actually was.

Inevitably, the headline writers, knowing of my job and faced with three deaths in which I was alleged to have served the men in my life a lethal concoction, or anyway one that facilitated their deaths, took to calling me "the Cocktail Waitress"—just like that, with capital letters, one for each capital charge against me. It was a sobriquet that caught on, and one that has dogged me ever since. It is why I finally began taping this, so that my name might be cleared, and my children not be saddled with a shame and notoriety that I never deserved and they certainly do not.

Children—yes. But I've leapt ahead of myself.

Mr. Hoopes made his last impassioned statement to the judge late in the afternoon two weeks to the day from the date of my arrest, and I had the night that followed to stew and to wonder what the outcome would be. Would my case proceed to trial, and from there, if I were to lose, on to sentencing? I could practically feel the restraints closing on my wrists and ankles, the metal cap lowering over my brow, and if I slept a wink all night I didn't know it. But in the morning, word came down of the judge's decision: two words, *Insufficient Evidence*. And I was free.

34

I had everything on earth that I needed to make me happy then: besides my freedom, I had, it was true, enough money left, as well as a mansion to live in if I wished, and friends. Except that I did not have the one thing that I wanted, which was my little boy.

On my exit from the prison, before Mr. Hoopes could depart, I asked if he would come along with me for one more task. He eyed his wristwatch, but still flush with his victory on my behalf and no doubt computing the extra fee he could charge, he agreed. We drove straight to Ethel's house and pulled up in front of their drive just as they were packing bags into the trunk of their sedan. The judge's decision had leaked somehow and been picked up by the morning papers, and Ethel had lost no time in preparing her husband and Tad for a trip, perhaps a long one, perhaps one-way. If I'd delayed even by half an hour, if I'd even gone home to change my clothes first or shower, I'd have arrived at an empty house, my son vanished.

But as it happened, I spotted him seated in the back seat of the sedan and ran over to the door and flung it open. I heard Ethel shout my name, but didn't care, for Tad was in my arms and I was swinging him up in the air, showering him with all the kisses I'd been forced to store up since I'd held him last. I had tears streaming down my face, and frightened by it, he began to bawl, but I cooed at him and wiped my eyes and told him not to be afraid, that Mommy was back to stay.

While I was doing all this, Jack Lucas stood looking on, a trunk in each hand and a guilty expression on his face, aware of what it looked like that we'd caught them on their way out. But there was no guilt showing on Ethel's face, only rage.

"Put that child down, Joan. You're not taking him away."

"...I am. I have. He's taken."

"What court will let you keep him, Joan? A notorious murderess?"

"I'm free, Joan. The judge found me innocent."

"Like hell. I read the article. He only said there wasn't enough evidence to prove you guilty. That doesn't mean you're not. There's not a person in this state who doesn't know you did it."

"I'll thank you, Ethel, not to speak ill of me in front of my boy," I said, cupping one hand over Tad's ear. "And if you're serious about wanting to fight for custody, I'd like to introduce you to my attorney, Mr. R. Harry Hoopes."

Hoopes came forward, enough steel in his stare to arm a battalion. "Why don't we talk, Mrs. Lucas, Mr. Lucas—why don't we just go inside and talk?"

The next several days were consumed with meetings. I was seeing lawyers, realtors, and bankers. The lawyers were probating Earl's will, and had things I had to sign. The realtors hoped, despite all the attention, to sell the mansion, but on that I hadn't made up my mind, and anyhow, it had to wait on the lawyers, until their work with the will was done. The bankers were Earl's partners—they owned only a minority of his firm, but knew how his business was done, and I would have been a fool not to bulge up their share, so they would carry on. I did, the thing was put on paper, in a new agreement that I signed, and then lo and behold, I was a 40% partner in a prosperous banking concern—EKW Associates, as they decided to call themselves.

I had requests, too, from the papers and the newsweeklies, and from radio and television—more than I could count. But I ignored them all, and had Araminta go out front twice to beg all those who had gathered there to leave, out of respect for the young child in the house if not for me. They didn't leave. Which meant no playing on the lawn for Tad, and no trips outside for me—except for one.

I learned, to my horror, that Tom's body had remained all this time in the morgue, unclaimed. Of course, I knew his parents were deceased, and that he had no wife or siblings. But it had never occurred to me that he had no one at all. In time, I guess, he would have been given a public burial of some sort, perhaps in some municipal graveyard, and I couldn't bear that. For all that he'd done wrong, he still deserved better than a pauper's grave.

So, I claimed the body, and called the undertaker, and made arrangements, and rode once more to a funeral with Tom by my side, only this time I was sitting with him in the back of the hearse, not a limousine, and he wouldn't be returning with me after.

I'd worn a black dress, conservative and sober, with elbow-length gloves and a hat, both also black, as befit the occasion. I wore, too, the dark glasses from our trip to the airport together, not to prevent the reporters and photographers from recognizing me, as that was hopeless, but to prevent them from seeing me cry, and capturing it with their cameras.

As it was, photos of me from the service did run in all the major papers—the first photos of "the Cocktail Waitress" since her controversial release from prison. I only regret one thing, which was my decision at the last moment before I left the house to rouge my lips, for it got commented on in every piece of coverage without exception. But I felt I needed a little color, so as not to look like a corpse myself.

We didn't hold a separate service, just went direct to the cemetery and met up there with the one clergyman I'd found who had been willing to do the honors. He kindly glossed over Tom's suicide in his remarks, and also kept them brief, and for his pains took home a fee healthy enough to refurnish his church, or his home if he preferred.

Liz was there, and Bianca, both of them weeping copiously at the loss. "I can't believe he did it," Liz said. "It's my fault, Joanie, all my fault." I tried my best to reassure her that it wasn't, but I was afraid my words rang hollow to her. So I just held her tight and let her cry and patted her shoulder. When she finally let go, I saw a woman standing behind her that I didn't recognize at first, but knew that I knew. Then I realized it was Pearl Lacey. I hadn't thought she'd known Tom so well, but then remembered she'd been fond of him. I went over to shake her hand. "Shocking, shocking," she said. It was the only word she spoke to me the whole time.

I want to say you know the whole story now—what happened, and how it happened, and why. But there's one more piece I haven't told, and that's what happened when I got home from Tom's funeral. I realized something, walking through the door, and began to cry, not weeping softly as I had at the cemetery while looking down into the freshly dug grave, but sobbing so hard I could barely catch my breath. Araminta rushed me a glass of water from the kitchen and I almost choked getting it down.

Then I asked her, gasping, for a calendar. She brought one, a tiny thing she kept pinned to the front of the Frigidaire with a magnet. I turned back a page and counted, though I hardly had to. I'd missed my period this time for sure.

Since that day, nine months have passed, nearly; my due date is tomorrow. The doctor who will deliver my baby is the same one who came when, in the first heat of panic, I called and begged him to bring over to the mansion whatever apparatus he needed to perform a test on the spot. He came, he performed the test, and sure enough, this time it wasn't a delay caused by stress, though god knows I'd had stress enough to dry me up for a lifetime. No, it was a baby, and I've carried her ever since.

Of course I don't know it's a girl—not so I can be sure. But I have a feeling about it. I've had dreams in which she's spoken to me, and in all of them it's been a little girl's voice. Who knows if that's reliable, the doctors say no, but some women I've talked to take a different view.

It's been a difficult pregnancy, with lots of morning sickness and bed-rest needed. Little Tad has been an angel about it, but it hasn't been easy on him, for sure. Of course we now have the money to hire ten caretakers if need be—but that isn't the same as having Mommy there to pick you up and whirl you around the room.

Fortunately, I had some of Hilda's pills left—a few—and they helped me through the worst of it. I couldn't ask a doctor for more, of course. Any pills but those, perhaps; but if it got out that the Cocktail Waitress had asked for more Thalidomide— god help me, the newspapers would have a field day with it. As it is, the coverage has picked up, people interested in the story again now that the baby's almost due. A KILLER'S CHILD, read one headline I passed on the street. I didn't know if they meant me or Tom. But that night I began recording this. To make sure the truth gets told.

I can't wait to see my little girl, to hold her in my arms. Tom's baby. With a father like him…she's bound to be a beauty, a perfect little beauty, and I want her to have the life I never did, and that even Tad lost out on, the first four years of his life. He's a good boy, but every now and again a frightened one, you can see he's one who's known pain. But his little sister—I pray she'll be spared all the cruelties we've endured.

I seemed to be all taped up—that must be all.

For now.

AFTERWORD

by Charles Ardai

When people talk about James M. Cain these days, it tends to be in reverential tones—he's earned a spot as one of the 'big three,' the giants of hardboiled crime fiction whose works are considered classics (the other two being Dashiell Hammett and Raymond Chandler). Cain's books have been taught in universities, even Harvard. People write dissertations about them.

But back when Cain started publishing his lean, tough novels in the 1930s and 40s—and even on into the 50s and 60s—he was seen very differently: as a dabbler in sin and scandal, a purveyor of the lurid and the low. The *Saturday Review of Literature* famously said, "No one has ever stopped reading in the middle of one of Jim Cain's books," a line that has been quoted on several generations of Cain paperbacks, but it was a backhanded compliment, acknowledging his books' explosive popularity with readers more than their quality. *Time* magazine, meanwhile, sneeringly called his books "carnal and criminal" and their author a "hoary old sensation-monger," opining in 1965 (with more than a whiff of envy) that

> *For 30 years, novelist James M. Cain has worked a literary lode bordering a trash heap. Even his best works—*The Postman Always Rings Twice, Mildred Pierce, Double Indemnity—*reeked of their neighborhood, and no doubt as a consequence were made into movies.*

They were indeed made into movies. One, Billy Wilder's *Double Indemnity*, scored a Best Picture nomination upon release and has since been named one of the 100 best American films of all time by the American Film Institute. Cain's books also sold millions of copies and were translated into eighteen or nineteen languages. All of which just goes to show how little critics' opinions count for if you've got readers in the palm of your hand (which, god knows, Cain did), and if your books are actually good (which, god knows, Cain's are).

But it would be a mistake to completely ignore the reception Cain got in his heyday, because it tells you something about what it was Cain was doing. The fact is that Cain *was* a scandalous, shocking writer—even a dangerous one, insofar as any novelist can be called dangerous. He shook up the social order of his day, delighting in pricking over-inflated balloons and watching them go pop. He brought matters into popular fiction that weren't the subject of polite conversation back then (some still aren't even now)—adultery, incest, depravity of all stripes, sexuality of all flavors. He had an underage temptress stealing her mother's lover a decade before *Lolita*. He had murders so brutal, so visceral, that even reading them today your gut twists. His books were banned. Is there any wonder that he attracted readers by the carload, or that they read his books breathlessly to the last page?

But unlike a mere sensationalist, Cain put this shocking material to work in the service of larger aims: showing us life as it is lived, language as it is spoken; the dreams and hungers and despairs of ordinary people in dire situations; the impact on the human soul of crisis and the ability of the human animal to give up its humanity under duress. Cain's characters sweat, and have reason to. And when you read about them, he makes you sweat alongside them. You want to know what it feels like to be trapped in a loveless marriage, yearning hopelessly for something better and grabbing desperately at a way out even if it's cruel and repellent and doomed? Read *The Postman Always Rings Twice*.

If you feel you need a shower afterwards, that's to its credit, not a criticism.

Cain did spend rather a lot of his time in the gutter and dealing with gutter matters, it's true, but his books are great not in spite of this but because of it. As a consequence, unlike the work of many contemporaries that have since been forgotten, Cain's books drew a powerful response, and continue to draw one. From ordinary readers, from critics, from other writers, from everyone who encounters them. In Cain's day, that reaction was sometimes revulsion, abhorrence—but make no mistake, that's a reaction, and a worthwhile one. At the end of Albert Camus' masterpiece, *L'Étranger*—a novel Camus said was inspired by Cain's work—Meursault goes to his execution hoping that "there should be a huge crowd of spectators and that they should greet me with howls of execration." Execration! Cain knew his share. But the greater punishment by far for an author is for his work to inspire indifference. And no one ever accused Cain of that.

Which brings us to *The Cocktail Waitress*, Cain's final novel, and one that shows us that even at the end Cain still had the ability to disturb, to trouble, to shock.

In 1975, James M. Cain was 83 years old; in two more years he'd be dead. His star, which had risen so meteorically in the 30s and 40s had fallen just as meteorically. He'd moved back east from Hollywood to Hyattsville, Maryland, where he suffered from a painful and debilitating heart condition—angina. He was an old man and getting older, in failing health and aware of it. But he was still a writer, goddam it, and every day he put pen to paper and the words flowed.

Some of these late efforts were attempts to branch out into other areas of fiction—a historical novel, a children's book. But at the very end, when he knew he most likely had only one more book in him, he decided to go back to his roots and write a James M. Cain novel again.

Clearly he put elements from his own life into the book—the Hyattsville setting, Earl K. White's angina, the nitroglycerine pills White carries (Cain carried them, too). He also returned to themes from his earliest and most successful books. From *Postman* and *Double Indemnity* there's the idea of a young, attractive woman, married to an unattractive but well-heeled older man, who meets a new man, young and handsome, who's ultimately implicated in the husband's death. From *Mildred Pierce* he took the premise of a female protagonist in severe economic straits, just getting out of a bad marriage, who has to take a degrading job as a waitress in order to provide for her child. The result of combining these elements is a classic Cain *femme fatale* story that's told for once from the *femme fatale*'s point of view.

Of course, no *femme fatale* thinks she is one, or admits it if she does. Which presents an interesting problem for a book told in the first person. In fact, Cain began writing *The Cocktail Waitress* in the third person, along the lines of *Mildred Pierce*, and got more than one hundred pages into the manuscript before abandoning the approach and rewriting the whole thing in his patented intimate first-person style. It was a good decision. The book springs to life when we see events through Joan Medford's eyes and hear them in her voice. But putting the story into Joan's voice means we hear only what Joan wants us to hear. And as she perceives things, or at least as she tells them, she's innocent of any wrongdoing—a hapless victim of circumstance, surrounded by deaths she neither caused nor contributed to. It's up to the reader to decide whether to believe this self-portrait or question it, and the resulting ambiguity makes *The Cocktail Waitress* one of Cain's most unsettling, unstable books.

It's the inherent contradiction in any work of fiction, the one we all conveniently ignore each time we sit down to enjoy a novel: Can we believe what this narrator is telling us? Well, no, of course not—it's all lies, it's all made up, that's what fiction is. But *within* the fiction, you say, if we imagine ourselves inhabitants of the characters' world instead of our own, can we believe what we're being told then…? Most of the time you assume the answer is yes: You can trust what Huck Finn tells you; Ishmael isn't lying to you about what went on between Ahab and Moby-Dick. But *why* do you believe that? How in the world do we know that Ishmael didn't kill all his fellow seamen and then wreck the *Pequod* himself to cover his tracks? After all, he's the only survivor; we're dependent on his account to know what happened. In *The Cocktail Waitress* we're just as dependent on Joan's. Is she really an innocent or a multiple murderer? It's up to you to decide.

Cain worked on *The Cocktail Waitress* pretty much up until his death. He never published it, though he did show drafts to his agent and his publisher. He wasn't satisfied and kept tinkering; even his typed manuscripts contain corrections and changes in his nearly illegible handwriting. The book's ending in particular bothered him, and after writing multiple versions he warned his publisher it might change again: as quoted in the biography *Cain*, he wrote to them, "If you're dealing with me you may as well get used to it. I work on an ending ceaselessly."

But no one works on anything ceaselessly. With Cain's death, the unpublished manuscripts of *The Cocktail Waitress* disappeared among his voluminous papers like the crate into the warehouse at the end of *Raiders of the Lost Ark*.

How did it get rediscovered? Well, there were passing references to the book's existence here and there—in interviews Cain gave toward the end of his life, in which he mentioned he was working on it; in the biography, where its premise is briefly summarized; in some of Cain's records and correspondence. In April 2002, back when Hard Case Crime was just a glimmer in the eyes of two writers with a crazy notion that old-fashioned pulp crime fiction needed to be revived, I began corresponding with Max Allan Collins, the award-winning author who has gone on to be one of our most prolific contributors. In addition to agreeing to write some books of his own for our line, he had suggestions for other authors, living and dead, we might consider publishing. Cain was a favorite of his, and as it happened, a favorite of mine, too. Since picking up a creased copy of *Double Indemnity* on a used book table while a freshman at Columbia, I'd hunted down copies of every book Cain had ever written and read them all—even the obscure ones, even the weaker ones, even the ones no one had read in decades. But Max had heard about one I never had: *The Cocktail Waitress*.

I spent the next nine years tracking down the book and securing the right to publish it.

The first problem was locating the manuscript. As it turns out, certain drafts—some partial, some complete—were housed in the Manuscript Division of the Library of Congress, where nearly one hundred boxes hold papers from all stages of Cain's life. But I didn't know that then (this was before the Internet made finding everything in the world so simple), and I spent the first couple of years canvassing friends and contacts in the publishing field, book collectors, academics, anyone I could think of who might have a lead. But no one did. Finally, when I learned that my Hollywood agent, Joel Gotler, had inherited the practice of an old-time agent named H.N. Swanson— "Swanie," to his friends, colleagues and clients, one of whom was none other than James Mallahan Cain—I asked Joel if he might be willing to look through Swanie's old files and see if anything turned up. Joel looked—and a few days later I got an envelope in the mail containing the manuscript of *The Cocktail Waitress*.

Talking to the *New York Times* later, I described the moment of opening that envelope as feeling like a scene out of a Spielberg picture—to stick with *Raiders* as our touchstone, like opening a tomb sealed for centuries and seeing the Lost Ark peeking out at me. But this moment turned out to be just the start of the quest, not the end. Because it became apparent quickly that there was more than one *Cocktail Waitress* to be found.

Sometimes a writer dies with his current work in progress unfinished. Then the challenge a publisher faces is finding another author to complete the work, and the results are rarely any good. Plenty of people loved Robert B. Parker when he was writing his own fine detective novels, but almost no one had a kind word to say about the job he did completing Raymond Chandler's unfinished final Philip Marlowe manuscript, *Poodle Springs*. Much the same can be said for the various attempts to complete Charles Dickens' *The Mystery of Edwin Drood* (although at least the musical version was fun).

But the situation with *The Cocktail Waitress* was different. We not only had a complete and finished manuscript, we had several, as well as several partial manuscripts and fragments, some consisting of no more than a few lines on a single sheet of notepaper, others going for a dozen pages or a few dozen. None of the manuscripts were dated, making establishing their order difficult (though one—the third-person draft of 107 pages—was labeled "O R I G I N A L"). Many contained the same scenes, only arranged in a different order; some had the same scenes only written slightly differently, with the differences sometimes being purely stylistic and sometimes being of great import to the book. (Example: After her first conversation with Mr. White, in one draft the scene ends with Joan thinking, "I knew I'd made a strike that could be important to me, but what stuck in my mind was: I wished I liked him better"; in another, Cain penciled through "I wish I liked him better" and wrote in, "Pale or not, he was very goodlooking and I liked him." Quite a difference!)

Cain liked to explore variations. He tried out different names for his characters. Earl K. White was, at various times, Earl P. White, Earle D. White, William Gilbert, and Leonard Gilbert. Joan Medford was Joan Keller. Liz Baumgarten was Liz Daniel and Lida Zorn. Ethel was Harriet. Interestingly, Jake the bartender was always Jake, the same name Cain used for the bartender in *Mildred Pierce* (also the one in his memorable short story "Mommy's a Barfly"—I can't help wondering if he actually knew a Jake who served him his drinks in his salad days). He tried out different titles for the book—at one point it was going to be called *American Beauty*, which in turn was going to be the name of the bar where Joan gets her job waitressing, rather than the Garden of Roses. And he tried out, endlessly, different versions of his opening scene—there must be a dozen, all taking place at the funeral of Joan's first husband, but some continuing with Joan meeting Tom there for the first time and others with Joan meeting Mr. White there instead:

> *That I was Miss Death, presiding at Ron's funeral, was a fancy that crossed Bill's mind that dreadful day at the cemetery, as he later confessed to me, and to prove to myself I'm not is why I'm taping this. I may as well admit. I wouldn't be telling the truth if I didn't say tragedy stalked us, morning, noon, and night, from the moment we met. From the beginning, the outcome was in the cards, as they say—it had to come, one way or the other. But did it? The answer to that tortures me, but for the moment I'll try to stop talking about it and get into what actually happened—and believe me, plenty did...*

I first met Leonard Gilbert at Ron's funeral, or half met him, perhaps I should say, as neither of us saw what the other looked like, or had any idea of what the encounter would mean in our lives. Ron's family, the Medfords, had gone ahead with the arrangements, as I couldn't possibly do, being left penniless, and their original idea, apparently, was to do nothing about me at all, to leave me out altogether. It was the under-taker who balked...

I first met Leonard Gilbert at Ron's funeral, or half met him, we could say, as neither of us could see what the other looked like, or had any idea what we'd mean to each other later. And how that came about was Ron's family. The Medfords had taken charge of things, as I couldn't possibly do, as I'd been left penniless, and their original idea, apparently, as they blamed me for Ron's death, was to leave me out alto-gether. But at such treatment of a widow the undertaker balked...

I first met William Gilbert and he first met me at Ron's funeral, though I didn't know it and he didn't know it until we'd got re-acquainted after meeting again, differently. And how that came about was: I was standing a little apart while Dr. Weeks read the graveside service when I became aware of someone behind me, and when I looked it was a man who had appar-ently been visiting the next burial plot and was now ready to leave. I stood aside for him to pass but he gestured he would wait and I turned back to our service. And the reason I didn't know him later and that he didn't know me was: I was veiled, so I couldn't see his face very well, and the reason he didn't know me was that he couldn't see mine at all...

"I am the resurrection and the life, saith the Lord; he that believeth in me, though he were dead, yet shall he live; and whosoever liveth and believeth in me, shall never die."*

The words held the thunders of Judgment Day, the voice quavered and shook, as its owner, gray locks thin and bare to the afternoon sun, stood by a casket atop an open grave, and read from an open prayer-book. Yet all heads suddenly bowed here in a flower-strewn cemetery: of two couples, one middle-aged, the other younger, making a group of four; eight or ten young men and girls, in windbreakers and slacks; and a girl in her early twenties, on the other side of the grave from the others, in short charcoal-black dress, with two men, under-taker's assistants apparently. She was medium in size and goodlooking, especially as to the tawny blonde hair in ringlets over her neck, and a strikingly beautiful figure...

And so on. Not only did Cain try out multiple variations of key scenes, he went back and forth with regard to his choices, with apparently later drafts sometimes reverting to match earlier ones, undoing changes introduced in drafts that appear to come in between.

All of this leaves an editor in the somewhat odd position of having to choose the version of each scene—where there are multiples—that works best in and of itself and also fits best into the overall architecture of the plot. And that means deciding what pieces to leave out, a painful set of decisions. Editing the book was difficult for other reasons as well. Some lines and paragraphs needed to be excised or altered for consistency (are Mr. White's stepchildren two men and a woman or two women and a man? did his first wife die one year ago or six years?) or

---

*Readers of *Mildred Pierce* will remember that Cain quotes this same passage in the funeral service in Chapter VIII of that book. Echoes of his earlier work abound here. But it's not mere repeti-tion—the funerals that begin and end *The Cocktail Waitress* serve a very different function from the one in *Mildred Pierce*.

for pacing and focus (a digression about Maryland architecture went, as did one about Maryland weather). Some vestigial bits from the earliest drafts, when the book had more of a political dimension, needed to go as they no longer made sense in the final version. On the other hand, a few excellent scenes Cain wrote in his first draft inexplicably didn't make it into the later drafts and I took the opportunity to fit them back in. And some sections throughout had to be carefully and respectfully edited to ensure that the story flowed logically and effectively from one end to the other, and that the various seeds Cain took such pains to plant early in the book were able to bear the fruit they were meant to by the end.

To be fair, this sort of editing is no more or less than I've done with the manuscripts of numerous living authors who have written novels for Hard Case Crime—as any of them could confirm, I am a believer in the old-fashioned role of the editor, in which he doesn't just acquire a book and toss it out onto store shelves to sink or swim but works closely with the text and with the author to hone every chapter, every line. But this is obviously harder when an author is deceased, doubly so when there are no relatives or friends of the author alive to consult (as there were, for instance, when I edited posthumous work by Roger Zelazny and Donald E. Westlake and Lester Dent and David Dodge).

That said, it's an editor's duty to do the best he can by any book he publishes, and it was a privilege to do so in this case. I gave particular care to the sections Cain worked over the most himself, aided by the notes he left behind, which ranged from details of setting ("Does girl launder, or have laundered, any part of uniform?…Does she serve from tray, or carry drinks by hand?…What is normal attitude of owner toward passes &c being made at girls?") to chapter-by-chapter breakdowns of events and motivations ("Her effort to deal with the $50,000—

Purchase of house across the street—Purchase of car—However, if she quits job, means just hasn't enough—if she keeps job + employs sitter, Harriet will take her to court") and notes on atmosphere ("Whole book should turn on the hot, close, sweaty, female smell of the cocktail bar…Joan's setting the theme—her walk, her attachments, the contours of her legs, her smell…"). It almost felt—almost—like having Cain sitting there with me at the keyboard, watching over my shoulder, keeping me on the straight and narrow.

When I finished editing the book and read it over from end to end, I was reminded of why I fell in love with Cain's writing in the first place. When I was 18 and cracked the slim spine of that first Cain volume I'd found, he stirred something inside me—enough so that I felt compelled to track down and read every word the man ever wrote. That voice, reaching out to me across half a century, grabbed me by the lapels, or perhaps by the throat, and it hasn't let go yet. If it weren't for Cain, there would be no Hard Case Crime. There would be no *Little Girl Lost* or *Songs of Innocence*, the two books I've written about tormented characters wrestling with their own grim circumstances of desperation and despair. There might, it's true, be less dirt on bookstore and library shelves, and less sweat, less blood—but also less honesty, less art, and we'd all be the poorer for it.

The brilliant, exquisitely talented Raymond Chandler, Cain's contemporary and peer (and incidentally the co-author of the Oscar-nominated screenplay for *Double Indemnity*), was one of those who loathed Cain. He wrote, with characteristic eloquence and pungency, "He is every kind of writer I detest…a Proust in greasy overalls, a dirty little boy with a piece of chalk and a board fence and nobody looking." But Chandler had it wrong. He thought this description of Cain was a condemnation, when in fact it was a badge of honor. And everyone was looking.

One last note, a historical one, on the subject of Thalidomide.

For anyone who lived through the 1950s, 60s, 70s, no introduction to this drug is needed—the horrors of children born with truncated arms and legs, or no arms or legs, or other terrible deformities, to mothers who had taken Thalidomide as a sedative or a treatment for morning sickness will be burned irrevocably into their memory. But many readers today may not even know the name.

In 1975, when Cain began writing *The Cocktail Waitress*, readers would have known. The drug was introduced in the late 1950s and became known as a "wonder drug," until being banned in the early 1960s after thousands of children who had been exposed to the drug *in utero* were born with birth defects. Thalidomide was never approved for sale in the U.S., but millions of tablets were distributed to U.S. doctors as part of a clinical trial. In England, the drug was approved.

Today, Thalidomide is used to treat leprosy.